the journey abandoned

the journey abandoned

The Unfinished Novel

Lionel Trilling

Edited and with an introduction by Geraldine Murphy

Columbia University Press   New York

Columbia University Press
Publishers Since 1893
New York   Chichester, West Sussex
Copyright © 2008 James Trilling
Introduction, notes, bibliography, appendix copyright
© 2008 Columbia University Press
All rights reserved

Library of Congress Cataloging-in-Publication Data
Trilling, Lionel, 1905–1975.
   The Journey abandoned : the unfinished novel / Lionel Trilling ;
edited and with an introduction by Geraldine Murphy.
      p.   cm.
   Includes bibliographical references (p.   ).
   ISBN 978-0-231-14450-6 (acid-free paper) —
   ISBN 978-0-231-51349-4 (electronic)
   1. Young men—Fiction. 2. Conduct of life—Fiction.
3. New York (N.Y.)—Fiction. I. Murphy, Geraldine. II. Title.
   PS3539.R56J68   2008
   813'.54—dc22
   2007034884

c 10 9 8 7 6 5 4 3 2 1

References to Internet Web sites (URLs) were accurate at the time of writing.
   Neither the author nor Columbia University Press is responsible for URLs
   that may have expired or changed since the manuscript was prepared.

To Richard and May

contents

Acknowledgments   *ix*
Introduction   *xi*
A Note on the Manuscript and Related Materials   *xliii*
Trilling's Preface   *xlv*

The Unfinished Novel   *1*

Trilling's Commentary   *155*
Appendix: "The Lesson and the Secret"   *163*

acknowledgments

When I tell other academics that I discovered an unpublished novel by Lionel Trilling, they ask questions about the work, yet they invariably return to my "eureka" moment. "Where'd you find it? There's got to be a story in *that*!" I live in Morningside Heights in New York City, a few blocks from where the Trillings lived, and I wish I could satisfy narrative expectations: "I was walking by 35 Claremont Avenue, the super was throwing out boxes, and I spotted a sepia-edged manuscript typed on an old manual. I don't know why, but I stopped to examine it, along with other papers destined for the Dumpster, and slowly realized what I held in my hands—" That's not what happened, of course. This unfinished novel has been housed with the rest of Trilling's papers in the Rare Book and Manuscript Library of Columbia University since Diana Trilling deposited them there. Although I first discovered it among unsorted material, at some point it was catalogued as "Novel [untitled]"; since then, even the most casual researcher could have found it. In short, *I* have no story here. This is Trilling's story—not only the novel but also the novel interrupted. Did he lose faith in it? Did he merely shelve it indefinitely, hoping to return to it? In my introduction I speculate on what might have happened, but the end of Trilling's career as a creative writer is as much a mystery as the fate of his characters, the Young Man on the rise and the Old Man of distinction.

Trilling never gave this novel a title, so I've borrowed the word "journey" from his other novel, *The Middle of the Journey*, following the example of Diana Trilling, who called her memoir *The Beginning of the Journey*. The journey in each case, however, refers to something different: a political life, a marriage, a writing career. I hope Trilling would be gratified that this novel, at least its beginning, has finally found its way into print, and I'm pleased to acknowledge those who have made this possible.

I'm grateful to the librarians and staff of Columbia's Rare Book and Manuscript Library, especially Tara Craig and Jenny Lee. At my home institution, the City College of New York, CUNY, Nana Abeyie, Dixon Ansong, and Steven Gonzalez converted sixty-five-year-old typescript into editable Word documents for me, a task far beyond my skills. I'm glad for the opportunity, finally, to acknowledge Carl Hovde's gracious intercession on my behalf with the Trilling family, Diana several years ago and James more recently. Jonathan Arac was kind enough to read my introductory essay, and for this and many other instances of professional generosity, I am deeply thankful. Similarly, Morris Dickstein has been remarkably supportive since I was a student in his NEH Summer Seminar on the 1930s. I have learned from his own writing on Trilling and from his comments on mine. His friendship and advice have been invaluable to me, and this project would not have been realized without his guidance. I'd also like to thank my friends Kathleen Diffley, for reading, and Fred Reynolds (who is also my dean), for prodding. At Columbia University Press, I'm grateful to my readers, to Clare Wellnitz for her advice at a critical moment, and especially to Jennifer Crewe for her attentiveness, support, candor, and judiciousness through a long and circuitous route to hard covers. She has been a wonderful editor. My deepest gratitude is extended to James Trilling for granting permission to publish.

Finally, I'd like to thank my family, to whom the book is dedicated— my husband, Richard Braverman, and our daughter, May—for the beginning, middle, and future of our own fine journey.

introduction

Lionel Trilling is best known today as a literary critic, but he thought of himself as a writer, a novelist, foremost. Just as Milton considered prose the work of his left hand, so Trilling regarded his own critical writing. It "was always secondary, an afterthought," he revealed at the end of a distinguished career in the academy, "not a vocation but an avocation."[1] In a perceptive essay on Trilling's "buried life" as a novelist, Cynthia Ozick describes his notebook reflections—on the death of Hemingway, on a conversation with Allen Ginsberg about Jack Kerouac's work—as "the ruminations not of a teacher or a critic but of a writer of fiction desperate to be in the running." Trilling felt that hostile reviews of *The Middle of the Journey* (1947) were motivated by anger at his presumption in writing fiction at all. "He did not presume again," says Ozick. "There were no other novels."[2]

This is not precisely the case. While Trilling published only *The Middle of the Journey*, he was at work on another novel in the 1940s and heartened by its prospects. To Columbia colleague Richard Chase he confessed his dissatisfaction with *The Middle of the Journey* as it went to press. "I think the next one will be better," he wrote, "—richer, less shaped, less intellectualized, more open."³ Trilling did not finish this other, untitled novel, however; he reached an impasse after completing the first third of it. According to his assessment (see "Trilling's Commentary" in this volume), "the intermediate part of the story does not present itself.... What is making the difficulty is that I have not yet got a new point at which to aim. That once got, I think I can depend on the unconscious process working out a series of connecting and interesting incidents."⁴ Although Trilling never found that new point, the substantial first third of the novel, more than 200 pages long, merits publication as is. The quality of the writing equals that of *The Middle of the Journey*, and the subject, the profession of letters, provides a more intimate perspective on the Trilling of the 1940s. Trilling examines his own vocation through three men at different stages of their careers: the young Vincent Hammell, the more mature Harold Outram, and the elderly, distinguished Jorris Buxton.

It is, perhaps, the fate of any novel written by an academic to be treated as a *roman à clef* regardless of the author's intentions—that is, to be shaken down by inquiring minds in the same business for biographical paydirt. This one does not escape. I consider the ways Trilling drew on his own experience and that of his contemporaries for Hammell, Outram, and Garda Thorne, his one woman of letters. Buxton, however, is a composite character modeled on literary figures. The conscious, original inspiration, according to the author, was the minor Victorian poet Walter Savage Landor, but Trilling draws more richly and vitally (although perhaps gradually, as the novel evolved) on Henry James and his brother William. To be more precise, the figure of Buxton conflates the vigorous, middle-aged "political" and "realist" James of *The Bostonians* and *The Princess Casamassima* period with the Master of the late phase. At the same time, Buxton, who in mid-career abandoned the humanities for science, conflates William James with his brother Henry, the man of action with the man of art. Through these men of letters, particularly the newly masculinized version of Henry James, the unfinished novel participates in the larger argument that Trilling delineated in the early years of the Cold War between a "Stalinized" liberal mind and the "liberal imagination."

In the manuscript's preface, Trilling provides the germ of his story. He had been reading a biography of Landor, and a scandal of the poet's old age intrigued him. A Mrs. Yescombe encouraged Landor's affection for Geraldine Hooper, a sixteen-year-old girl in her charge, and proceeded to defraud Landor on the basis of it. When he publicly attacked the Yescombes in pamphlets and poems, they brought libel charges against him; Landor fled to Italy, where he lived the remaining few years of his life. What interested Trilling was the situation of a romantic living on into the Victorian age, which is to say, a heroic personality acting once again on the grand moral scale, though in a slightly ridiculous cause. The drama lay not so much in Landor's defense of the girl—his "senile obsession," as Trilling called it—as in its impact on a circle of admirers dismayed by the unseemly jousting of their resident genius.[5]

The time frame and setting of this novel are similar to those of *The Middle of the Journey*: the late 1930s, in the fictional New England town of Essex. Landor has metamorphosed into Jorris Buxton, a distinguished eighty-year-old with a remarkable professional history. A successful classical scholar like Landor, Buxton was also a poet, a painter, and a novelist. He nevertheless gave up the artistic life at the age of forty to become a mathematical physicist and then went on to make groundbreaking contributions to his second field. "He went to M.I.T. and his doctoral thesis is still famous," boasts Harold Outram (60). A literary man in his mid-thirties with his own interesting history, Outram is one of the principal figures in Buxton's circle. Currently the director of the wealthy, influential Peck Foundation (possibly modeled on the Ford Foundation), he has been instrumental in naming Buxton's official biographer. The other distinguished member of this group is Garda Thorne, a woman in her early forties and the author of exquisitely crafted short stories. Mrs. Claudine Post, whom Outram and Thorne despise, is the Mrs. Yescombe figure, and her protégée—a nubile, guileless sprite named Perdita Aiken, the Geraldine Hooper of Trilling's narrative—is her bait to ensnare Jorris Buxton. In addition to these characters, Buxton's entourage includes Philip Dyas, the kindly headmaster of a private school; Marion Cathcart, an opinionated young woman who takes care of the Outram children and appears to be modeled, in part, on Diana Trilling; and Linda and Arthur Hollowell, wealthy fellow travelers who resemble Arthur and Nancy Croom in *The Middle of the Journey*.[6] The central consciousness of Trilling's novel, however, is not the eminent Buxton nor any member of his coterie but an untried young man, a newcomer on the scene: twenty-three-year-old Vincent Hammell, who, through a stroke of remarkable luck (or so he thinks), has been named Jorris Buxton's official biographer.

Two Men and a Woman of Letters

Vincent Hammell is the classic young man from the provinces who sets out from an unnamed midwestern city to make his fortune. Idealistic and ambitious, he sees the life of letters as both a labor of love and a path to upward mobility. Before Outram arrives from the East with his fabled offer, we learn a good deal about Vincent's origins and his efforts to sustain an intellectual life in an inauspicious environment. The novel opens with a tennis match between Vincent and his childhood friend, Toss Dodge, at the local club (the Dodges are members, the Hammells are not). Toss has graduated from Yale, where he cultivated an interest in eighteenth-century literature and political liberalism as well as sympathy for Soviet Russia. The boys dreamed of attending Yale together, but as Vincent's parents could not afford an Ivy League education, he had to live at home and commute to "the City University." Vincent Hammell is a more daringly autobiographical character than John Laskell, the protagonist of *The Middle of the Journey*. His college crowd, for example, sounds like a midwestern outpost of the New York Intellectuals; its members included "a rather raffish group of Jews, an Armenian who was regarded with awe as a genius in Renaissance scholarship, an Irish boy whose father had had two conversations with Yeats and one with Joyce, and a poor boy from the farm country whose passion for sociology made it inevitable that he should be thought of as a new Thorstein Veblen." They were "in all things complex and complaining minds" (12). Trilling thus develops a contrast between the antiquarian Dodge and the modern, theoretical Hammell that rehearses the familiar opposition between the genteel "Stalinist" fellow traveler and the avant-garde intellectual from the wrong side of the tracks. Although Trilling went to Columbia, his first choice was Yale, which his wealthy German-Jewish friends from high school attended. "German Jews," said Diana Trilling, "had to suffice as Lionel's Guermantes."[7]

The opus on which Vincent is at work before the biographical project is offered to him is a history of American literature in the second half of the nineteenth century, the period Trilling regularly taught at Columbia in the 1940s. Living at home, supporting himself by teaching and occasionally writing for the local newspaper, Vincent works on his project in obscurity. He is aware of time passing, fears it is passing him by, and suffers bouts of self-doubt and despair. His father, an optometrist who reads Spinoza, is an ineffectual dreamer. His more resourceful and present-minded mother is Vincent's ardent supporter, listening for the sound of his typewriter and fretting when it falls silent.[8] It is hardly surprising, however, that her faith irritates and oppresses her intellectual son. Teddy Kramer, Vincent's former professor, is nearly as devoted as Mrs. Hammell. He contemplates each step of the young man's development as though Vincent were in training for knighthood, considering, for example, the wisdom of a girlfriend at this stage, but not marriage. The former student, for his part, is affectionate but patronizing toward this "timid, suspicious, but resistant"—and Jewish—paterfamilias:

> He would lecture on the literature of modern Europe as he had learned to love it in his rebellious youth.... As he talked, his stature would grow and he would forget his old-fashioned Jewish pride, which Vincent had come to see as consisting of the belief that being Jewish meant being a physically small man of such scrupulous intellectual honesty that he could bring no work to a satisfactory conclusion. (28–29)

The irony here is not just Vincent's. Trilling may have had Elliot Cohen, editor of the *Menorah Journal*, in mind, or at least the "positive Jewishness" that the journal endorsed. Having served his apprenticeship on the *Menorah Journal* in his twenties, Trilling came to see its program as "provincial and parochial."[9] Furthermore, in the mid-'40s, while Trilling was working on this novel, Cohen tried to lure him onto the contributing board of his new journal, *Commentary*, an effort Trilling interpreted as an "impulse to 'degrade' me by involving me in [a] Jewish venture—." He recorded in his notebook "how little hesitation or regret" he felt in turning Cohen down.[10] Vincent's plight is similar to Trilling's: stuck in the provinces, trying to come to terms with the tradition of American letters, he is the fair-haired boy of a doting mother and a mentor he has outgrown.

If Vincent's character bears trace elements of Trilling the neophyte, the figure of Harold Outram reflects the disillusionment and cynicism of a successful man of letters for whom "culture" has become a business proposition. A brilliant, handsome, scholarship boy who completed his Ph.D. in his early twenties, Outram published remarkable essays and a good novel at the beginning of his career and then became a Leftist—"the pet of a hundred committees, clubs, leagues, and guilds," so Vincent tells Toss. After being a proletarian writer for a year, Outram renounced the Communist Party and suffered a nervous breakdown. He made a superb comeback in magazine journalism and was then appointed director "of the great new Peck Foundation with power to dispense at discretion those incalculable millions for the advancement of American culture" (16–17). Neither Vincent nor Trilling sees Outram as a success, however; "something *Time*-ish and *Fortune*-ish, with something of a less anonymous nature," Trilling wrote in his preface, would signal Outram's compromised talent.[11] Twelve years older than Vincent, Outram is a cautionary figure; after the brilliant beginning of his literary career, he has sold out for a large salary and the trappings of the literary life.

The binaries of being a writer versus "selling out"—to *Time* and *Fortune*, to cultural foundations, or, for that matter, to the academy—have little relevance in contemporary intellectual life, but they haunted Trilling. "Suppose I were to dare to believe that one could be a professor and a man! and a writer!" he wrote in his notebook in 1948, "—what arrogance and defiance of convention" (Notebook 9:145). By 1951 he had extricated himself from the graduate program in English, concluding that while there was no "escape from the university," he would lead "a hidden life" within it. In his view, he fell "between the two categories of the academic and the men of genius and real originality, but better to make a full attempt toward 'genius.'" At the same time, he recognized that he was intimidated by the "fierce and charismatic writers" he regularly taught (Notebook 11). Trilling is about the same age as Outram, and the latter's mordant reflection on his generation's obsession with the novel expresses Trilling's own anxiety about his literary ambitions:

> In my time it was novel or nothing. We spent our days getting ready for it, looking for experience. An *honest* novel it had to be—honest was the big word. And always one novel was what we thought of. Only one, very big, enormous. Thus having laid this enormous egg, I suppose we expected to die. It had to be big and explosively honest—you'd think we were collecting dynamite grain by grain, you'd think we were constructing a bomb. We expected to blow everything to bits with our honesty. (54)

Outram tells Vincent (who reasonably asks Outram why he doesn't write Buxton's biography himself) that he's washed up as a writer, a fate that Trilling, through the writing of *this* novel, is hoping to avoid.[12]

The groundwork for the meeting between Vincent and Outram is carefully laid. First, Vincent tells Toss Outram's history, and he is exasperated that his friend cannot grasp the moral tragedy of letters it represents. "You have to see, Toss, what it means to our cultural situation that a man should throw away so much talent, just for money."

"I *don't* see it," Toss said, making his voice as coarse and practical as he could. "I suppose I'm crass and dumb, but I just don't see it. The man was free to do what he wanted. He took a flyer at being a writer, and he took a flyer at being a radical. All right, he didn't like either one. Now he's got a job where he can do some good to mankind at large and you talk as if he had committed the—the unpardonable sin. No, I don't see it. He has my respect." (17)

The morally hyperbolic Teddy Kramer takes neither the pragmatic nor the tragic view of Outram; instead, he casts him as the Prince of Darkness. Once his acquaintance, Kramer now blanches at the mention of his name: "that man, if you let him, that man will corrupt you—corrupt you to Hell," Kramer warns Vincent (34). Having written to Outram with the vague hope of finding a more worldly and powerful mentor and now secretly buoyed by the luncheon invitation he receives in response, Vincent smiles at his professor's melodrama. "Kramer was fighting for souls, Vincent's and his own. He was defending the dark castle of six small rooms which housed his virtuous wife, his two unruly children and the book that must never be finished" (31). Vincent keeps his appointment with Outram, who, as director of the Peck Foundation, has come to visit Meadowfield, a lavish new center for the arts in Vincent's hometown.

The two discuss the younger man's work at the Athletic Club. This watering hole of the midwestern corporate elite is *terra incognita* to Vincent, who feels that he has entered the halls of power. His best published essay, "The Sociology of the Written Word," is a meditation on the life of letters as a profession, like the clergy or the military, by which an ambitious young man might choose to rise in the world. It is "the most treacherous" career, however, because the writer as a "moral authority" opposes the status quo, yet, bent on success, he must simultaneously win society's favor. Vincent's essay outlines several "Ways" that the writer negotiates this paradox; Outram mentions one, presumably his own, that Vincent has overlooked, "The Way of the Darling" (48–49). Outram also asks about Vincent's book and acknowledges the wisdom of his choice: "The American subject—it's in the cards. There's going to be an enormous boom—there is already.... If you tone it right, you may have a great success." Vincent wants to answer "that nothing in the world interested him so much as the American mind in its effort to comprehend the American complexity," but he doesn't because Outram's remarks "suggested to him how much his intellectual passion was interwoven with his vulgar will to be 'successful.'" Despite the older man's gracious interest in him, Vincent senses "the pain, the wild sense of loss, and the consequent desire to destroy" that the barely stable Outram feels; this new mentor might not have his best interests at heart (55–57). In time, Vincent comes to suspect that his youth and inexperience, which would presumably make him easier to manage, were more attractive to Outram than his critical acumen.

At the fateful luncheon, however, Outram makes Vincent the offer he can't refuse. After hearing a litany of the elderly Buxton's accomplishments, Vincent realizes that he is about to be given the position of official biographer. "As solid and real as a hunk of mineral placed on the table, the opportunity was before him." When Outram mentions Garda Thorne's involvement, Vincent is euphoric. "If the mineral had been wonderful in its solid reality, it now began to glow with light" (61). Vincent not only admires Thorne's exquisite short stories but also takes her as his model of literary virtue and integrity. Unlike Outram, Thorne has not sold out.

Garda Thorne—or at least Garda Thorne's fiction—first made an appearance in a short story by Trilling, "The Lesson and the Secret," published in 1945 in *Harper's Bazaar*. In this episode lifted from the unfinished novel, Vincent teaches a creative writing class at the new cultural center. (Trilling no doubt drew on his experience as a lecturer to suburban women's groups in the early 1930s.) The students are wealthy matrons whose highest aspiration is to sell to the slicks. Vincent reads to these disgruntled women, who feel they are getting nothing from their "theoretical" and "very modern" instructor, a story by Garda Thorne about two American girls who, on a trip abroad, visit the local priest of an Austrian village. The priest is called away suddenly, and the girls grow bored waiting for him. Finally, one takes off her stockings and steps into a nearby vat of new wine. Her friend follows suit, and the girls splash about merrily. They quickly tidy up as best they can before their host returns. When he does, he serves them the wine they've been cavorting in "and their manners were perfect as they heard him say that never had he known the wine to be so good." The story acts like a benediction upon the class, but the spell is broken when a student asks whether Thorne's stories "sell well."[13] When Vincent finally meets Garda in Essex, at the Outrams', she does not disappoint. Lively and beautiful, the older woman charms him. But he learns that Garda became Buxton's mistress many years ago at the age of seventeen, and since she has letters in her possession invaluable to Buxton's biographer, her relationship to Vincent promises to be a complicated one.

With her slim, tensile figure, dark hair, and expressive eyes, Garda Thorne bears a physical resemblance to Mary McCarthy, who traveled in the same Left literary circles as the Trillings in the late 1930s and early 1940s. Lovely and iconoclastic like Thorne, McCarthy also shared her reputation as a writer's writer. While she started out as a reviewer, McCarthy began to publish the stories that would be collected in *The Company She Keeps* (1942) around the same time and in the same venues (*Partisan Review* and *Harper's Bazaar*) where Trilling's "The Other Margaret" (1945), "Of This Time, of That Place," and "The Lesson and the Secret" appeared. The unnamed story by Garda Thorne that Hammell reads to his students in "The Lesson and the Secret" touches upon McCarthy's subjects, the Church and female sexuality, if not her treatment of them. In Trilling's story within a story, the transgression against religious authority (stepping into the priest's vat of new wine) is a naughty lark; wine represents Christ's blood, but here, spattered on young, female thighs, it connotes passion, the loss of virginity, fertility, and childbirth, and stands for sensual rather than sacred blood. The story, in short, is charming, innocently and obliquely erotic and thus a far cry from McCarthy's graphic depiction of Meg Sargent's sexual encounters in "The Man in the Brooks Brothers Shirt" (1941), "Portrait of the Intellectual as a Yale Man" (first published in *The Company She Keeps*), and "Ghostly Father, I Confess" (1942). On the other hand, Thorne's liaison with the middle-aged Jorris Buxton when she was seventeen ("And a very tasty little thing I must have been," she says) smacks of McCarthy's sexual adventurism (88). In 1937, at the age of twenty-five and already twice divorced, McCarthy left the relatively unknown Philip Rahv for a prominent man of letters seventeen years her senior, Edmund Wilson. After Vincent has met Garda Thorne, he reconsiders the virginal innocence of at least one of the girls in the story.

Finally, McCarthy's contempt for the Yale man was congenial to Trilling. There is an affinity between Jim Barnett, the college Marxist of McCarthy's "Portrait of the Intellectual as a Yale Man," and fellow Eli Toss Dodge. The Popular Fronter's "Gee, whiz" appreciation of Marxism is something both Trilling and McCarthy send up, though from different perspectives. The "modernist" Hammell, with his finer face, frame, and sensibility, is the foil for the crude, practical, "American" Dodge—a fictional contrast consistent with the critical one Trilling drew between Henry James and Theodore Dreiser in "Reality in America." Barnett, newly married with a pregnant wife, has a brief, self-serving affair with Meg Sargent, a political maverick who defends Trotsky, when they work together at a Left-wing journal. As he moves toward the mainstream, financial security, and middle-class respectability, Barnett cannot get Meg out of his system, yet he blames her for his own bad faith. Like Outram, Barnett goes to work for the capitalists (the Luce empire), but this is no tragedy of letters, nor have we arrived at any dark and bloody cross-roads of literature and politics that Trilling might recognize. Jim Bar-nett secretly likes his fate. Scratch a Stalinist and you'll find a Rotarian, both Trilling and McCarthy believed, but only the latter framed Left politics as erotic satire and tragicomedy. Meg Sargent, the independent Leftist, is the one screwed by Marxism *and* capitalism—in the person of Barnett. According to one of McCarthy's biographers, Barnett was mod-eled on John Chamberlain (a book reviewer for *The New York Times*), Dwight Macdonald, Malcolm Cowley, and Robert Cantwell.[14] One or two of these men may have served Trilling as models for the briefly proletarian Outram.

In the tight frame of "The Lesson and the Secret," the cultural cen-ter where Vincent teaches his class does not come in for comment, but in the novel, in leisurely, deadpan fashion, Trilling skewers Meadow-field and what it represents: a complex of 1930s cultural trends associ-ated with the Popular Front. "In addition to its training of professional artists and craftsmen," the narrator observes, "Meadowfield reached out to touch the city's life at many points. With great success it introduced the pleasures of community singing. It taught adults the art of finger-painting and clay-modelling and instructed housewives in interior dec-oration." The center drew its faculty "from the nations which had a just and exacerbated sense of national suffering and national destiny"; con-sequently, these instructors "had a quick response to the young musi-cians who wished to write compositions entitled *Prairie Suite* and to the ideas of young painters who, tired of theories, wished to record the lives of what they called their own people" (39–40). Meadowfield owes its existence to a Babbitt figure: a local philanthropist, Gilbey Walter,[15] bequeathed his millions not to the city university, as everyone expect-ed, but to the creation of a cultural center that blurred the boundaries of art and craft, endorsed a populist, celebratory approach to the arts, and nurtured the nationalism of an Aaron Copland and the neorealism of a Thomas Hart Benton. Vincent Hammell—theoretical, cosmopoli-tan, and modern in sensibility—displeases his students, and he will be fired from the Meadowfield faculty after one semester. His victimiza-tion at the hands of a feminized, philistine culture articulates the New York Intellectuals' hostility to "mid-cult." Outram knows of his immi-nent dismissal at their lunch meeting because he met that morning with Rykstrom, the anti-Semitic director of Meadowfield. Fortunately,

Vincent is spared the humiliation by Outram's offer. Miss Anderson, his most sympathetic student, sees him in a new, martial light due to his prospects, and her final words to Vincent are the last sentence of Trilling's chapter: "I hope," she said, "oh, I hope you can remember to be fierce" (74).

The Master

Thus far, I have been avidly pursuing biographical parallels between Trilling and his principal characters, especially Vincent Hammell. Although Trilling was not attempting a fictionalized autobiography, the novel is very much about the life of letters—"There really cannot be too much objective comment on Vincent's profession," Trilling observes—so his own experience naturally provided material (156). Now I turn to the literary dimensions of the novel and consider them in light of the prevailing themes of *The Liberal Imagination*. *The Middle of the Journey* was Jamesian in its commitment to the nuanced observation of Left manners. In this novel, the example of Henry James is more variously and palpably evident. Indeed, the Master has a walk-on part, for the third and most distinguished man of letters, Jorris Buxton, owes as much to Henry James—or Trilling's anti-Stalinist version of James—as he does to Walter Savage Landor.

On his first appearance, Buxton is described as not tall but "satisfyingly bulky," with a short beard. The elderly James, of course, was clean-shaven, but he did wear a beard in middle age. In one long, elegant sentence of *A Backward Glance*, Edith Wharton combined these two: "the bearded Penseroso of Sargent's delicate drawing, ... the *homme du monde* of the eighties" of her first acquaintance and the elderly, intimate friend whose once-compact figure had acquired "a rolling and voluminous outline ... while a clean shave had revealed in all its sculptural beauty the noble Roman mask and the big dramatic mouth." Buxton has "the keen grey eyes" that James's secretary, Theodora Bosanquet, recalled and is also a sentient observer in the Jamesian mold.[16] "In whatever way Buxton judged what he saw, he certainly saw a great deal" (144). While his mild, dignified manner and deliberate social grace also recall the novelist, a more obvious clue to Buxton's origins is the name of his servile amanuensis, "Brooks Barrett." This repellent character links Van Wyck Brooks, a progressive critic who disparaged James's cosmopolitanism, with William Barrett, an editor at *Partisan Review* with whom Trilling and

Chase sparred over liberalism in 1949.[17] Thus Trilling literally subordinates obtuse liberal critics to the Master.

The imaginative appeal to Trilling of being a biographer—of being James's biographer—is easy enough to see. His study of Arnold had been an intellectual biography, and Trilling tended in any case to extend his admiration of a literary text to its author. James was not so far removed from Trilling as he is from us. Trilling was eleven years old when James died; the novelist could have been his grandfather, just as Buxton could have been Vincent's. In reviews, Trilling complained that the personal note was precisely what was missing in James scholarship: Matthiessen's study of the major phase lacked intimacy, and the first volume of Edel's biography wanted greater "intellectual intensity."[18] In fiction, in Vincent and Buxton's relationship, Trilling's intimate and profound engagement with James in the 1940s could find richer, truer expression. Furthermore, the role of the biographer is something of a leveler since it licenses Vincent to probe, judge, and evaluate, regardless of the difference in their ages and their accomplishments. Buxton half jokingly tells the young man how frightening it is to meet his biographer. Challenging the Master with his own formidable powers of observation and analysis was no doubt a compelling fantasy for Trilling, who still hoped to be known as a novelist first.

Certain elements of Trilling's unfinished narrative echo the situation in *The Aspern Papers* (1888): an ambitious young critic, an author "of long comparative obscuration," and a cache of valuable letters controlled by a former lover. Garda Thorne will allow Vincent access to her letters from Buxton only under certain unspecified conditions and tantalizingly assures him that "there aren't any to equal the ones of Jorris Buxton" (88). Of course Trilling's Aspern (Buxton) is not quite dead, and his Juliana (Thorne) is not quite menopausal; perhaps Vincent was meant to succeed in the campaign, ostensibly literary but metaphorically sexual and military, that James's unnamed narrator botched. The circle of Shelley and Byron provided the inspiration for *The Aspern Papers*. James describes in his preface to volume XII of the New York edition his discovery that Claire Clairmont, stepsister of Mary Shelley and mother of Byron's Allegra, had been living in Florence as his elderly contemporary and how charmed he was by the intimacy with the romantic era that she, a living representative, provided. James alludes to the efforts of Captain Edward Augustus Silsbee to acquire papers of Shelley's from Miss Clairmont, even stooping to make love to a younger niece in her household. This, to James, represented "a final scene of the rich dim Shelley drama played out in the very theatre of our own 'modernity.'" His "delight in a palpable imaginable *visitable* past"[19] is precisely what intrigues Trilling in *his* preface to the unfinished novel whose germ is the somewhat tawdry entanglement of another romantic poet, Walter Savage Landor. As an early modern, James inhabited Trilling's own "visitable past" as James had inhabited the past of the romantics. James wrote *Hawthorne* (1879) for the "English Men of Letters" series, and Trilling was one of the editors of the "American Men of Letters" series while he was working on this novel. Where James (like Arnold and Landor) sustained a dual identity as a creative writer and a critic, Trilling feared he could become, like the narrator of *The Aspern Papers*, a "publishing scoundrel" exclusively, someone closer to Harold Outram than to Jorris Buxton.

Initially Vincent is annoyed that the odious assistant Brooks Barrett remains for the first meeting between the biographer and his subject, but he has a "strange moment of perception, that the mind of Buxton contained them both [Hammell and Barrett] and brought them to a strange equality." Vincent recalls Aristotle's belief "that intellectual activity transcended in the human scale even the activity of morality. But what Vincent saw was that from this movement of intellect came something very like morality itself" (105). He records in his journal the feeling that Buxton inspired as "the emotion of pure disinterestedness, the emotion of contemplation." It provides a kind of heavenly balance, "a perfect poise of the energies without the alloy of personality," a "perfect equilibrium of the impulses and powers" (106). In a letter to Teddy Kramer he compares his experience to reading Wordsworth's poem on the leech gatherer.[20] Trilling has a good deal invested thematically in Vincent's epiphany; in his commentary he refers to "that curious Aristotlean business" that "endows Buxton with a great meaning for him" (160), but the grounds for such an extravagant response are lacking. There is no remarkable movement of Buxton's intellect on display, and Barrett's continued presence may well be due to an old man's oversight. Furthermore, despite the detailed reflections lavished on Vincent's perception—at the moment it occurs, in his journal, and in his letter to Kramer—the meaning of the "Aristotlean business" remains obscure, at least within the terms of the novel. It becomes clearer, however, in the context of *The Liberal Imagination*.

In an often-cited passage in "Reality in America," Trilling celebrated classic American authors like Melville, Hawthorne, and Poe who "contained both the yes and no of their culture." Being of two minds about something, entertaining ambivalence, ambiguity, conflict, and paradox, was the hallmark of the liberal imagination. In essay after essay, Trilling extolled "negative capability" and brought to bear all of his rhetorical resourcefulness to show how a kind of transcendence, both intellectual and moral, was achieved through the drama of the mind's dialectic. The essay on James's *The Princess Casamassima*, typical in this respect, is worth considering in some detail, for it has rich affinities with Trilling's unfinished novel. "The Princess Casamassima" (1948) has been esteemed by Daniel O'Hara as a piece that "illuminates the major elements in Trilling's writing at the time" and by Michael E. Nowlin as "possibly the most compelling essay of his career," yet it has had its detractors as well. Trilling's "anti-Jacobite" contemporary Maxwell Geismar scoffed at both *The Princess Casamassima* and Trilling's overinflated assessment of it, while more recent commentators, notably Morris Dickstein and Mark Krupnick, have criticized Trilling for enlisting James in his own cause.[21]

The six sections of the essay constitute movements, almost musical in composition: in the first, Trilling establishes the novel's relevance for a contemporary audience in light of "our grim glossary of wars and concentration camps."[22] In the second, he traces the literary genealogy of the novel, seeing it as a classic European *bildungsroman* in the tradition of *The Red and the Black*, *Père Goriot*, *Great Expectations*, and *Sentimental Education*. Hyacinth Robinson, the protagonist, is the archetypal "Young Man from the Provinces" who sets out to make his fortune and establish himself in society. It is no coincidence that Vincent Hammell, Trilling's Young Man from the Provinces, keeps the three French novels on top of his bureau (20). Hyacinth is a type for Buxton as well, but in what Trilling liked to call "qualities of mind" rather than in social station or condition.

Part IV of "The Princess Casamassima" addresses what Trilling calls "the autobiographical element." According to Trilling, Henry James identified with Hyacinth Robinson, the illegitimate bookbinder caught between the revolutionary politics associated with his maternal heritage and a conservative respect for the cultural accomplishments of European civilization, the legacy of his aristocratic father. In *The Princess Casamassima* the novelist revised the James family dynamic on his own terms, casting William as the aggressively masculine Paul Muniment and Alice as the Princess. Henry's "revenge" was to exalt Hyacinth as a tragic figure and thereby vindicate his own choice of Europe, aesthetic contemplation, and reverence for the past over William's commitment, as a man of action, to America and the future. Here, as elsewhere in *The Liberal Imagination*, Trilling makes the figure who embodies the yes and no of culture a tragic hero, investing his ambivalence with danger, glamour, and virility. Hyacinth Robinson is a difficult test case due to his youth, his diminutive stature, and his asexuality; it is his commitment to art, as it is James's, that masculinizes Hyacinth, for artistic creation is associated with aggression, power, and the Napoleonic will. Having drawn the distinction between the man of action (William) and the aesthete (Henry), Trilling turns the latter into the former—or rather claims James does when he puts his surrogate, Hyacinth, at the heart of the revolutionary drama and consigns Paul and the Princess to the periphery.

By the end of the essay on *The Princess Casamassima*, Trilling has turned his attention exclusively to the heroic qualities of James rather than Hyacinth, approaching them through the concept of moral realism. Defined in characteristically elliptical fashion, moral realism is discriminating yet magnanimous. According to Trilling, James never condescends to his working-class characters (in contrast to contemporary liberal fiction, which "pets and dandles" them); he "could write about a workingman quite as if he were as large, willful, and complex as the author of *The Principles of Psychology*" (83). That all of his characters are fully realized, from Paul Muniment to the Princess, is due not only to James's powers of observation and analysis but also to his capacity for love. Indeed, the ground for such a full and fine-grained understanding is love. "People at the furthest extremes of class," says Trilling, "are easily brought into relation because they are all contained in the novelist's affection" (84). Trilling's extraordinary claims for James's *caritas* illuminate Vincent's extraordinary response to Jorris Buxton, or rather the mind of Jorris Buxton, which could bring two such disparate people as Vincent Hammell and Brooks Barrett to "a strange equality." What Trilling calls the "Aristotlean business" in his own novel is called moral realism in "The Princess Casamassima." The "perfect poise," the "perfect equilibrium," the morality that arises from "this movement of intellect"—all those qualities that Vincent takes such pains to describe and understand—suggest a continuum of tragic cultural heroes and moral realists, from Hyacinth and James to Buxton, Hammell, and Trilling.

Jorris Buxton's career, bridging as it does "the two cultures" of art and science, also recalls the essay on *The Princess Casamassima*. In Buxton, Trilling merges Henry with William James, the consistently bearded and symbolically "masculine" brother. Artist and scientist, observer and actor, Europe and America are now literally one. (Like William, Buxton was a painter as well as a writer before he turned to physics.) Buxton doesn't just dabble in psychology and medicine, however; he goes to the heart of matter as a theoretical physicist. "Do you know," Outram asks Vincent, "that there are men who with paper and pencil construct the plan of the universe down to its subtlest, most secret aspects, sitting alone, with no tools but their minds?" (60). This question was posed in the late 1930s, the time frame of the novel. A few years later, of course, mathematical physicists with paper and pencil would be planning the *destruction* of the universe down to its subtlest, most secret aspects. Buxton's career in this respect recalls that of J. Robert Oppenheimer, the head of the Manhattan Project, who was commonly known as "the father of the atom bomb" and who after the war became the director of the Institute for Advanced Study at Princeton. Perhaps Trilling was aware that Oppenheimer considered becoming a classicist, a painter, and a poet before he settled on a career in science; certainly he knew of Oppenheimer's literary cultivation and philosophical bent. By the early 1950s the physicist was deemed a security risk and subjected to a federal investigation. In a lengthy essay on the Oppenheimer case, Diana Trilling resorted to the breathless style of a Harlequin Romance in describing the scientist as "something of a culture hero" to American literary intellectuals:[23]

> Our contemporary scene does not offer many figures so exciting and sympathetic to the humanistic imagination as this most theoretical of physicists so apt for decisiveness in practical affairs, this genius of science who knows how to read and write English, this lean handsome aristocrat bred in the indulgent Jewish middle-class, this remote man of civilization called from the academy into the fiercest of worlds—a world of inventions to destroy civilization—only to return at will into that purest of academies, the Institute for Advanced Study at Princeton.

In the unfinished novel, again the man of action is in fact the man of contemplation. William is really Henry, and Trilling confirms his sexual and social potency by making Jorris Buxton a symbolic grandfather of the atom bomb.[24]

Making a Man of Henry James

Many critics have pointed out that at the beginning of the Cold War the New York Intellectuals—Trilling in particular—refashioned James in their own political and cultural image.[25] The discussion above on Buxton and Hyacinth shows how crucial the masculinization of James was to that project. Three times in the essay on *The Princess Casamassima* Trilling disparages the "vulgar and facile progressivism" that could confidently assume "James's impotence in matters sociological" (71, 77, 84). In the novel, the virility of Vincent and Outram is implied by their warlike names: Vincent, the victor and conquerer; Outram, the aggressor. In the opening chapter, Vincent sings Leporello's aria from *Don Giovanni* but jokingly substitutes the word "Narcissismus" for "la piccina"—the women, the countless conquests of the master lover. The day he leaves home to seek his fortune in the East, however, he sings Mozart's original lyrics, thus linking his literary quest to sexual maturity and potency. Outram, on his first appearance, is described as tall, erect, and vibrant. He has blonde hair, "but not so light as to seem less than masculine. If there was a hint of late Greek in the full mouth and the rounded chin, this was contradicted by the solidity of the skull, the expanse of the forehead and the restless, repressed energy of the eyes" (45). The novel insists most strenuously, however, on Buxton's manhood.

Mrs. Outram, the first of the Essex circle to receive Vincent, tells him that "the one thing about Mr. Buxton is that he's a *man*" (83). And the elderly man's masculinity is almost semaphorically signaled at the initial encounter of the biographer and his subject. The first thing Vincent notices is the beard. "It was the best kind of beard that a man can wear, it was short and firm and jutted a little forward. It gave a base to the head and did not mask the face. It suggested fortitude and the possibility of just anger.... The beard was all alive, it was the great classic symbol of strong age, of masculine power not abdicated." Buxton's handshake is firm, the hand itself "warm, strong and pleasantly calloused." When the elderly man calls him "Hammell," leaving off the "Mr.", Vincent rhapsodizes about a form of address "preserved by Buxton from a past in which manners were less intimate and more masculine" (99–100). If Trilling had continued writing the novel according to plan, Buxton, who had taken a seventeen-year-old lover at the age of fifty-five, would be acting on the grand romantic scale, at the age of eighty, as the heroic defender of a sixteen-year-old nymphet. Vincent, who has regular meetings with Buxton to discuss his papers (love letters among them), has a young man's squeamishness about any derogations into "senile lubricity," yet the narrative takes pains to affirm that Buxton is, as May Outram says, a *man*.

In insisting on the James figure's virility, Trilling counters the earlier Parrington–Brooks paradigm of Henry James as an effete aristocrat whose expatriation emasculated him as a writer; his demolition of Parrington in "Reality in America" is well known. Yet by the mid-'40s, Trilling was hardly a voice in the wilderness. The James revival was at its height, and the New Critical appreciation of James (signaled by the 1934 issue of *Hound and Horn*) had already challenged earlier dismissive attitudes. In a 1948 *Partisan Review* symposium on "The State of American Writing," Trilling continued to exaggerate Parrington's importance, calling him the "essential arbiter" of contemporary literary tastes and deploring the destructive influence of one "who so well plows the ground for the negation of literature."[26]

It seems puzzling that a critic as sensitive to shifting cultural winds as Trilling would continue to level his sights on Parrington. It was not the twilight of Parringtonism that concerned Trilling, however, but the resurgence of Popular Frontism during and after World War II, a Left "renaissance" in which F. O. Matthiessen played an important role. Indeed, Parrington was a screen for Matthiessen, who preempted Trilling in *The Major Phase* (1944) by recasting James in conventionally masculine terms as a heroic modernist writer.[27] Throughout *The Liberal Imagination*, however, Trilling ignored this complicating factor and recuperated James not only from Parrington and company but also from the postwar Popular Front that Matthiessen represented. In doing so, he participated in the larger project to feminize and homosexualize the Left, a rhetorical move that, according to Robert J. Corber, "enabled Cold War liberalism to emerge as the only acceptable alternative to the forces of reaction in postwar American society."[28] Trilling's anti-Stalinist reclaiming of James through Hyacinth Robinson—and Jorris Buxton—challenged the Left's charge of sociological impotence; it dismissed all talk of the obscure hurt and patronizing Williamite attitudes toward poor, dear Harry. Hyacinth is not "unmanly," says Trilling, but merely "too young to make the claims of maturity" on, say, Millicent Henning or the Princess (72). By the same token, the elderly Buxton is neither a grinning lecher nor a smooth-faced, balding old queen. He is the lion of Essex, just as the elderly James, in Sussex, was the "lion of Lamb House."[29]

In carrying out his project of masculinization, Trilling became something of a matchmaker. While the character Garda Thorne recalls certain features of Trilling's contemporary, Mary McCarthy, the name itself belongs to a character in *East Angels* (1886), a novel by Constance Fenimore Woolson. A grandniece of James Fenimore Cooper, "Fenimore" (as

James called her) sought James's acquaintance and finally met the novel-ist in Florence in 1880. Woolson and James renewed their acquaintance in 1883 when they both lived in London. Together in Florence in the first months of 1887, they occupied separate floors in the Villa Brichieri, which Woolson had leased. Leon Edel has characterized her as a lovelorn spin-ster and a second-rate local colorist: "that Henry should have bestowed upon work as regional and as 'magazineish' as hers the discriminating literary taste which he had hitherto reserved for the leading European writers of fiction, or upon figures such as Hawthorne or even Howells, strikes one today as curious," he muses and concludes that "Miss Wool-son" (1887), the essay that James published in *Harper's Weekly* and col-lected in *Partial Portraits* (1888), was an act of professional charity.[30] A generation of feminist critics has challenged Edel's views and reconsid-ered Woolson and James's complex friendship and mutually creative in-fluence on each other's fiction, reading in it a record of sexual politics by other means. According to Lyndall Gordon, Woolson and James's stories "debate the issue of dominance with a fury that was a counterpoint to mutual graciousness.... If we align their works in chronological order, what seems to come into focus is a debate of the sexes, high-powered on both sides."[31] Trilling and Edel rarely saw eye to eye, critically speak-ing, yet Trilling probably shared the hierarchy of aesthetic value his fel-low Jamesian described: European writers at the apex, followed by Haw-thorne and Howells in descending order, with American women writers at the bottom. Why, then, would Trilling borrow from Woolson the name of one of his principal characters—a name too unusual, too idiosyncratic to be a coincidence—especially as none of the other characters' names in Trilling's novel is taken intact from another source?

The answer to this question leads not into Woolson territory but back to James and, more particularly, to Trilling's need to fashion a manly—heterosexual—James for the 1940s. Trilling's adoption of "Garda Thorne" mimics James's adoption of "Tita," from Woolson's first novel, *Anne*, as the name of Juliana Bordereau's niece in *The Aspern Papers*. (James changed the name to Tina in a later edition, after Woolson's death.) It is possible that Trilling never read *East Angels*, but certainly he read James's assessment of Woolson in *Partial Portraits*. Her subject, says James, is loss and renunciation, and these have been more successfully realized in the character of Margaret Harold in *East Angels* than in *Anne*'s Tita, who "vanishes into the vague" after her marriage. "Garda Thorne is the next best thing in the book to Margaret,... conceived with an equal clearness," James continues. Garda does not renounce, however; she consummates.

Childlike though she is, she marries twice, and "nothing is more natural than that she *should* marry twice," James observes, "unless it be that she should marry three times."[32] Trilling's Garda Thorne—who writes fiction, who has had a long love affair with the Master, Jorris Buxton—subtly but surely points to Woolson; in borrowing the name of one of her characters, Trilling allows for the possibility of a romantic relationship between Woolson and James.

The queer James of contemporary scholarship has made this notion even more anomalous today than it was to Trilling's contemporaries. But Trilling was writing a novel and did not need to prove his case; in the absence of evidence to the contrary, he preferred to interpret the facts his own way. In the 1940s, Jamesian sources on the relationship between the two novelists were slim. There is one reference to Woolson in a letter from James to William Dean Howells in Percy Lubbock's 1920 edition of James's letters: "you are the only English novelist I read (except Miss Woolson)."[33] If Trilling had read Alice James's diary (first published in 1934), he could have learned that Katharine Loring, Alice's companion, visited Woolson and that Loring was reading Woolson's "Dorothy" to Alice before the latter lost consciousness on her deathbed. In short, he could have discovered that James respected Woolson as a writer and that she was friendly with his sister.

The two books on Woolson available to Trilling were *Constance Fenimore Woolson* (1930)—compiled by her niece, Clare Benedict, and containing excerpts of Woolson's letters, journals, and published work—and John Dwight Kern's *Constance Fenimore Woolson: Literary Pioneer* (1934). In a letter written from Florence in the spring of 1880, when she first met Henry James, Woolson describes "the old world feeling ... [which has] taken me pretty well off my feet! Perhaps I ought to add Henry James. He has been perfectly charming to me for the last three weeks." James was her knowledgeable guide to the art and architecture of Florence. To her correspondent, Woolson confided, "it is going to take some time for me to appreciate 'the nude.' I have no objections to it, I look at it calmly, but I am not sufficiently acquainted with torsos, flanks, and the lines of anatomy, to know when they are 'supremely beautiful' and when not."[34] This is what Hollywood calls "the cute meet," Victorian style: a lady writer fresh from the wilder shores of America being educated by her cosmopolitan countryman, who finds the torsos and flanks of Renaissance nudes "supremely beautiful." Kern notes that Woolson's "A Florentine Experiment," which traces the complicated courtship of Margaret Stowe and Trafford Morgan, draws on the knowledge acquired from James. "In fact, the comments of the lovers on painting and on life," says Kern, "are probably very similar to those exchanged by Miss Woolson and Henry James in their walking tours of Florence."[35] Had Trilling read "A Florentine Experiment" (1880), "The Street of the Hyacinth" (1882), or "At the Château of Corinne" (1880, published 1887), he would have seen James depicted as a lover in the character of Trafford Morgan, Raymond Noel, or John Ford, respectively. For that matter, if he had skimmed *East Angels*, he would have realized that James was the model for Evert Winthrop, the man with the keen gray eyes and short brown beard in love with Margaret Harold. As Trilling well knew, having reviewed *The Legend of the Master*, there were countless reminiscences of Henry James as a friend, a writer, and a literary monument, but here was James in his early middle years, still vigorous, still bearded, and at least fictionally capable of getting the girl and transcending the obscure hurt.

Novel and Romance

In his discussion of the Young Man from the Provinces in "The Princess Casamassima," Trilling finds the origins of this narrative of testing and initiation in older, more "primitive" modes such as folktale, fable, and legend. Although the *bildungsroman* is thoroughly modern in its representation of class, money, and upward mobility, "through the massed social fact there runs the thread of legendary romance," he claims, "even of downright magic" (61). James, he continues, "was always aware of his connection with the primitive.... He loved what he called 'the story as story'; ... and he understood primitive story to be the root of the modern novelist's art" (62). Trilling adopts what he asserts is James's view of romance in his own work. Entering the debate over the death of the novel in "Art and Fortune" (1948), he advocates a return to the romance and folkloric roots of the genre as a way to invigorate it, citing James's distinction between novel and romance in the preface to *The American* to illustrate his point.[36] In his earlier study of Forster (1944), Trilling valued the romance elements of his contemporary's novels, and in his preface to his own novel he notes that the Yescombe incident "satisfies my very strong feeling ... that a novel must have all the primitive elements of story and even of plot—suspense, surprise, open drama and even melodrama." Echoing James a few pages later, Trilling insists that his work "is to be above all a *story*. The fable, I think, is of a kind that will inevitably throw off ideas.... But this is not to be a 'novel of ideas.'... As for the manner of the novel, that will be as simple as possible. I will attempt no 'devices,' have no foreshortenings, no tricky flashbacks; it will move from scene to scene in the old-fashioned way" (xlviii–xlix, lii). As a novelist (and as a critic) Trilling prefers nineteenth-century examples in touch with their inner child—the romance—to experimental modernist masterpieces. Perhaps to counter charges about the sterile intellectuality of *The Middle of the Journey* (a "novel of ideas"), he turned to literary "biology" just as he was beginning to adopt a Freudian "biology" as a touchstone for his criticism in the 1950s.

Whatever the reason, Trilling assiduously invokes fable, legend, romance, and magic in his unfinished narrative. A terrific storm at the end of Vincent's second evening in Essex deepens the intimacy between Buxton and his young biographer. It is impossible for the old man to return to his home, so he sleeps at the Outrams' in the guest bed intended for Vincent. Buxton has a phobia about thunderstorms and summons the young man, to the surprise of the rest of the dinner party, to his bedside as "the comforter of his agony and, so far as biology would permit, its partaker" (124). Although Buxton is not out in the elements as "a poor, bare, forked animal," the storm underlines an association with King Lear that is suggested elsewhere. In the preface, Trilling compares Landor to Lear, and Philip Dyas, the headmaster, who playfully typecasts Vincent as "the foundling son of the king—the young man who has the giants to deal with, who is going to do *deeds*," insists that Buxton "is the king himself and always was" (132, 133). In the planned narrative, Buxton, like Lear and Landor, is a grand, leonine figure who succumbs to flattery that he should see through, yet neither the scandal nor the death of the "ruined old man" nor "the resolution of the young hero's own life" that Trilling plots in the preface (lii) was written. Trilling's novel leaves off with Claudine Post bringing Perdita Aiken to sing for Buxton.

If Buxton is the king and Vincent the tragic young hero and foundling son, Perdita Aiken (aching loss?) is overdeterminedly the princess. With her mass of blonde ringlets, huge eyes, slim figure clad in a green (verdant) dress, and her "two little apple-like breasts," Perdita, or Perdy, "looked as if she had stepped from the illustrations of a book of fairy tales." All her lovely, clichéd attributes suggest to Vincent "the expectable details ... of any well-known picture-book princess.... His heart quickened with astonishment and excitement, for he was seeing here in reality the pictured fantasy of his early boyhood" (149). Mrs. Post too is cast as a figure from folktales; Vincent first perceives her as "giant size," like an ogre. Earlier, Garda Thorne had called her "an enchantress," "a dragon" and warned Vincent, "You must be crafty and you must be strong!" (XIII:2–3). If the novel were to follow the script of the fairy tale, Vincent would slay Mrs. Post and marry the princess, yet that doesn't appear to be Trilling's design. At Mrs. Post's direction, Perdy sings "*Voi che s'appete*"—the canzone that Cherubino sings in *The Marriage of Figaro*—for Buxton. The elderly man calls her performance "very charming," but Vincent finds her voice wholly inadequate. By the end of the visit, he sees her as sweet but ordinary.

Even though Perdy is not the princess, or at least not Vincent's princess, Trilling is not merely satirizing the archaic genre he so pointedly invokes. Vincent's Old World apprenticeship; the archaic flavor of the "Ways" of the young literary man's quest for worldly success; the psychomachia that Kramer, the moral absolutist, predicts in defense of his cramped little castle; the temptation represented by the irresistible glowing mineral; the allusions to King Lear and late Shakespearean romance (*The Winter's Tale*, Perdita); the escalating references to foundlings, kings, heroes, enchantresses, witches, and princesses—all situate the reader in the realm of romance. Trilling's concept of romance would be developed by Richard Chase in *The American Novel and Its Tradition* (1957), and American romance would become one of the most influential paradigms of postwar Americanist criticism. Here, however, Trilling is *writing* romance, putting his critical assertions to the test in his own fiction.

The End of the Novels

Trilling continued to work on his first novel despite the critical reception of *The Middle of the Journey*. After bitter reflections on his reviewers, he commented in the same notebook on a lucky break that Irving Howe received (an offer from *Time* based on a handful of promising reviews) and exclaimed, "How right for my Vincent!" (Notebook 9:102). As late as 1952, Trilling was still thinking about the first novel. Apparently he planned to enrich the issue of Jewish identity that was first limned in the character of Teddy Kramer by making Vincent Jewish as well. "I begin to see it something like this," he says, in the opening lines of Notebook 12: "Our young man is specifically Jewish, but not 'to the ostent of the eye.' Here we can count on the older sense of Jewish to establish his *passability*...." (The archaic "ostent" means outward appearance. Trilling is probably misquoting Whitman in *Democratic Vistas*: "To the ostent of the senses and eyes.") The contrast between the young man and his friend, between "intellectual" and "business man," must now "be more complicated and subtler." While ideas for stories continue to appear, even a reference to a short-lived *nouvelle*, comments about the Hammell–Buxton novel cease.

All but the last chapter of Trilling's unfinished novel is exposition. If Henry James came to displace Landor as the inspiration for Trilling's heroic old man, as I have suggested, then the idea of the elderly, magisterial Buxton committing a passionate, quasi-romantic indiscretion along the lines of Landor's may have been too anomalous to carry out. It may be too that as the larger political climate changed, James had done his work for Trilling. The introduction to *The Bostonians*, published in 1953, rehearses some of the same polemics as the one to *The Princess Casamassima*, but there is a perfunctory quality to them, as though Trilling were simply going through the motions. When after a long hiatus he returned, indirectly, to James in "Hawthorne in Our Time" (1964), Trilling's attitude was more ambivalent. Finally, and most importantly, however, Trilling may have abandoned this novel, and novel writing altogether, because he could not learn the lesson of the Master.

Trilling was accurate when he described his novel in progress, to Richard Chase, as "richer, less shaped, less intellectualized, more open" than *The Middle of the Journey*. He wanted to move beyond the political novel of ideas, and the life of letters as a subject had potential for broadening his scope. It permitted him to mine his own experiences in the character of Vincent Hammell; to reflect on his literary generation's development through Outram and Thorne; and to engage the mind, the *oeuvre*, and the model of Henry James more intimately. Trilling's powers of observation and chaste prose provide rewarding moments here as they do in *The Middle of the Journey*. When nothing is at stake thematically—when he is tapping his own past for the leisurely description of Vincent and Toss's boyhood friendship or reflecting on the tourist's experience of old New England—Trilling is at his best. Intelligent reflection, however, does not alone make a novel; the same weaknesses that marred the first novel are still evident. Leslie Fiedler called *The Middle of the Journey* "a schedule not a unity of those things from which a novel is compounded," unfavorably comparing it to Saul Bellow's *The Victim*, in which "the passion and the idea are unified, because they have never been separated."[37] In a thoughtful yet ultimately damning review in *Commentary*, Robert Warshow had said something similar the year before: "the problem of feeling—and thus the problem of art—is not faced." Contemporary reviewers of *The Middle of the Journey* often noted the influence of both E. M. Forster and Henry James on Trilling's fiction, especially Forster. According to Warshow, Trilling learned to employ the melodramatic incident from Forster, but never to good effect because of his "tendency to place upon the material a greater weight of meaning than it can bear."[38] A good example of bad Trilling from the second novel is Vincent's epiphany about Buxton. On his first meeting, because the elderly man allows his amanuensis to stay, Vincent intuits Buxton's dialectical imagination, moral realism, and tragic heroism. The incident is not equal to the burden of significance Trilling heaps upon it, and so Vincent's insight is not one the reader can share. Here and elsewhere in the unfinished novel—Garda Thorne's epiphany of middle age is another example—Trilling violates the first rule of the creative writing workshop to show, not tell. He was a Jamesian observer but not a Jamesian dramatist.

Trilling could have continued to write short stories, where his inability to develop the narrative stakes would not present the problem it did in longer works. Indeed, he continued to record ideas for stories in his notebooks into the 1960s. Or, again following the example of James, he could have tried his hand at the memoir or travel writing, genres equipped with a narrative framework.[39] He would have been offended by any suggestion that he stick to lesser forms, however. Despite all his talk of novel writing as a trade, Trilling never managed to demystify the Great American Novel; for better or worse, he shared the assumptions of his generation. As Harold Outram says, "it was the novel or nothing." The aria that Trilling sings to James's moral realism in "The Princess Casamassima," the extravagance and passion of his claims on behalf of the Master, voice his own affirmation as a novelist in defiance of reviewers such as Warshow. "How dared I presume?" he sarcastically asked in his notebook in 1947, as he was "presuming" again in another novel (Notebook 9:101). In the late 1940s and early 1950s, he still dared to be "a professor and a man! and a writer!" conflating masculinity and novel writing in his own professional identity as he had in James's. One of his most poignant notebook reflections written during this period sounds a rare note of confidence in his creative powers and his unfinished novel:

> There comes the impulse to take myself more seriously, for although measured against what I admire I give myself no satisfaction, yet against what I live with I have something to say and give and might really interest myself—and all this gives to the novel a new validity—the notion is right and I

begin to see it substantially—for that old man of mine represents all that I am feeling. (Notebook 11)

When Trilling reached his impasse, however, he gave up being a "writer," according to his own lights. It was the novel or nothing.

Notes

1. Lionel Trilling, "Some Notes for an Autobiographical Lecture," in Diana Trilling, ed., *The Last Decade: Essays and Reviews* (New York: Harcourt Brace Jovanovich, 1979), 227.

2. Cynthia Ozick, "The Buried Life," review of *The Moral Obligation to Be Intelligent*, Leon Wieseltier, ed., *The New Yorker*, 2 Oct. 2000, 120.

3. Lionel Trilling to Richard Chase, 1 June 1947, Richard Chase Papers, Columbia University Library.

4. Lionel Trilling, "Novel [untitled]," Box 40, Folder 7, Lionel Trilling Papers, Columbia University Library. In addition to the novel, the folder includes a twelve-page prospectus ("Trilling's Preface"), and a ten-page evaluation written well into the novel's composition ("Trilling's Commentary"). For a more detailed discussion, see my "Note on the Manuscript and Related Materials." Trilling's difficulties in moving forward in the novel, quoted in the text, appear in the commentary, 161. All subsequent references to the novel, the preface, or the commentary will be cited parenthetically in the text.

5. In the preface, Trilling compares the impact that Buxton's folly will have on his admirers to the situation in "Of This Time, Of That Place" (l). In this 1943 story, probably Trilling's best known, an assistant professor named Joseph Howe empathizes with but finally withdraws from an intelligent but eccentric and disturbed student, Ferdinand Tertan. In the novel it is the mature figure, Buxton, who is "insane" and the young man, Hammell, who must face the moral dilemma of extricating himself. In both narratives, the protagonist feels vulnerable; his purchase on the profession he has chosen is tenuous, held on sufferance. He has too much to lose in his association with the misfit whom he both identifies with and must exorcise.

6. Vincent observes Marion trying to swim in the Outrams' pool, and in some handwritten notes accompanying the manuscript, Diana Trilling mentions learning to swim in friends' pools in 1948 and again in the 1960s. Obviously, she saw a connection between herself and Marion. Marion's nickname, moreover, is "Marry." The initial reaction of Vincent and Marion to each other, however, is mutual antagonism. Regarding the parallel between the Hollowells and the

Crooms, Trilling refers to Mr. Hollowell as Julian in the preface, but he is called Arthur in the novel proper.

7. Lionel and Diana Trilling in the first decade of their marriage were financially insecure. No doubt "the City University"—that is, City College—and the ranks of the lower middle class haunted Trilling as his unhappy fate should he lose his precarious hold at Columbia. See Diana Trilling, *The Beginning of the Journey: The Marriage of Diana and Lionel Trilling* (New York: Harcourt Brace, 1993), 163–73, 266–70.

8. Vincent's family situation resembles Trilling's own. Born in London, Fannie Cohen Trilling was a cultivated woman who encouraged her son's literary interests. (When he was first rejected from Columbia, she managed to get him admitted.) David Trilling was sent to America in disgrace for forgetting his bar mitzvah speech and ruining his chance for the rabbinate. Although he became a successful tailor, he failed in the manufacturing business, and Lionel was obliged to support his parents during the depression (D. Trilling, *Beginning*, 18, 24–25, 31–34, 39).

9. D. Trilling, *Beginning*, 145; Mark Krupnick, *Lionel Trilling and the Fate of Cultural Criticism* (Evanston, IL: Northwestern University Press, 1986), 22–25, 31n.

10. Notebook 7, Lionel Trilling, Notebooks, ms., 2001 Addition, Lionel Trilling Papers, Columbia University Library. The notebooks have been numbered (not by Trilling); they are rarely paginated. Subsequent references to them will be cited parenthetically in the text by number; citations of Notebook 9 will include page numbers. Some excerpts were published in *Partisan Review*; the editor points out that the notebooks "were not a conventional diary. They contain comments on books, people and happenings in his life, records of certain important events, suggestions for stories and novels." "From the Notebooks of Lionel Trilling," *Partisan Review* 3–4 (1984): 496n.

11. Outram's career prior to the Peck directorship seems to be a composite, alluding to Whittaker Chambers (the model for Gifford Maxim in *The Middle of the Journey*), Dwight Macdonald, and possibly Robert Cantwell. Chambers wrote for *Time* after he broke from the Communist Party, and Macdonald, the maverick *Partisan Reviewer*, worked at *Fortune*. An acquaintance of F. W. Dupee, Trilling's colleague at Columbia, Cantwell published a well-received radical novel, *The Land of Plenty* (1934), and wrote for Luce publications; in the early 1940s, he suffered a nervous collapse.

12. In her autobiography, Diana Trilling echoes Outram's commentary on the novel's importance for her and Lionel's generation. "Ours was a society in which there could be few more significant accomplishments than to write a novel. Young writers did not talk of the slow difficult process of building a literary career or producing a body of work but only of 'a' novel, the single much-to-

be-heralded volume which would justify a life and no doubt remake the world" (*Beginning* 127). Lionel Trilling, in "Art and Fortune" (1948), describes how the novel had come to be overvalued in American cultural life: "*the* Great American Novel ... was always imagined to be as solitary and omniseminous as the Great White Whale" (*The Liberal Imagination: Essays on Literature and Society* [1950; New York: Harcourt Brace Jovanovich, 1979], 261).

13. Lionel Trilling, "The Lesson and the Secret," in Diana Trilling, ed., "*Of This Time, Of That Place" and Other Stories* (New York: Harcourt Brace Jovanovich, 1979), 69–71.

14. Carol Brightman, *Writing Dangerously: Mary McCarthy and Her World* (New York: Clarkson Potter, 1992), 224.

15. In the late nineteenth century, Walter Gilbey was a successful businessman of Essex, England. Trilling has transposed his name for an American Essex businessman.

16. Wharton's and Bosanquet's recollections appear in Simon Nowell-Smith, ed., *The Legend of the Master* (New York: Charles Scribner's Sons, 1948), 6, 7.

17. William Barrett, "What Is the 'Liberal Mind'?," *Partisan Review* 16 (1949): 331–36, and Lionel Trilling, Richard Chase, and William Barrett, "The Liberal Mind: Two Communications and a Reply," *Partisan Review* 16 (1949): 649–65.

18. Lionel Trilling, "The Head and the Heart of Henry James," review of *Henry James: The Major Phase* by F. O. Matthiessen, in Diana Trilling, ed., *Speaking of Literature and Society* (New York: Harcourt Brace Jovanovich, 1980), 205–6, and "The Personal Figure of Henry James," review of *Henry James: The Untried Years, 1843–1870* by Leon Edel, *The Griffin* 2 (1953): 3.

19. Henry James, "Preface to *The Aspern Papers*," in Richard P. Blackmur, ed., *The Art of the Novel: Critical Prefaces* (New York: Charles Scribner's Sons, 1937), 163, 164.

20. The old man, who appears at first to be a rock, recalls Trilling's comments in "Wordsworth and the Rabbis" (1950). "Wordsworthian courage,... the courage of mute, insensate things," says Trilling, is represented by the Leech Gatherer, "who is like some old, great rock" (*The Opposing Self: Nine Essays in Criticism* [1955; New York: Harcourt Brace Jovanovich, 1978], 114–15).

21. Daniel O'Hara, *Lionel Trilling: The Work of Liberation* (Madison: University of Wisconsin Press, 1988), 111. Michael E. Nowlin, "'Reality in America' Revisited: Modernism, the Liberal Imagination, and the Revival of Henry James," *Canadian Review of American Studies* 23 (1993): 17. Morris Dickstein, *Double Agent: The Critic and Society* (New York: Oxford University Press, 1992), 74–75. Krupnick, *Fate of Cultural Criticism*, 71–72.

22. Lionel Trilling, "The Princess Casamassima," in *The Liberal Imagination*, 58. Subsequent references to this essay will be cited parenthetically in the text.

23. Diana Trilling, "The Oppenheimer Case: A Reading of the Testimony," *Partisan Review* 21 (1954): 619.

24. Buxton's nuclear capabilities bring to mind Outram's description of the novel as one, big, enormous bomb that would blow the world to bits and also the job offer (extended to Hammell) that glows like a radioactive mineral. Trilling appears to be recasting Jamesian fantasies of Napoleonic will for the atomic age.

25. Alfred Habegger associates "the Master's" appeal with their political disillusionment. "The Partisan Reviewers loved James," he says, "because his fiction supplied the ideal material prop—highbrow fantasy masquerading as realism—for mandarins on the margins of American political life" (*Gender, Fantasy, and Realism in American Literature* [New York: Columbia University Press, 1982], 295). Nowlin more sympathetically argues that James provided a way to address the relationship between high culture and politics. These critics saw the experimental, antimimetic tendencies of modernism as inherently revolutionary, as opposed to the reactionary realist aesthetic of the official Left. In his "formal ingenuity" and "integrity of vision," James anticipated this revolutionary modernism. Initially, at least, the recuperation of James was an adversarial project of critics who were just beginning to identify themselves as American (see "'Reality in America' Revisited" 3–4). Elaborating on the immigrant theme, Jonathan Freedman has recently advanced the provocative and highly nuanced argument that Trilling reconstructed James as a Jew in order to reconstruct himself as Henry James, thereby legitimizing his own authority as a cultural spokesman and "mak[ing] 'culture,' as an idiom, and the pursuit of literary high culture, as a practice, safe for postwar Jewish intellectuals" (*The Temple of Culture: Assimilationism and Anti-Semitism in Literary Anglo-America* [New York: Oxford University Press, 2000], 199, 192–99 passim).

26. Lionel Trilling, "Our Culture: Expostulation and Reply," in *Speaking of Literature*, 244.

27. Richard Henke, "The Man of Action: Henry James and the Performance of Gender," *The Henry James Review* 16 (1995): 227–41.

28. Robert J. Corber, *Homosexuality in Cold War America: Resistance and the Crisis of Masculinity* (Durham, NC: Duke University Press, 1997), 3.

29. F. W. Dupee, Trilling's colleague at Columbia, called a chapter of his *Henry James* (New York: Sloane, 1951) "The Lion of Lamb House," and the title of Trilling's review of Nowell-Smith's *The Legend of the Master* was "The Legend of the Lion" (*Kenyon Review* 10 [1948]: 507–10).

30. Leon Edel, *Henry James: The Middle Years, 1882–1895*, vol. 3 (Philadelphia: Lippincott, 1962), 203–7.

31. Lyndall Gordon, *A Private Life of Henry James: Two Women and His Art* (New York: Norton, 1998), 172.

32. Henry James, "Miss Woolson," in Leon Edel, ed., *The American Essays* (Princeton, NJ: Princeton University Press, 1989), 166, 173.

33. Henry James to William Dean Howells, 21 Feb. 1884, *The Letters of Henry James*, vol. 1, ed. Percy Lubbock (London: Macmillan, 1920), 105–6.

34. Clare Benedict, *Constance Fenimore Woolson* (London: Ellis, 1930), 184–85, 187.

35. John Dwight Kern, *Constance Fenimore Woolson: Literary Pioneer* (Philadelphia: University of Pennsylvania Press, 1934), 118–19.

36. Trilling, "Art and Fortune," 251–53.

37. Leslie Fiedler, "The Fate of the Novel," review of *The Middle of the Journey* by Lionel Trilling, *Kenyon Review* 10 (1948): 526.

38. Robert Warshow, "The Legacy of the 30's: Middle-Class Culture and the Intellectuals' Problem," review of *The Middle of the Journey* by Lionel Trilling, *Commentary* 4 (1947): 543, 544.

39. According to Diana Trilling, her husband had started to work on an intellectual memoir just before his death (*Beginning* 23–24)

Bibliography

Arac, Jonathan. *Critical Genealogies: Historical Situations for Postmodern Literary Studies*. New York: Columbia University Press, 1987.

Barrett, William. "What Is the 'Liberal Mind'?" *Partisan Review* 16 (1949): 331–36.

Benedict, Clare. *Constance Fenimore Woolson*. Vol. 2 of *Five Generations (1785–1923)*. London: Ellis, 1930.

Brightman, Carol. *Writing Dangerously: Mary McCarthy and Her World*. New York: Clarkson Potter, 1992.

Corber, Robert J. *Homosexuality in Cold War America: Resistance and the Crisis of Masculinity*. Durham, NC: Duke University Press, 1997.

Dickstein, Morris. *Double Agent: The Critic and Society*. New York: Oxford University Press, 1992.

Dupee, F. W. *Henry James*. New York: Sloane, 1951.

Edel, Leon. *Henry James: The Middle Years, 1882–1895*. Vol. 3. Philadelphia: Lippincott, 1962.

Fiedler, Leslie. "The Fate of the Novel." Review of *The Middle of the Journey* by Lionel Trilling. *Kenyon Review* 10 (1948): 519–27.

Freedman, Jonathan. *The Temple of Culture: Assimilation and Anti-Semitism in Literary Anglo-America*. New York: Oxford University Press, 2000.

Geismar, Maxwell. *Henry James and the Jacobites*. Boston: Houghton Mifflin, 1963.

Gordon, Lyndall. *A Private Life of Henry James: Two Women and His Art*. New York: Norton, 1998.

Habegger, Alfred. *Gender, Fantasy, and Realism in American Literature*. New York: Columbia University Press, 1982.

Henke, Richard. "The Man of Action: Henry James and the Performance of Gender." *The Henry James Review* 16 (1995): 227–41.

James, Henry. Letter to William Dean Howells, 21 Feb. 1884. *The Letters of Henry James*, 2 vols. Ed. Percy Lubbock. London: Macmillan, 1920, 1:103–6.

———. "Miss Woolson." In Leon Edel, ed., *The American Essays*. 1956; reprint, Princeton, NJ: Princeton University Press, 1989, 162–74.

———. "Preface to *The Aspern Papers*." In Richard P. Blackmur, ed., *The Art of the Novel: Critical Prefaces*. New York: Charles Scribner's Sons, 1937, 159–79.

Kern, John Dwight. *Constance Fenimore Woolson: Literary Pioneer*. Philadelphia: University of Pennsylvania Press, 1934.

Krupnick, Mark. *Lionel Trilling and the Fate of Cultural Criticism*. Evanston, IL: Northwestern University Press, 1986.

McCarthy, Mary. *The Company She Keeps*. New York: Simon and Schuster, 1942.

Nowell-Smith, Simon, ed. *The Legend of the Master*. New York: Charles Scribner's Sons, 1948.

Nowlin, Michael E. "'Reality in America' Revisited: Modernism, the Liberal Imagination, and the Revival of Henry James." *Canadian Review of American Studies* 23 (1993): 1–29.

O'Hara, Daniel. *Lionel Trilling: The Work of Liberation*. Madison: University of Wisconsin Press, 1988.

Ozick, Cynthia. "The Buried Life." Review of *The Moral Obligation to Be Intelligent*, Leon Wieseltier, ed. *The New Yorker*, 2 Oct. 2000, 116–27.

Trilling, Diana. *The Beginning of the Journey: The Marriage of Diana and Lionel Trilling*. New York: Harcourt Brace, 1993.

———. "The Oppenheimer Case: A Reading of the Testimony." *Partisan Review* 21 (1954): 604–35.

Trilling, Lionel. Papers. Novel [untitled], ts. Box 40, Folder 7. Notebooks, ms. 2001 Addition. Columbia University Library, New York.

———. "Art and Fortune." In *The Liberal Imagination*, 240–63.

———. "From the Notebooks of Lionel Trilling." *Partisan Review* 51 (1984): 496–515.

———. "The Head and Heart of Henry James." Review of *Henry James: The Major Phase* by F. O. Matthiessen. In Diana Trilling, ed., *Speaking of Literature and Society*. New York: Harcourt Brace Jovanovich, 1980, 202–6.

———. "The Legend of the Lion." Review of *The Legend of the Master*, Simon Nowell-Smith, ed. *Kenyon Review* 10 (1948): 507–10.

——. "The Lesson and the Secret." In Diana Trilling, ed., *"Of This Time, of That Place" and Other Stories*. New York: Harcourt, Brace Jovanovich, 1979, 58–71.

——. Letter to Richard Chase. 1 June 1947. Richard Chase Papers. Columbia University Library, New York.

——. *The Liberal Imagination: Essays on Literature and Society*. 1950; reprint, New York: Harcourt Brace Jovanovich, 1979.

——. *"Of This Time, Of That Place" and Other Stories*. Ed. Diana Trilling. New York: Harcourt, Brace Jovanovich, 1979.

——. "Our Culture: Expostulation and Reply." In *Speaking of Literature and Society*, 239–48.

——. "The Personal Figure of Henry James." Review of *Henry James: The Untried Years, 1843–1870* by Leon Edel. *The Griffin* 2 (1953): 1–4.

——. "The Princess Casamassima." In *The Liberal Imagination*, 56–88.

——. "Reality in America." In *The Liberal Imagination*, 3–20.

——. "Some Notes for an Autobiographical Lecture." In Diana Trilling, ed., *The Last Decade: Essays and Reviews*. New York: Harcourt Brace Jovanovich, 1979, 226–41.

——. "Wordsworth and the Rabbis." In *The Opposing Self: Nine Essays in Criticism*. 1955; reprint, New York: Harcourt Brace Jovanovich, 1978, 104–32.

Trilling, Lionel, Richard Chase, and William Barrett. "The Liberal Mind: Two Communications and a Reply." *Partisan Review* 16 (1949): 649–65.

Warshow, Robert. "The Legacy of the 30's: Middle-Class Culture and the Intellectuals' Problem." Review of *The Middle of the Journey* by Lionel Trilling. *Commentary* 4 (1947): 538–45.

Woolson, Constance Fenimore. *East Angels*. New York: Harper and Brothers, 1886.

a note on the manuscript and related materials

The unfinished novel in the Lionel Trilling Papers at Columbia University is accompanied by two prefaces by Trilling. The first, twelve pages long, appears to be a book proposal, although it is not clear whether Trilling drafted this for himself or a particular editor. The second, ten pages long, in rougher draft than anything else, is an appraisal of the project at a slightly earlier point in its composition than the extant twenty-four chapters (names and narrative details differ, and nothing beyond chapter 20 is mentioned). In the present volume these documents are called, respectively, "Trilling's Preface" and "Trilling's Commentary." A few short notes in Diana Trilling's hand are also enclosed in the folder, and notes in her hand appear on the margins in chapter 4 and chapter 11, pointing out the repetition of a descriptive paragraph about Vincent's neighborhood.

The novel itself is 239 pages long, in mostly clean typescript; it is composed of 24 chapters identified by roman numerals, with each chapter paginated separately. Two different chapters are identified as chapter X, and there is no chapter XXI. I have dispensed with the roman numerals, called the chronologically "second" tenth chapter chapter 11, and numbered the rest of the chapters consecutively. Chapter 21 may be lost, or Trilling may have misnumbered his manuscript, as there is no obvious narrative gap between chapters 21 and 23.

I have silently inserted Trilling's handwritten corrections when they occasionally appear and indicate blanks where he left them. I have also corrected typos, inconsistencies in capitalization and spacing, and the rare misspelling; my occasional emendations are enclosed within brackets. In chapters 1 and 2 especially there are some underlined or circled words and some phrases enclosed in parentheses. Possibly Trilling had started another cycle of editing, but as his intentions are ambiguous, these markings are neither represented nor addressed here. Trilling hyphenates "to-morrow" as well as compound words such as dining-room, dance-card, bed-lamp, and plate-glass; on the other hand, he does not hyphenate "middle class" or "oaklike." I have retained his hyphenations, and nonhyphenations, for their period flavor. Because Trilling's punctuation is a characteristic of his style, I have not inserted commas after introductory elements, between coordinating adjectives, before the coordinating conjunction in a compound sentence, or after the penultimate item in a series. The one exception to this policy is quotation marks. Trilling often, but not consistently, puts the period or comma after the closing quotation marks, following the British style; however, I conform to American usage and put them within.

The short story Trilling published from the manuscript, "The Lesson and the Secret," helps date the composition of the novel, but the question then arises whether the novel gave birth to the story or vice versa. A close examination of the notebooks reveals that the former was the case. Trilling started writing this novel a few years before *The Middle of the Journey*. There are notes on Walter Savage Landor dating from around 1940 (Notebook 4), but Notebook 7, which fortunately is dated by Trilling, October 1944–September 1945, provides evidence that the novel was well under way and the characters established. About one third of the way through, there are a number of working notes on specific characters: "For Philip Dyas—have him struggle against tobacco"; Linda Hollowell "is too simply pretty," she should be "more angular." Trilling filed away elder colleague H. R. Steeves's appearance—"lips reddened & swollen" from some illness—for Buxton, and he also noted with satisfaction that an engaging elderly man he'd met, W. A. Nilson, "substantiates admirably my view of Buxton's age and manner." A character Trilling refers to as "E." appears to be an early version of Garda Thorne. In this notebook, Trilling also recounts with frustration a lunch with William Maxwell of *The New Yorker*, who apparently rejected "The Lesson and the Secret."

trilling's preface

I am sure there is no need for me to explain why I do not want to make a precise formulation of my novel so early in the game. A novel must eventually be conceived through its writing even more than through its originating idea and an abstract statement of the story's impulses at this point might well freeze them and make them useless. But perhaps I can sufficiently indicate the intention of the novel by giving something of the history of its development. I should warn you that this is only an account of how the idea was generated and does not undertake to be anything like a literal description of the form the idea will take as I write it.

The ideas came to me as I was reading a new life of Walter Savage Landor. The sad grotesque incident which concluded Landor's life immediately presented itself to me as a remarkably attractive theme for a novel for it has a classic and tragic simplicity, yet at the same time it is beautifully fitted to accommodate whatever detail I might want to supply it with. It is a coherent and dramatic story of mounting intensity, bound to shape and control whatever variety I might want to invent for it.

The Landor story is a tangled one and I shall not try to give it in all its bewildering detail. In essence this is what happened:—Landor was a man of naïve, passionate energy; both in political and in personal matters he had a huge indiscriminate generosity of feeling. From his own family, however, he was unable to win any reciprocal emotion. His wife, many years his junior, had long been unfaithful to him; and she had come to hate him intensely. His children, whom he adored, had been turned against him by their mother, and although Landor seems to have done everything possible for their welfare, even to making over to them the larger part of the income from his estates, they despised and mocked him. He was literally persecuted in his own home. Unable to endure such a family life, Landor left Florence, where he had been long established, and came to England, settling in Bath.

Landor was sixty-three when he returned to England. His age is important to the story; he was nearly ninety when he died and the incident which attracted me took place when he was in his eighties. In his old age he was often ill but he was always mentally vigorous—his great *Hellenics* appeared when he was seventy-two, some of his best *Imaginary Conversations* when he was seventy-eight; two of his best poems are "On His Seventy-Fifth Birthday" and "To My Ninth Decade."

Although Landor's fame had always been rather esoteric in the romantic period to which he properly belonged (he was born only five years later than Wordsworth), in the Victorian time he began to be more widely esteemed. To many young people he was a kind of monument of the great days of romanticism, a bridge to the heroic time of poetry. He made many friends among the young literary people of both sexes. They gave him admiration and affection and he gave them what may well have been all the paternal feelings that had been frustrated in his own family. Perhaps just as he was a monument for the young, they stood for him as the memorials of his own youth.

The last young person to whom Landor became attached was a certain Geraldine Hooper. She had been introduced to Landor by a neighbor in Bath, the Hon. Mrs. Yescombe. Mrs. Yescombe had no real right to the Hon. which she sported—she improperly retained it from her first marriage to the younger son of a lord. She was now married to a clergyman of vague character and function who nevertheless, in so far as he figures in the story, manages to emanate an aura of subtle corruptness. It seems pretty clear that Mrs. Yescombe introduced young Geraldine to Landor with a motive. She knew Landor's weakness for young people and there is little doubt that she was using Geraldine as a bait to accomplish her own purposes with Landor. In all that followed Geraldine seems to have been foolish, passive and innocent. She was only sixteen, she was not very bright and she had been put into Mrs. Yescombe's care as a paying guest by parents who were not able to cope with some sort of emotional difficulty from which she suffered. Landor liked to be generous with gifts; in order to advance Geraldine's career in music, he made her several presents of money. He also gave her some of his Italian paintings. These were actually not of great value, for Landor was always being fooled about old pictures, but he believed that they were priceless and Mrs. Yescombe, who seems to have accepted his valuation, was most eager to secure them. Landor's gifts to Geraldine were usually made through Mrs. Yescombe; they seldom reached their destination. And the lady was apparently after more loot and even had hopes of figuring in Landor's will.

From here on the story gets indescribably complicated; I summarize at the cost of innumerable details.

Landor began to suspect Mrs. Yescombe. He heard stories to her disadvantage—of her cheating servants, of her filching petty sums from shopkeepers' tills. He began to believe that she steamed open his letters and took out money. He believed that she was trying to manipulate his actions. He learned of the misappropriation of his gifts to Geraldine. He also began to believe that Mrs. Yescombe's influence over Geraldine was a malign one; and it is almost certainly true that Mrs. Yescombe had corrupted the girl sexually.

Landor, having conceived a moral horror of Mrs. Yescombe, found that all his passion for justice, all his fierce romantic morality dictated to him the conviction that he ought to expose and denounce her, no matter what the cost to himself. He made statements, wrote letters, threatened public denunciation. Mrs. Yescombe and her husband pleaded with him to be lenient and keep silence; but he was adamant. He prepared a pamphlet and could not be persuaded by John Forster (the prudent friend, business agent and censor of Dickens and later the inaccurate biographer of Landor himself) from having it printed. He wrote epigrams against Mrs. Yescombe, some of them obscene in the Roman satiric manner, and these he included in his newest collection of poems.

The Yescombes brought suit. On the advice and under the pressure of friends—Forster chief among them—Landor yielded, and the case was settled out of court by his reluctant retraction and apology.

But after a time Landor received further evidence against Mrs. Yescombe, including a confirmation of his suspicion that she had corrupted Geraldine. He now felt that, come what might, he must wipe out the Yescombe infamy. He knew that if he published again he would certainly be adjudged guilty of libel. If guilty the obloquy as well as the financial penalty he would face would be so great as to drive him from England. Were that to happen, his only course would be to return to Florence and become dependent on his persecuting family.

He decided that he must publish the truth and take the consequences. He was eighty-one years old.

Landor's decision was in the tradition of his youth. He was still the man who, at thirty-three, had raised and armed a regiment to support the Spanish revolutionists against Napoleon and he himself had been its colonel. But it is clear that his unshakable determination in the Yescombe matter was an insane obsession. His obduracy brings to mind Wordsworth's poem about the flower that had outgrown its ability to fold itself against the storm:

> It doth not love the shower, nor seek the cold:
> This neither is its courage nor its choice,
> But its necessity in being old.

Yet Landor's action has all the *appearance* of courage and choice; and certainly it would not have been undertaken by anyone who was not by past temperament eminently courageous.

The case came to trial, the trial went against Landor, the court-room scene was horrible, the response of the press was ferocious; he was everywhere denounced as a vicious and obscene old man and the Yescombes were vindicated.

There was little that Landor's friends could do. Some did that little, others slipped quietly away. Now the return to Florence was inevitable. And by now he had surrendered the last vestige of economic hold over his by now depraved family. His worst fears were quite confirmed—the old man was so badgered that, one day, unable to endure any longer, he fled the house and Robert Browning found him roaming the streets of Florence dirty and deranged. Through Browning's efforts he was comfortably established for his last days. Up to his death he was obsessed by Mrs. Yescombe's iniquities, maddened by the thought that she now enjoyed his money, tortured by the world's foolishness and injustice.

This—possibly with some inaccuracy, for I have not bothered to check my memory of the details—is the story that attracted me. I scarcely need point out that I do not plan to "re-create" this story, nor to tell it in any literal historical way. For one thing, my novel is to be a novel of contemporary life; the 19th century episode simply suggested an idea which satisfies my very strong feeling (I have expressed it critically in my *E. M. Forster*) that a novel must have all the primitive elements of story and even of plot—suspense, surprise, open drama and even melodrama.

My first interest in Landor was in the heroic size of the man—he was physically big, and then there was his careless fighting past (his middle name was used as a descriptive nickname: he could be savage), the great age to which he lived, the hugeness of his classical scholarship (he wrote Latin more easily than English), the breadth of his emotions, the intransigence of his poetical and political ideals, the absoluteness of all his passions. Inevitably he suggests King Lear by his "kingliness," his leonine qualities, his absoluteness; and morally by his utter refusal to submit to reality; and then of course by the external facts of his story. Like Lear's, his story is about justice. But Lear learns about justice through suffering, which is brought on by his acting with absolute passion, while Landor's absolute passion from which he suffers is, from the first, exactly a passion *for* justice.

Such a man was startling enough in Victorian England. I began to think what a really heroic person like him might be in modern America. Interesting in himself, he would be even more interesting in his effect upon the people around him. Such a person would become enshrined in the minds of lesser people; a circle of admirers would naturally form around him and draw a kind of life from him. Such people would admire him not so much for his present power—they would perhaps assume he had none—but for his being a symbol of past power, the way everyone gets to admire a dead revolutionist; his quiescence would be the condition of their love.

Suppose such a man, made into a legend and monument of himself. Suppose him now to begin to act on his own great scale and according to the lights that made him admired, his action being one like Landor's, just and right, but naïve, scandalous and impossible, an action that makes a perfect dilemma. It would be like an extinct volcano suddenly erupting; among the people who lived on its slopes a mighty disturbance would be caused. And if these people were, as they could be, significant of the life of the period, the disturbance would bring out in a dramatic way the real assumptions—what in current jargon is being called the "mystique"—of their various positions.

The dominant figure of my story is to be such a character. He will have much of the quality and temperament of Landor—a very old and very impressive man who had lived richly and daringly and had accomplished much; his existence beyond the life of his own generation gives him the appearance of the naïveté and simplicity we like to associate with "the heroic." Around him there is to be a group of people, all of considerable stature, though looking to the old man for the secret of strength and dignity.

Of this group, there is one member whose relation to the old hero is particularly interesting and significant. He is a young man, just starting in life as the old man is approaching his end. This relation to the whole affair, to the "disturbance," is a critical factor in his life, for such a young man, if he lived in a group like the one I have in mind, would be presented with all the materials of an "education," not in the usual novelistic way of giving the young hero a linear series of adventures but by involving him in an intense dramatic incident in which characters of some meaning in our civilization are also involved.

The social group I have in mind will be located in a New England town of considerable tradition, inhabited by old families but also by New Yorkers of some importance. We might imagine Concord, Deerfield, Lennox, with a population something like that of Westport. In the district there is a famous school which is to provide some of the characters, among them a significant Headmaster, as well as a significant teacher and his wife (for the Yescombe-characters?) [sic].

We have, then, a great central figure with his aura of heroism and heroic morality, and all the implications about human personality which are raised by his senile obsession—implications similar to but larger than those that arise from my story, "Of This Time, Of That Place." Then we have a young hero at the crucial point in his moral development. And we have the sketch for a social group.

Our young man, as I now think, will enter the story at the point of his entry into the social group, which to him is to seem complex and difficult. This is his first real step into the world. Born and brought up in a large middle-western city, he has been put at a considerable disadvantage by his parents' lower middle class poverty. Yet within a narrow ambit he has made a certain place for himself. His ambitions are intellectual and, at twenty-four, he has won some intellectual distinction in his own city. Think of him as doing a variety of unsatisfactory jobs—he has a part time teaching position at the local college, he reviews books, he gives lectures on modern literature at women's clubs, he writes a little advertising copy for a local art dealer, and sometimes he interviews literary notables for a local newspaper. Think of him as practical, energetic, not a dreamer or a mooncalf. He has real talent and he does not have the mechanical "shyness" of a sensitive young hero; indeed, one of the notable things about him is his active charm. He has what in a young man passes for maturity. He is decent, generous; but he is achingly ambitious. He has considerable insight into the conditions of his society, he wishes to be genuine, a man of integrity; yet he also wishes to be successful. His problem is to advance his fortunes and still be an honest man. He is conscious of all the dangers; he is literate and knows the fates of Julien Sorel, of Rastignac, of Frederic Moreau—all the defeated and disintegrated young men of the great 19th century cycle of failure. He, for his part, is determined not to make their mistakes.

His entry into the story is effected by a character as yet unnamed—call him X. In his late thirties, X is brilliantly established in the world by a complication of professions; it is at least a question if he has not made his success by some compromise with his best talents. (This presents a nice problem of invention to suggest something *Time*-ish and *Fortune*-ish, with something of a less anonymous nature.) He visits the city of our young hero, who is sent to interview him.

Our young man quite consciously sees X as a possible instrument of escape from his provincial situation, but he is only half conscious of the method he uses to involve X with himself. For X is caught by the young man's innocence—it suggests his own at that age (or so he imagines)—and he is also caught by the boy's possibility of duplicating his career, thereby justifying its falsifications. As for our young man, he responds both to X's feeling for his innocence and to X's feeling for his corruptibility. And so, in a rather tense scene, the two proceed through antagonism—the hero jealous of the older man's power, X jealous of the younger man's youth—to a complex involvement. And when our young man, knowing that X is a member of the community in which the old hero lives, speaks, with a quickly conceived intention, of his admiration for our Lear-Landor character and of his desire, never felt before this minute, to write a biography of the hero, X undertakes to further this scheme by bringing the young man to the old one. Through his friendship with the Headmaster of the school, he procures our young man a teaching job with the express purpose of enabling him to be near Landor-Lear and to undertake the biography.

In this way our young man, both provincial and sophisticated, both honest and scheming, is introduced with some drama into the scene in which the action takes place. The nature of the society in the town is such that he must inevitably meet people who can help him better himself—and tempt him.

What we now have is the young man in intimate relation to the old hero (assume him accepted as official Boswell-Eckermann); we have him in relation to X, a person of considerable stature and complexity; and we have him necessarily in relation to the Headmaster, a young man of pronounced spiritual views whose part in the story will be large.

What is needed now is the filling out of the social picture (there are as yet, it will have been noticed, no women in these notes) and the adaptation of the Landor story to suit the requirements of the novel and of modern sensibility.

Speaking in the most general way, the story follows this sequence: the entrance of the young man into the new social world and his first meeting with people of importance; his love experience; his relations with the ancient hero; the developing scandal; the complex responses of the community to the scandal; his own feelings and action in the case; the formal resolution of the story in the death of the ruined old man; the resolution of the young hero's own life.

The young hero, then, is to be the carrier of the thread of the story; he is not, however, to be perfectly the center of the interest—clearly the old man will dispute that with him, not to mention X, the headmaster, the several women, the Yescombe-and-Geraldine characters, and others that are knocking for admission.

From this point further detail isn't possible. But I can say a few things about the quality of the story as I want it to be.

First, it is to be above all a *story*. The fable, I think, is of a kind that will inevitably throw off ideas; and the characters are articulate, intelligent and embody certain moralities. But this is not to be a "novel of ideas." The fable was chosen because it is inherently dramatic, and the characters are shaping themselves toward size and the ability to act.

As for the manner of the novel, that will be as simple as possible. I will attempt no "devices," have no foreshortenings, no tricky flashbacks; it will move from scene to scene in the old-fashioned way. The prose is to be equally simple, as unobtrusive as possible and not "internal" to any one of the characters. A great deal in this narrative will depend on the nature of the prose; it must create the right attitude to the characters—it must be at once objective and warm, something like the prose of the story of mine I referred to.

The time of the story will be what, since the war, we can call the recent past—that is, the late thirties: the period when the intense consciousness of the Depression had faded and when the war had not yet become a perfect certainty. The novel will have, I hope, political—that is to say, moral, cultural—reverberations, but no specific political content. The length of the story I of course cannot estimate, but 400 pages seems a desirable length; the nature of the story suggests at least this much expansiveness.

chapter 1

The Tennis Club was a modest affair of six good courts and a small frame clubhouse. It was not far from the heart of the city but it had a pleasant little lawn and a fine large tree shading the verandah. On the farthest court two elderly members were playing their daily game. They were admirable players, quite the pride of the club. Their trousers were of the whitest flannel and they stroked with so grave and rhythmic a skill and they kept the ball so long in play that their game was like a figure in a ballet. A rather noisy game of doubles occupied the court nearest the clubhouse. Two young men, Toss Dodge and Vincent Hammell, were playing on the third court.

Vincent Hammell could usually beat Toss Dodge, but not always. Dodge was really the better player but he was in a relation to Hammell that hurt his game. He could play very well against an opponent who did not make him feel stupid. Even with Hammell he sometimes forgot about himself and then his real game came through. When that happened, Vincent Hammell played far below his own real game because he felt unhappy at having up to then beaten a better man by what amounted to guile.

Tennis was always important to Vincent Hammell and the bad days and the good ones were alike significant. There were certain days when some newly-gained sense told him just where the ball was going to be. On these days it was as if a small brain had established itself in his wrist—without any conscious intention, his racket sent the ball where, if there had been time, reason would have suggested. Usually such days were also the ones when he had before his eyes the correct pattern of the service and could make his body conform to it.

Today he had been granted all the magics. He kept very much to himself on his side of the court, protecting the mystery of his skill from any interruption by his opponent. He also had to protect it from any interruption by himself. If he became too conscious and interfered with it, the favor of this beautiful coordination would vanish.

The first set had gone to Vincent, then Toss Dodge had won the second set, and in the third set Vincent was ahead, three-two. He was getting ready to serve when the doubles game on the first court ended and one of the players, Francis Hammell, his distant cousin, walked over to him. Francis was the night city editor of the *Advertiser*. Vincent held his service and waited for his cousin to come up.

Francis said, "Can you give us a day to-morrow? Malcolm is sick."

Vincent was glad to have the work but he said nothing more than "Sure." Usually he was careful with Francis. The cousinship was vague and there were a few small things that Francis could do for him. But today he handled himself carelessly. He found that being a guest at the club made a difference. So did being flushed and physical and playing well. He was less anxious to be pleasant to Francis than to have Francis leave the court before the pattern of the service should get uncertain in his mind. And Francis, who never treated him with quite enough respect, had now to understand the rights of a man in action. He said, "I'll be seeing you then," and turned to go.

Vincent found that with the racket in his hand and the heavy sweat on his face he did not have to make any answer. He took his position at the baseline. It was not often that all the parts of his young mind and body made so perfect a whole as they did at this moment. Suddenly he felt the impulse to put the inspired moment to some larger use. He decided to believe that if he beat Toss Dodge he would gain something momentous from his interview with Harold Outram. The letter from Outram, sufficiently momentous in itself, was safe in his jacket in the locker room.

He did not know what he could possibly gain from Outram, but he needed help and perhaps Outram was the man to give it. There was enough chance of Toss's beating him to make the game a true hazard. Toss was really the better player but Vincent knew that he could beat Toss if he went about it right. If he allowed Toss to beat him, it could only mean that his intention was not strong.

This wager that Vincent Hammell made with himself was partly fanciful but also partly serious. Young men who consciously thirst for greatness often keep the superstitions of their boyhood and are sometimes impelled to test the power of their stars.

Toss Dodge had not been able to overhear the brief conversation between the Hammell cousins. The world was depressingly full of secrets for Toss and he lost the next game at love. But with the set going his way at four-two, Vincent grew cautious. He began to think about his strokes and Toss took the next game and then the next. Vincent told himself that winning or losing the set could make no real difference. Yet he did not believe this and he was right not to, the wager having once been made.

Early in the next game Vincent had Toss well out of position and the point seemed inevitably his. But he drove the ball wide and lost the point. Toss called out in a large and genial way, "Thank you ever so much."

Vincent was about to make some reply, such as "You're quite welcome, I'm sure," but he checked himself and said nothing. He walked in silence from the net to the baseline. An answer was called for by the tradition of the game's banter, by the habit of his old friendship with Toss, by his conscious desire to be kind, by the very air of mid-western America that he breathed. But he kept silent. He could plainly see Toss's hurt perplexity, but he did not relent. He was able to win the last game easily and take the set.

In the locker room Vincent Hammell shucked off his shorts and shirt and stood before the mirror for a view of himself. He was pleased enough with what he saw. At twenty-three he was just weighty and hairy enough for maturity, yet he was slim enough to make chiefly the impression of youth.

"Narcissismus," he said aloud.

"What did you say?" Toss called from his locker down the aisle.

"Narcissismus!" Vincent called back, not explaining and knowing that Toss would not ask again.

He was in a good humor with himself. He began to sing the grotesque clinical German word to the music of Leporello's aria in *Don Giovanni*. Where Leporello sings "La piccina, la piccina, la piccina," informing us that his master prefers young girls to all other sorts of women, Vincent Hammell sang, "Narcissismus, Narcissismus, Narcissismus," mocking himself. But in Spain, in Spain alone, said the song, there had been a thousand and three—peasant girls and chambermaids, citizenesses and countesses, marchionesses and princesses, femininity of every degree. It was a song not only about women but also about scope and possibility, about a superabundance that never sated, although the joy was in the mind of the servant who counted up the delights, not in the mind of the master who had had them.

When they had showered and dressed, Toss Dodge invited Vincent to a drink. Vincent liked sitting on the club verandah. The club had a good tone although it was not snobbish—he could belong any time he could spare the fifty dollars a year, but that was a long way off.

chapter 2

The friendship between Toss Dodge and Vincent Hammell was nearing its end. They had known each other for twelve years and there was a good chance that neither of them would ever again have a relation with a member of his own sex that would be so pervasive and so pleasurable. They had met when Toss was twelve and Vincent eleven, two mannerly boys and very grave, approaching each other on a sidewalk not so much warily as shyly. They had their manners in common, for the Dodges had come down a little in the world at the time of their meeting and the Hammells had always been rather superior to their own financial position, which, as a matter or fact, was then not too bad.

Mrs. Dodge, who was from the East, with Southern connections, and who did not like or trust this great, "new," shambling city, had spied young Vincent Hammell the day she moved in. She was struck by the admirable shape of his head and the dark handsomeness of his intelligent look. She called him to the attention of her son, who was roving bored and restless amid the moving-in, prowling among the furniture that was being so shamelessly exposed on the sidewalk. "That looks like a nice boy," Mrs. Dodge said, "Why don't you get to know him?"

It was summer and Vincent Hammell had less to do with his days than he needed. There were very few children in the neighborhood and Mrs. Hammell did not like him to wander far from home. Mrs. Hammell was a lonely woman[;] she had become reconciled to her loneliness, believing it to be inevitable at her age, but she was touched by her son's lost fidgeting through the long summer afternoon. Having observed the furniture of the new family with approval of its quality, she saw young Toss Dodge with pleasure and relief.

Her feeling was for Vincent's sake, for the new boy looked like a promising friend. But she was pleased for another reason. Although the new people were moving into a newer and more desirable house than the one the Hammells had, and although their furniture was clearly more elegant than the Hammells', she saw at once that their superiority ended there. When it came to sons, the new family could not equal the Hammells. The new boy was undoubtedly a nice-looking boy, but as he stood watching the van-men, it was clear to Mrs. Hammell that he did not have Vincent's distinction.

And when Mrs. Hammell met Mrs. Dodge, she understood how the difference had originated. Although the boys were almost of the same age, something more than a decade separated the mothers. Mrs. Hammell was in her forties, Mrs. Dodge in her thirties. The decade between them was more than a difference in age. It was part of a difference in culture. Even at Mrs. Dodge's age, Mrs. Hammell had thought of herself as no longer young. But Mrs. Dodge was clearly a young woman. This was apparent not only in her nice figure and pretty legs but also in her bright, cropped hair, her perfume and her way of speech. Mrs. Hammell knew that it was not only because Mrs. Dodge had been born into a more generous time which allowed women to be young longer. It was also because her social class was more fortunate. "Fortunate" was the word, not "better," for Mrs. Hammell thought of her own family as plain but good. Her father had, for a short time, served as a city magistrate and she took pride in her own training and service as a school teacher. But certainly more fortunate, and that accounted for Mrs. Dodge's early marriage and motherhood, as well as her present youth. They were all part of the social establishment that Mrs. Dodge had had in her youth and expected to have again. The two women never became really friends but they respected each other and learned something about each other's past. And the difference in their pasts, far more than any difference in character, accounted to Mrs. Hammell for the difference between their two sons. For Mrs. Hammell saw how relatively little a son *meant* to Mrs. Dodge.

She had to envy, a little, the advantages Mrs. Dodge had had, but she could also see how much Mrs. Dodge had lost by them. For Mrs. Dodge's Toss was but a casual person, a person like any other. But into Vincent had gone the desire, the tension of Mrs. Hammell's own life, the delayed marriage, the delayed and difficult pregnancy, all her will in overcoming difficulties. And the result was to be seen, she felt, in the fineness of her own son's appearance, the alertness and demand of his whole being.

Mrs. Dodge might drink cocktails with her husband before dinner—thus forcing Mrs. Hammell to modify her views, derived only from the newspapers, of the sordidness of illegal liquors—or be playfully spanked by Mr. Dodge in greeting or farewell, or kiss certain men friends who came to visit. And Mr. Dodge, with his long legs, his white shirts with buttoned-down collars and his suits that, as Toss told Vincent, came from "Brooks," with his schemes and his trips and his rolls of blueprints, he might be very different from Mr. Hammell, so quiet a man, who lived his life as an optometrist with so scholarly a reserve. Yet all that fine and rather enviable flair of the Dodge parents had not been able to produce what Mrs. Hammell saw in her own son.

It was not merely motherly pride that made her judgment of Vincent, of that Mrs. Hammell was convinced. She was rather short sighted and a little absent-minded and more than once she had seen the figure of a boy on the street which would strike her with its distinction, so much, indeed, that in her admiration she would feel a pang of jealousy for her own son, until suddenly as the boy came nearer, she would see with gratitude and relief that it was Vincent himself. She was as confirmed as she needed to be in the objectivity of her opinion.

The two boys, Toss and Vincent, when their attention was called to each other, naturally did not directly accept their mothers' suggestion to make acquaintance. Vincent stood on his part of the sidewalk and looked at the newcomer, who looked back and then turned his attention to the moving-men. Vincent kicked his way over to the curb and examined something at the edge of the road. He looked at it with a deep, rather amused curiosity. He touched it with the toe of his shoe. The object, whatever it was, engaged his attention as a Naturalist, a person to whom all things were significant. Actually he was examining nothing at all. But to justify his attention, he picked up a fallen seed-pod, peered at it a moment with a discerning eye, then threw it away, shaking his head in mild disappointment—nothing, after all, out of the ordinary. Meanwhile Toss had taken up a position of responsibility near the van. He stood with his hands behind his back, superintending with quiet vigilance the operations of his men. He said nothing but he was sharp-sighted and a slight frown showed that he was not to be imposed on by his subordinates.

They were both now established in sufficient importance and could acknowledge each other.

Vincent said, "Hello," carelessly, take it or leave it.

Toss answered in kind.

"You moving in?" said Vincent.

"Uh-huh. You live here?"

Vincent showed the direction of his home by a backward movement of his head. He had his mother's consciousness of the superiority of the house the new boy was to live in. But he was not disturbed by that. He held strongly to the belief, which was helped to formulation by certain doctrinal discussions in school, that considerations of social position were contemptible. Still, he was taking the difference into account, just as, when he learned about Toss's New York past, he took that too into account.

They exchanged names. Toss's name, it came out, was really George and he said he did not know why he was called Toss, it was what he had always been called. Much later, when the intimacy had developed, he admitted that he was called Toss because that was the way he had first pronounced his own name. They exchanged ages. Toss took it as a matter of advantage that he was older than Vincent by a year. But Vincent felt the advantage or being the junior and ultimately he enforced this view upon Toss.

Within a few weeks the intimacy between the two boys grew until it reached the point of surfeit. They found that they could not do without each other. Then suddenly it seemed that they could scarcely endure each other's sight, so bored and disgusted did they become. But they survived this period as they survived others of the kind that were to come—their intimacy would reach so far that they expected more from each other than either could supply. They gave each other much, the loyalty, the almost fanatical chivalry that can be given by boys whose parents have been able to spare them the imminent prospect of having to make their way in the world.

It was assumed between them that on the whole Toss was the more practical of the two, the more hard-headed. But they were more inclined to stress the similarities rather than the differences of their characters. For example, they agreed that they were equally idealistic. Toss inaugurated the venture into radio as well as the venture into stamp-collecting. Vincent was not really interested in either activity, but he was willing to go along. He had, as boys do have, an almost ritualistic sense of what was becoming to boyhood. Toss took these commitments to boyish propriety rather more seriously than Vincent. Yet he too actually lived the double life. To the adult world they appeared engagingly enough as "real boys." But the adult world would have been astonished by the gravity and scope of their conversations. Boys then still wore knickerbockers and black stockings and that costume made the discrepancy between their appearance and their talk even greater. They were indefatigable moralists. They judged everything and were great partisans of justice in all things, in their relations with each other, in the discipline of school, in the dealings of shopkeepers and their parents, and even in politics.

When it was time for one of the pair to leave the other's house, he would always make an appeal to be "walked home" and, after some resistance, the appeal was always granted. But then the one who had walked the other home had to be "walked back," and so they would go back and forth, sometimes in the bitter cold, each struggling against being the one to take the last walk alone, until they settled the matter by separating at a point which they believed to be precisely median between the two houses.

At some time in their first year of high school, there was an incident for which Vincent never forgave himself. A Shakespearean company came to town and there were reduced tickets for the Saturday matinees. It was Toss who proposed that they see *Macbeth*. It was Vincent who suddenly felt oppressed by the prospect. "Oh—we're too young for that sort of thing. Tragedy!" he said. And Toss had replied, calm and lofty and priggish, "It's part of the education of a gentleman." Vincent did not know why he had said what he had. Perhaps it was part of the ritual of boyhood, carried too far. Toss's rebuke was humiliating. Vincent felt that in their relation to literature, it was he himself who had the intimacy, that there was something merely assumed in Toss's attitude about tragedy. Later, Toss remembered that remark of Vincent's and used it against his friend.

Who could have known how seriously they lived the heroic life?— how on Saturdays when they had gone off for the day to some wooded place with their knapsacks and had made and eaten one of the two messes they had learned to make from a work on camp cookery (one being of dried beef, the other of canned tuna-fish), they were Martin Arrowsmith and his fierce friend Terry Wickett, toiling together for the pure sake of science in a cabin in Vermont, fiercely contemptuous of all social elegance, despising the distractions of convention. Or they were Dick Heldar and *his* friend Torpenhow before the light failed, exposed to the dangers of the desert and the Mahdi's men—what was the Mahdi?—for the sake of truth and art. They did not, of course, act out these dreams, only used some catchword from the book to indicate their understanding of what they were up to. Each of them was at the same time both Martin Arrowsmith and Terry Wickett, but when it came to *The Light That Failed*, Toss was rather on the Torpenhow side, while Vincent rather fancied the tragedy that was to overtake him as Dick Heldar. It was from the Kipling book, with its strange charm of being far-off in time, yet near in spirit to their boyhood, that they learned their most persistent fancy, of being foreign correspondents who would see and know everything. They dreamed of "travelling light," by which they meant that their "kits" would be cut to a bare minimum of equipment and also that they would have no human ties except, of course, their partnership with each other.

Lust itself was no less involved in their sense of the heroic and it was *The Man Who Laughs* that led them to talk, guardedly, of their sexual hopes. They never confided to each other how frequently and how seriously the scene of Gwynplane in _____'s [blank in original] bedroom engaged their nocturnal thoughts.

[One line blank in original]

but they drew closer together in their response to that wonderful moment, relieving the shame of their secrecy by coolly and maturely discussing the future realization of their hopes.

Yet it was over this novel of Victor Hugo's that a certain rift in their friendship developed, to grow with the years. Toss extravagantly admired the opening of the story. "Ursus was a man. Homo was a bear." "God," said Toss, shaking his fist in inexpressible enthusiasm, "that's *writing*." He had a tendency to admire what he called the "true to life" and the "natural" in books, by which he meant a certain brusqueness or a familiarity in the author's prose manner. Vincent did not know why, but he found something irritating in the excessiveness of Toss's admiration of these things, especially of the Hugo passage. It was the first occasion on which Toss seemed alien, a human object to be looked at and considered, not a part of himself.

Together the two boys fought their way forward in the intricate political life of a great high school. They were great admirers of *Babbitt* and *Stalky and Co.* and they kept in their private lives together a certain area in which they mocked all the talk of "service" to the school. But it was their life and they were properly endowed to live it. Neither was heavy enough to think of real football, but they gallantly offered themselves for the form teams which played without helmets or shoulder-pads and they came home bruised and battered from practice. There was the great hierarchy of "squads," which began with the Sanitation Squad, went on to the Traffic Squad and culminated in the almost awful Control Squad which was made up of boys and girls of the most frightening sexual maturity. To this last pinnacle Toss eventually arrived, though neither could ever have dreamed of the possibility of this in the days when both were "humble freshm[e]n."

"Humble freshman" was one of the clichés of the school literary magazine that Vincent fought against when he became its editor-in-chief. Some feeling that he never wholly formulated kept Vincent from wishing to join the Control Squad, although Toss assured him that he could "make" it if he wanted to.

Together they began their experience of girls. Guided by shyness and class feeling, they were attracted only by the nicer girls. Toss was inclined to like girls of a rather passive prettiness, while Vincent preferred girls in whom special charms were to be found by him alone, girls in whom a lack of merely obvious beauty suggested a spiritual or intellectual interest. In their senior year they made the discovery, and pooled their information, that even the well dressed girls Toss knew and even the intellectual girls Vincent knew were accessible and curious. It filled their days with wonder that the hopes begun in the time of *The Man Who Laughs* might yet be fulfilled.

Toss's father was a Yale man and that had decided Toss's choice of a college, which in turn decided Vincent's. Even when the Dodges were not doing well there had been no question but that Toss would go to Yale, for a wealthy uncle was to be relied on. But the uncle was not needed, for Mrs. Dodge came suddenly into the inheritance of a very considerable estate of an aunt of hers, and Mr. Dodge himself, in the very midst of the depression that was making it bewilderingly difficult for Mr. Hammell to approximate his own usually comfortable income, became indisputably a success. The two boys had planned Yale together and they had dreamed of their rooms in Harkness even when the bleak, staring fact in the Hammell home was that the family was no longer in comfortable circumstances. It was for Vincent the first real deprivation of his life that Toss went off to New Haven without him.

Then began the long ending of their friendship. The first year of their separation was no more than sad. They wrote long letters and were glad of the chance to do that. But when Toss came home for Christmas it was he who had had the experience of college and Vincent who had, in decency, to listen to all that his friend had learned. At the City University, which was all that the Hammells could afford for Vincent, there was a kind of "college life," there were fraternities and even an inferior kind of football spirit, there were activities and politics and "big men." But Vincent, thinking of Yale and the quadrangles and towers of Harkness, knew that there was no comfort for him in these imitations. He began to build his own myth of student days, moulding it closer to a French university than to an American or an English one, building it on intellectual activity. Toss, to be sure, was not without his own intellectual life. He had developed a Yale love of eighteenth-century literature and had settled on Smollett as his favorite. He bought a great many books and talked of the wonders of the Brick Row and the treasures of the Elizabethan Club. He even had acquired a political liberalism of which he was rather proud and was a great admirer of Soviet Russia. It was an intellectual life of which Toss was proud, but it did not match Vincent's whose circle at that time was beginning to form as a rather raffish group of Jews, an Armenian who was regarded with awe as a genius in Renaissance scholarship, an Irish boy whose father had had two conversations with Yeats and one with Joyce, and a poor boy from the farm country whose passion for sociology made it inevitable that he should be thought of as a new Thorstein Veblen. With these friends he played handball and enjoyed it, yet it was handball he played, and even though he remembered that it was the game that Stephen Dedalus played with Cranly in *A Portrait of the Artist as a Young Man*, still it was painful to remember that at Yale Toss was playing squash. He never introduced Toss to these friends of his, as much for Toss's sake as theirs, for he knew that they would have been hostile to Toss's polite antiquarianism and even to his good opinion of Russia, for they were in all things complex and complaining minds. They knew that Vincent had wanted to go to Yale and they used to tease him about the gentility of his desires, for they themselves were, or affected to be, pleased with the social inadequacies of the city university. That was the time when the Sterling Library at Yale was being built and Vincent followed the liberal magazines in making it the object of his contempt, what with its telephone booths designed to suggest the confessional booths of a cathedral. He even went so far as to say that Harkness with its English Gothic was a cultural falsehood, thus rejecting something he and Toss had loved together. He said that Connecticut Hall, where Nathan Hale had lived as a student, was the only honest building at Yale. Toss was angry not only because he was being attacked in his university but also because he felt snubbed by the false superiority of Vincent's new circle of friends, which he had never met. He spoke of his disappointment that Vincent should be so "weak" as to accept his opinions from a bunch of screwballs.

"And greaseballs," he had added, blinded by his anger.

It made the occasion of their first real quarrel, the fatal one, the quarrel that set them apart from each other, that established Toss as a man who loved fine leather bindings on his books—"why shouldn't a book be as beautiful as anything else?"—and who intended by his own efforts and his father's help to establish himself in life and in life's fine things, a man who respected the life of the intellect and owned two good Hogarths and a fine print of Fielding's big face; it established Vincent as a reader of Flaubert, Baudelaire and Joyce, a close and careful student of poetry according to the methods of critics Toss never heard of and was not interested in knowing about, a man jealous for the integrity of his own intellect and already planning to make his way by it, a willing wearer of shabby clothes—though here there was not much difference between the two, for the orthodox collegian like the intellectual collegian was already rather shabby in a careful way and Vincent was more elegant in his shabbiness than his own college friends.

What was happening between them happens every year to a few thousand young American men who discover that their special friend has ceased to have all his old value. The lines of communication grow fewer and more conscious. The thinning out of feeling is a slow one and it makes for great, if unspoken, bitterness between the young men. They never lose a kind of interest in each other, the bitterness is even the last stage of their affection, but they become members of different races. One becomes a "business man" and the other an "intellectual." Each one comes to believe that the facts of ingestion, procreation and death are not quite the same with this former friend, once so nearly another self, as with himself.

chapter 3

Even Vincent, who was the one who was aware that the real end must come soon, did not want the break between Toss and himself. They were at their best when they played tennis and did not talk much. This morning on the little verandah of the club, they felt relaxed and clubby. They were able to draw on all their old times together, their old happiness and regard for each other.

"Do you remember," Toss said, "when your cousin Francis looked like God Almighty to us because he was a newspaperman? He was a reporter then, a leg-man."

Toss used the professional phrase with the relish they had shared when, making their plans to be correspondents together, they had admitted that it might be necessary and even useful to begin as leg-men, learning the municipal secrets before they learned the secrets of chancellories.

"That was ten years ago," Vincent said in a large easy way.

"Yes, a good ten years."

They got a common pleasure, at their age, from being able to express their past in so full a figure. Vincent took a swallow of his drink and so did Toss.

"We used to think Francis was romantic," Vincent said. But the humor of putting their juvenile misconception in this particular way won no response from Toss.

"You're pretty friendly with him now, aren't you?" Toss asked.

"Friendly? Well ..." Vincent let his voice trail into dubiety. "Francis doesn't like me and I don't care for him, but he's a very proper fellow and he has a sense of family obligation, as he would call it, so he throws little things my way. Like his just asking me to fill in at the copy desk tomorrow."

Toss's face brightened as the secret transaction of the tennis court was explained. Vincent saw the relief he had given his friend and it made him feel friendly. He wanted to have back again the old relationship in which he and Toss shared every detail of their lives. He told Toss the momentous fact.

"I've had a letter from Harold Outram," he said. "He's in town and he's asked me to come to see him."

Toss responded well enough to the importance which the fact seemed to have for Vincent. He could not be entirely impressed because he did not know who Outram was. But he was genially willing to be told.

"Who's Outram?" he asked.

The question was frankly asked, without any of the sulky irony which lately touched Toss's questions. Vincent made up his mind to answer just as openly. He was aware of the risk. What he felt about Outram was the kind of thing he now found hard to tell Toss. It was part of the ethical certitude that had grown to dominate his life in the last few years. His consciousness of what Harold Outram's fate meant was exactly the kind of thing that was cutting him off from Toss. Yet this time he was determined that he would keep back none of his actual feeling. He would give Toss the story of Outram's career just as he really saw it.

In every large American city at that time there were certain young men who took great interest in such stories as the one Vincent Hammell told Toss Dodge. These were the precarious few, their talents unknown or untried, for whom art and intellect were salvation. Some taught in the high schools, some in universities, some served as librarians, or worked in department stores. A few held jobs from WPA but that was coming to an end. Whatever they did was only by the way—their gaze was fixed on what they would do. It had, that gaze of theirs, not merely a spiritual but a geographical direction. It was turned East, Europe in the hazy ultimate distance, New York closer in possibility but still far off. Time was of the essence of their deep anxiety. They cherished their youth, for they supposed their gifts to be bound up with it. They saw each unfruitful year as a loss not only of opportunity but of integrity. Hawk-eyed and with apocalyptic imaginations, they watched over the integrity of certain heroes and demi-heroes whose fates, as they felt, were a portent of their own. They had their martyrs; some cherished Scott Fitzgerald, some Hart Crane. For many of them, the new ethical fierceness of radical politics made their morality of art the more merciless.

Such young men would be well-versed in an American story like Harold Outram's. They believed they could trace it back in variant versions for some decades. They would certainly not find Outram's version exceptional. Still, it had a more than usually brilliant appeal to their imaginations because of the rumored vastness of the salary and the extent of the power for which Outram had, as they said, "sold out."

It did not take Vincent long to tell the story. He told it in a quiet voice, looking now and then into the glass he was holding. With every few sentences he renewed his determination to tell it as he really saw it, to believe that Toss would see its sad and perplexing meaning. He told first how Outram, a poor boy, had worked his way through college, winning unusual honors and a graduate fellowship. Of Outram's doctorate at twenty-three he spoke lightly, as if it were nothing more than an indication of the native power of Outram's mind and of his skill in using it. But he gave more weight to the critical essays which made the next stage of Outram's career. They had been very simple and unassuming yet they were marked by a degree of perception and personal feeling which were surprising in a man so young. A novel came next, not all it should have been, but so startlingly good that for a small group Outram became one of the legends of new American promise. Not long after this, however, Outram had had a sudden experience of political conviction. His work had always been to some degree "socially aware," as people then said, and he even had the literary socialism of the time, mild and taken for granted. But now he moved far to the left. He became the pet of a hundred committees, clubs, leagues and guilds. He wrote very little and that little was of an "agitational" nature. Yet within a year he had descended to apostasy as dramatic as his conversion, and from that into a year of mental depression which quite incapacitated him. But his health had come back and within an amazingly short time he had made an almost legendary rise in magazine journalism. The climax of his career had come only recently. It was an event which beautifully completed his moral interest for the watchful young men. To the accompaniment of a brisk ruffle of newspaper drums, Outram had been appointed director of the great new Peck Foundation with power to dispense at discretion those incalculable millions for the advancement of American culture.

Vincent held to his resolve as he told this story. He told it to Toss just as he would tell it to that little group of his literary friends Toss so jealously hated. As he went on, he saw the sullenness set harder and harder on Toss's face. Yet he did not relax his determination. His effort was his last offering to his dying friendship with Toss.

"Well?" Toss said when Vincent finished. The blankness of his voice was heavily contrived. It was the trick of saying "Go on" to the man whose joke has been fully told.

Vincent was angrier with himself for giving the advantage than with Toss for taking it. "Silence and cunning," he warned himself, "silence and cunning!" It was a motto which, when he had been rather more flamboyant in his notion of himself, he had adopted from a once-favorite book. But he was no Stephen Dedalus. He could not aspire to the arrogance of the motto of the artist as a young man. Some generosity of his imagination made him see the subtle unhappiness which his large and stern considerations introduced into the mind of Toss Dodge. A recollection of their old boyhood creed of fairness, the code by which the shared candy-bar was bisected to the micro-millimeter, made him see that he was refuting Toss's life as much as Toss was denying his. And so he made his reply gentle.

"You have to think," he said, "of how great his talents were and what it means for a man like that to be made into an official, a stuffed shirt."

And he even went on to say, "You have to see, Toss, what it means to our cultural situation that a man should throw away so much talent, just for money."

Never before had he used with Toss the tone of forbearance. It was fatal.

"I *don't* see it," Toss said, making his voice as coarse and practical as he could. "I suppose I'm crass and dumb, but I just don't see it. The man was free to do what he wanted. He took a flier at being a writer, and he took a flier at being a radical. I have respect for both and you know it. I have respect for a sincere radical. All right, he didn't like either one. Now he's got a job where he can do some good to mankind at large and you talk as if he had committed the—the unpardonable sin. No, I don't see it. He has my respect."

Toss got up. In the movement, the edge of his jacket brushed against his glass and swept it off the table. The sound of its shattering gave to their difference of opinion a retrospective confusion and intensity. It made them feel that they had been even more deeply involved in passion than they had supposed.

Vincent knelt to pick up the fragments, expecting Toss to do the same. So often in the past they had knelt in guilty cooperation to gather the shards of their mothers' glassware or crockery. But Toss said, "Leave it, the houseman will sweep it up."

There was nothing at all unfriendly in Toss's voice. He had spoken, indeed, with a notable simplicity, as of an older man to a younger. Rich young people acquire certain of the manners of authority. In some ways they seem older than their years. But Vincent had never before heard from Toss the easy voice of a man who knows exactly how things are done and what is to be left to the servants. But neither had Toss ever heard from Vincent, as he had a moment before, the checked, considerate tone of one who conveys instruction. For the first time in their twelve years together they had condescended to each other.

As they walked to Toss's car, Toss said, "How do you know so much about this Outram?"

"Teddy Kramer knew him at college. They were friends."

As always, Toss kept a sour silence at the mention of Kramer's name. He had never met this former professor and present friend of Vincent's but he felt toward Kramer a deep antagonism. He said, "You say he wrote to you? What made him do that?"

"Well," said Vincent, "he answered a letter I wrote him."

"You wrote to him?" Toss was really surprised, but he made his surprise seem greater than it was. "*You* wrote to *him*? What did you write to him about?"

"I happened to read his collected essays and I liked them. So I wrote to tell him that I did."

"A fan letter," Toss said. His voice was friendly and even encouraging, so that his use of the phrase to summarize what Vincent had done had perhaps the look of a tentative amend. But then Vincent saw that Toss's handsome boyish face was taking on the air of archness which it assumed for one of those moments of finesse in which Toss sometimes indulged.

It was a trick of Toss's, acquired in the last few years, that Vincent hated. It always broke, if only for a moment, the connection between the two young men. Toss looked contemplatively into the far distance and drawled in a high juvenile irony, "Well, I hope it won't corrupt you, I hope it won't rot your soul that you picked such an influential sell-out to write a fan letter to."

And Toss laughed as if the old bond were now again in force. No doubt he wanted it to be. But the bond was not between them. What a year ago would have still been kidding, now reverberated as malice. They would meet again, but the friendship was finished. Vincent did not reply. He was too concerned with the meaning of this moment. He understood it fully and he marked it to himself by thinking in clear, articulate words, "My youth is over."

chapter 4

On the chiffonier in Vincent Hammell's room there stood four books, held upright by a pair of bronze bookends in the once familiar form of the straining elephants. The books were the yellowish white volumes of the Collection Nelson, the little French classics that are printed in Edinburgh. The sentimental whiteness of their binding and the limp festoons of violet and green which drooped down their spines belied their stern contents, for one volume was Flaubert's *Sentimental Education*, one was Balzac's *Père Goriot* and the others were the two volumes of Stendhal's *The Red and the Black*. They were soiled with much handling; within, their narrow margins were filled with vocabulary notes.

The carpentered bookcase against the opposite wall was not full— these books had not been placed on the chiffonier for lack of space but for a ritual purpose. They were here before the mirror to remind Vincent Hammell of the several fates which might destroy a young man. From the histories of Frederic Moreau, Rastignac and Julien Sorel, this young man of the American middle west had learned what he must be careful of.

The ritual position of these books was the key to the room, for everything here had a meaning for its occupant. Only two pictures hung on the walls. One was a reproduction of the Dürer engraving of the Prodigal Son. It represented a young man of strongly marked features kneeling in prayer among the swine. The other picture was a color print of the Henri Rousseau in the Hermitage at Moscow and it showed a large-bodied, big-faced allegorical figure, robed in purple, her hand raised in announcement or admonition, the other arm thrown about the shoulders of a man who wore a velvet jacket and under it an ugly brown sweater; he carried a very white quill pen in one hand and in the other a roll of manuscript and his heavy countenance was reflective and sour. Behind the figures was a tangled jungle and before them a lawn neatly set with flowers, and the picture seemed to mean that the Muse was leading a literary man out of the woods.

A small radio-phonograph stood on a carpentered stand of stained pine and beneath it were a few albums of records. On the desk was a portable typewriter and a pottery jar full of sharpened pencils. Among the books in the bookcase—there were about two hundred—were a Greek grammar, a French and a German dictionary, a college-text anthology of Latin poetry. Most of the volumes were the cheap books that a student buys, Everyman's Library, Modern Library or the Oxford Standard Authors, but there were also copies of Hopkins, Yeats and Eliot and the two volumes of Rilke that had at that time been translated.

Everything in this room was sparse and neatly arranged, for it was a fortress provisioned against siege. It was a matter of satisfaction to Vincent Hammell that two unopened reams of paper and a carton of cigarettes lay in a drawer and that an electric plate and a jar of coffee made him, in the solitary hours of the night, independent of his mother's kitchen.

The only discordant object in the room was the chiffonier on which the shrine of books was set. Its mahogany veneer had bubbled and had fallen away in a few places, exposing the soft white wood beneath. Its curves spoke of a defeated, and hopeless gentility. The chiffonier was an irritation in the military or monastic neatness of the room, yet Vincent Hammell felt that for this very reason it had its place here—it served to remind him of the everlasting enemy.

Vincent was laying his tennis things over the back of a chair when his mother looked in at the door. She was a handsome woman of fifty-six, lonely but always alert to her son. Vincent's room usually daunted her a little. She imagined it as the scene of intellectual mysteries from which she was unjustly barred. But now she saw what Vincent was doing and she entered boldly and snatched up the clothes into a moist bundle. "I'll take these," she said, "and hang them on the line."

She stood there, holding the damp clothes which momentarily gave her the license to be again his mother, in function as well as in fact. "My goodness!" she said. The clothes were very damp and they were beginning to smell strong. Vincent saw her face become happy as she deplored his being a man and a nuisance.

"You were working late last night," she said, "I heard your typewriter. It must have been nearly three o'clock."

Vincent said, "I'm sorry if I kept you up."

"Oh, you didn't. It was company for me, I couldn't sleep. I'd hear you get over the false starts and go along as if nothing could stop you and that made me very happy. What was it?"

He did not answer, for the knowledge that he had not been alone in the night made him feel unaccountably deprived. His moment of affectionate understanding of his mother passed. He felt caught and dull. Down upon his mind there descended the dark impotence, the marshy boredom that for so many months had been the chief condition of his life. The tennis court coherence left his body and all possibility and futurity passed from his world. What he felt is often felt by young men between their earliest youth and their maturity, when the college connections are broken and the world has not yet received them, not even badly, and especially by young men of a literary turn of mind, poor young men or those of the lower middle class. On spring nights that echo with the unheard whistles of transcontinental trains, or in the sunny emptiness of great summer afternoons, or in the large false brightness of thawing February days, these young men experience their respectable shabby neighborhoods as the localities of nightmare enchantment. It is they who can best understand the intention of certain pictures of Chirico, feeling the long shadows and the desperate emptiness like an inverse sensuality. "Life" presents itself to them not as an abstraction but as a simple great object to be seized by everyone else, only not by them. In their impotence they live with images of flight and death, and they can scarcely contemplate the great plans that had formerly given pleasure to their imaginations. Sometimes, in order to touch, to receive a response, to be able to influence, to do, to create, they turn to some love affair, finding the world made almost real again by a girl's quickened breath, and they even begin to think that the process of realization can be carried further by the very hardships and responsibilities of marriage, although only recently these very things had seemed the enemies of all their hopes.

To Vincent Hammell, the letter from Harold Outram had been a breath from the great world that really existed, from "life" itself. The letter had come the day before and last night, for the first time in many months, Vincent had been able to work. But now, suddenly, the letter had lost all its talismanic power.

When Mrs. Hammell did not receive an answer to her question, she asked encouragingly, "I suppose it's the book?—I'm glad you've started again," she said. She partly believed what Vincent had told her, that he might establish himself in the world by means of literature. It was beyond her knowledge of literature and of the world to be astonished at the project her son had undertaken. For at twenty-three Vincent Hammell was staking his life upon nothing less grandiose than a history of American literature in the latter part of the nineteenth century. Mrs. Hammell, having accepted this project as a somewhat unusual way of rising in the world, but one it was not for her to judge, gave it all her loyalty and was concerned only when it no longer seemed to be advancing. And for a good while now Vincent had met all questions and all questioning looks with silence and a shrug. As the weeks and months went by, she had learned to say nothing and even to look nothing. But now that the work seemed to have begun again, she thought that it could not be amiss to speak of it. "I'm glad you've started again," she said. "It sounded as if you were doing well."

"It's a flash in the pan," Vincent said with bitter energy. "Tomorrow I'll be as dry as a bone."

It was far easier, it was somehow even preferable, to recall the hostile, splenetic energies that had so long kept his mind immobile than to remember the bright sober emotions of the night. He turned sullenly from his mother and looked out of the window, holding aside the faded chintz curtains. He stared down at the narrow driveway between their house and the house next door. He saw with intentional literary sharpness the parallel tracks of concrete that led to their neighbor's garage, saw the ashes and weeds between the tracks. He spoke without turning, his eyes fixed on these saddening things. "I can't go on like this," he said.

His mother came up to him and touched him. "You're so young," she said, "and in a way you're successful already."

But his self-torture was stubborn. "Not so young any more," he said. "We can't go on forever thinking I'm young. I'm not so young any more."

He was being as cruel to his mother as to himself.

"I'm twenty-three and my fine success consists of a quarter-time job at the university, a couple of days a month for the *Advertiser*, oh yes, and the pleasure of instructing the ladies at Meadowfield in creative writing. Quite a success."

"There are your pieces in *The Prairie Review*."

"Who reads that except Kramer?"

Mrs. Hammell looked at her son with troubled eyes. He was making her unhappy, as he intended, but beneath her unhappiness she felt a flicker of warmth and animation. She was stirred by the impatient frustrated energy that filled him, even though it expressed itself in anger. She felt that it held promise and hope for him and for her.

She said, "This Mr. Outram who wrote you that letter. You're going to see him. Do you think that maybe?—" And she stopped, transparently diplomatic.

Vincent looked at her haughtily. She did not go on and he said, "Maybe what?" His tone was icily neutral, daring her to say what she meant.

She chose to defy him. "Maybe he could help you in some way." She knew this would bring them to a quarrel. But she had had the fantasy and now she clung to it.

"In what way, for example?" His voice was dangerously polite, excessively interested.

But she saw his young absurdity and it was she who spoke angrily first. "How do *I* know?" she said in exasperation. "How do I know what way? People help each other. A big man helps a young man to get a start in life. It happens all the time. What's wrong with it? And God knows we need it."

He said, "I suppose you think I wrote to him to get his help. I suppose you think that."

"I don't think anything. But suppose you did, suppose you did? What would be so terrible?"

"I don't need any help—I don't need his help or anyone's help. I'll get along all right."

"Yes, you'll get along." There was a simple admission in Mrs. Hammell's answer but also a touch of bitter irony—he would get along, being young, but who else in the house would, who else?

"Well, 'help' won't do it. 'Help' never helped *him* and God knows he asked for enough of it." Vincent, in his hatred of himself, threw into the battle with his mother the whole of his father's failure. Not until he had uttered the sentence did he know that he was accusing his mother of having chosen the wrong father for him, of having diluted with her husband's weakness the strength she had had to give him. She looked away, moved by what he implied but not daring to accept it. And as she turned away her head, like a young heroine in a romantic novel of her youth, there passed over her face a look of sadness at the failure of her life. Vincent, seeing it, knew it for what it was, and his anger dissolved into compassion. "Ah, don't let's fight," he said and put out his hand gently. His mother turned to him with a piteous look and embraced him. The antagonism of their deep connection was gone and its place was taken by a sad and chastened peace which made the quarrel quite worth having had.

"Don't worry, dear," Mrs. Hammell said. "You'll come out fine, I know it, Mother knows it. I'm very proud of you," she said and she stroked his back as she embraced him, renewing the old blessing of urgency and mission which had been her first and strongest gift to him, earlier even than love.

The avenue down which Vincent walked when he left his house was shabby. In a few years it would surely become sordid, but now it still held the memory of days when it was substantial, even fashionable. The new generation of the well-to-do lived in ample new suburbs and could scarcely imagine that these close-set heavy houses had ever represented comfort and standing. Manilla Boulevard had become a street of apartments and rented rooms, and, lately, of improvised stores, little hat shops and dress shops in which business was conducted with a confidential air. It was becoming too a street of specialists in certain technical services to the body, masseurs, podiatrists, electrolysis experts, beauty operators and undertakers. A few lawyers combined home and office and declared their existence by signs which represented them as Counsellors at Law.[1]

Yet the Boulevard still had its trees and its small lawns. Among its houses were some that kept a strict respectability of trim hedges and flower borders and a few of the very oldest families of the city stubbornly held their place. The freshness of the spring air, the trees, the few houses that still resisted degradation allowed Vincent to find a kind of beauty in the scene. He had trained himself to find beauty in American things not usually loved.

The City University toward which Vincent was walking had been founded in the era of America's strongest and naïvest faith in education. Richardson himself had designed its first building in 1883 and Beading Hall stood darkly red and squatly romanesque in the little plaza that had preserved it from the encroaching city. But the halls of the next ten years were now enclosed by the business district and the university had been forced to expand into offices and lofts, creating

---

[1] This description of Vincent's neighborhood will be repeated in chapter 11.

bright and cheerless classrooms by means of steel partitions on concrete floors. Vincent was glad that his work at the university, what little there was of it, kept him to Beading Hall. Richardson had built darkly but honestly, there was something sturdy and sullen about the place. It looked defeated and isolated, but proud.

There were for Vincent two ways of reaching Beading Hall. They were of almost equal length and convenience; the difference between them was that one went by his father's optometrical sho[p] and the other did not. Most days Vincent chose the way which did not take him by the place: in the language of the Hammell family it was always *the place*, never *the store*, and this was the latest and least of the many *places*—the word derived from the old genteel phrase, "place of business"—that Mr. Hammell had attempted since the days of prosperity had unaccountably passed. Today Vincent chose the unaccustomed route.

He looked in as he passed without much slowing his step and saw his father seated at the counter in which the spectacle frames were kept. As usual, Mr. Hammell was reading. The book, Vincent knew, was the *Ethics* of Spinoza. Mr. Hammell felt that the optical trade made a connection between him and Spinoza, though of course he did not grind his own lenses. When he read the *Ethics* he skipped the proofs of the propositions, but he believed that the propositions themselves calmed and ennobled him. Within the last few years he had lost the simple and militant agnosticism which a student of physics would have easily picked up in the early years of the century. He was beginning to look for what he called an "answer." He never stated clearly what the question was.

In the shop window were two framed colored pictures, the advertisements of a large optometrical company. One of them represented _____ discovering the _____, the other represented _____ inventing the _____ [blanks in original]. Vincent knew the pictures well. The sunlight of the seventeenth century was less gay than that of the eighteenth, though more significant, but both lights were historical and each illuminated its scene in a way to suggest a contrast with the sunken twilight of his father's place.

He felt a chill of the spirit. Year by year his father's income grew smaller. Already his father was beginning to treat him, not without resentment, as a partner in the failing family enterprise, beginning to look to him for strength and guidance.

Vincent said grimly to himself, "The child is father of the man."

Then it occurred to him to say, "The father is father of the man," and this heavy joke struck him as a heavy truth. He remembered that on the tennis court he had, half in jest, made a wager with fate. But "My fate sits there reading Spinoza," he said now. He said it almost aloud. There seemed no connection between himself and the young man who, invigorated by the breath from the great world, had been so whole on the tennis court. He hurried on to Beading Hall, eager to lose himself. As a community the university was not adequate, but it was better than being alone. Yet when he stood at the door of Kramer's office and knocked, his heart sank again and when Kramer called for him to come in, he entered elaborately surrounded by a joke.

"Professor Kramer, sir," he said, mimicking the politic voice of a graduate student, "Professor Kramer, sir, I've run into what might be called a little snag in my seminar paper and I thought you could straighten me out, sir."

chapter 5

Kramer's little Jewish face broke into its tentative smile. Vincent knew how much Kramer loved to be teased and how much he loved to be reminded that life might be careless. As best he could, Kramer broke through his magisterial gravity to meet the joke. He nodded his head in an owlish parody of himself. "Well, now, we must try to straighten this out, Mr. Hammell," he said elaborately, "we must look into this." He was being Professor Kramer, the careful, sympathetic teacher. An unkind observer would have found matter for satire even in his self-mockery.

Vincent was a little restored by Kramer's pleasure in the joke. Today or any day, Kramer too would be working his own way through darkness. But with how slim a chance for success. In a few minutes he would stalk into his classroom, a small man, stiffly and meticulously dressed, timid, suspicious, but resistant. He would lecture on the literature of modern Europe as he had learned to love it in his rebellious youth, arranging into careful categories the lessons of rebellion to be found in Ibsen, Sudermann, Schnitzler, Wassermann and Pirandello, referring to his careful notes in many languages, which actually included the Scandinavian. As he talked, his stature would grow and he would forget his old-fashioned Jewish pride, which Vincent had come to see as consisting of the belief that being Jewish meant being a physically small man of such scrupulous intellectual honesty that he could bring no work to a satisfactory conclusion. Before his mind Kramer kept forever the martyrdom of the artist and the seeker for truth. "Dedication" was the word he thought, "integrity" and "compromise" were the words he used.

Kramer, said, "Vincent, you look tired." His tone was admonitory, even querulous, and Vincent knew that in this way he expressed and masked the affection he was feeling.

"Do I?" The interest of his friend and former teacher made Vincent feel young and heroic. "I was working late last night."

"On the book?" Kramer asked. "Is it going again?" He spoke in an almost hushed voice and Vincent knew that Kramer was seeing the lonely light in the little room and was hearing the intermitted rattle of the typewriter. He knew that Kramer was having a vision of his young friend "wrestling" with his work, for only in this way could Kramer imagine the process of thought and creation.

At this moment Kramer would have liked to say that no idea of material gain, no glimpse of mere popular success must intrude to spoil the purity of the work. He wanted to utter his belief that Vincent's long months of sterility and despair were the marks of the virtue of his enterprise. He did not say what he believed, but his feminine solicitude shone from his face. All he said was, "I'm glad you've broken through again. That's bound to happen—the ideas find their place."

Then, shy of what he was about to say and making his manner objective to the point of dullness, Kramer said, "I've been thinking, Vincent. Now that you're in the clear—I didn't want to interfere before—it occurs to me to suggest that sometimes such difficulties are not entirely intellectual. Often they are emotional—psychological, you know. They are often—"

And Kramer looked straight and brave into Vincent's eyes. "They are often sexual. You used to have a kind of affair, as I remember, with a little undergraduate girl. But I gather that lately—. What I mean, of course, is not marriage. I shouldn't like that for you just yet, but a civilized—. You know, a boy like you should have many triumphs in his campaigns."

The old diction of love with its metaphors of warfare came easily to Kramer. He knew the long account of Goethe's amours, which, to account for genius, the scholars have told over so often, and he could conscientiously suggest to Vincent a line of action which would have been

[as] impossible to himself as cannibalism. But it was part of the tradition of his youth to war on puritanism.

Vincent smiled, feeling a tender amusement at his awkward friend. He thought he was unperturbed by Kramer's advice, yet he chose this moment to say, "I'm going to meet an old friend of yours."

Kramer noted that Vincent had refused the opening. He was of two minds about the sexual conduct of the Gentile world. On the one hand, he believed it licentious. On the other hand, he believed it hopelessly and symptomatically puritanical.

"An old friend?" and Kramer's eyebrows went up in genuine surprise. "Who could that be?"

"Harold Outram," Vincent said and heard in his voice not only the intention of surprising but also a certain readiness to be stubborn.

He had supposed that the name would have a considerable effect on Theodore Kramer, but he had not imagined so deep a stirring as actually took place. Kramer's little face went white and his eyes opened in an almost wild consternation. He seemed on the point of repeating the name incredulously. But then he said with a notable calm, almost a haughtiness, as if Vincent had committed a breach of etiquette which could be dealt with only by the grand manner, "And how, Vincent, did this come about?"

"Well," Vincent said and knew at once that that "well" had spoiled his reply, "I wrote him a letter."

"You wrote him a letter."

There was no question in Kramer's voice. But the question came now, the more accusingly for the delay.

"Why?" Kramer asked.

Why indeed? He had, he thought, written on an impulse, on generous impulse. He had liked some essays written when the author had been not much older than he himself now was. He had sent a letter, really a very graceful letter, to tell the author of his admiration. It was a common enough thing to do, people did it every day. To be sure, one does not often write in appreciation of work done ten years ago. Still, even that was not so strange. What was perhaps worthy of remark in his action was that the author was no longer a fine writer but a man who had been a fine writer, ten years before. That could, of course, bring his letter into something like ambiguity, making its impulse at least not an ordinary impulse.

"'Why?'" said Vincent, questioning the question.

But of course it was useless to pursue this line. He knew the answer. Apparently everyone else knew it before he did. He said, "I wrote to him because I read him and liked him. But you mean that I wrote for more reason than that. You mean that that 'more reason' wasn't entirely innocent. That I had—'an ulterior motive.' I think you're right."

He could not have said it with more simplicity. The moral fire in Kramer's eye banked itself. It occurred to Vincent that, to account for so complete a confession, there must be, beneath his affectionate superiority to Kramer, a stronger trust than he had ever supposed.

"An ulterior motive," said Kramer. He said it gently and sadly. He tasted each word drily, "*Motive. Ulterior,*" and shrugged as if he found them without any savor of meaning at all.

"Go see him, Vincent. You will learn something from him, I can assure you. You will see a man utterly corrupt. A handsome man, a charming man, and—I can guarantee—a man utterly untouched by life."

Vincent said, "Untouched? I thought from what you've told me that he had a hard enough time."

"Hard time? You mean he was a poor boy? Yes, *technically* I suppose he was. But when you have his looks and charm, you're not poor, no, you're by no means poor." Vincent knew that Kramer was saying that Outram had not been a Jewish poor boy. "He worked his way through college but people took care that the path should be smooth for him. I am sure you will see a man still young, untroubled. But let me tell you, Vincent, you will see a man utterly corrupt."

Kramer's voice rang with the passion of his bitterness. "Let it be a lesson to you, Vincent," he said.

Embarrassed by the nakedness of his friend's feeling, Vincent said in a worldly way, "It's quite a lesson—at thirty thousand a year." For that was the sum which, according to rumor, Outram received as director of the Peck Foundation.

But his irony did not lighten the situation at all. Kramer was fighting for souls, Vincent's and his own. He was defending the dark castle of six small rooms which housed his virtuous wife, his two unruly children and the book that must never be finished.

He was defending something else as well. How many cups of coffee or glasses of beer he had drunk with Harold Outram at college was hard to calculate, because each cup of coffee or glass of beer provided Kramer with more than one memory and had been seen by him from more than one point of view. Kramer's accounts of the early friendship varied according as he was bitterly proud or proudly bitter. Vincent, in his mind's eye, saw the young Harold Outram bending his brilliant head toward the young Theodore Kramer, in the companionship, or its simulacrum, from which Kramer had not recovered. But never until this moment had

Vincent understood how intense that variable memory was to his friend, how involving, passionate and enduring it was, or how torturing.

Kramer rebuked Vincent's frivolity. "Quite a lesson," he said with a large homiletic sadness, "yes, Vincent, quite a lesson. To have been Harold Outram, to have had his gifts, to take a doctorate at twenty-three, to write essays and a book like his—quite a lesson indeed. All right, Vincent, I am very intelligent, a good scholar, a very exact skeptical mind. And you are a very intelligent young man. I'll say it: the best student I ever had, and you know the kind of hopes I have for you, the kind of work I expect you to do. But Vincent, let me tell you that the two of us together couldn't touch Harold Outram when he was young."

The pulpit tradition of Kramer's childhood was not a good one, but the unconscious memory of all the rabbinical sermons he had once despised came to Kramer's aid now. "The biggest lesson of all, I assure you, Vincent," he said, wagging his head with sad wisdom, "the biggest lesson of all is what a few years can do, what life can do to a man. To give up such talents, to pervert and prostitute them! For what? For a contemptible few thousand dollars a year. Our money economy knows what it wants, believe me. It knows what it wants and it gets it. Our profit system knows how to buy the best. If the Peck Foundation wants a commissar of culture it buys itself a Harold Outram—*after* he is corrupted by that magazine he worked for! Such a magazine! At fifty thousand a year—is that what he gets?—he coordinates culture in America. A grant here, a grant there, could such an artist and scholar go wrong?"

Then, getting down to business, he said briskly, "You think he can help you, Vincent? You think one of those grants could be for you?"

"Oh, come on now, Ted," Vincent said, with an expansive and worldly note of protest, "aren't you letting this thing run away with you? After all, I only wrote the man a letter. He invited me to come to see him—I never suggested it. And you know that the Peck Foundation only puts its money into institutions."

Kramer dismissed the practical objection. "A man like that has the power to help anybody. You ought to know that money isn't everything in things like that. He has what's better than money—he has power." Then he said as if standing back from the situation, as if he understood that in this world there are many things one must do to survive, "Vincent, I don't blame you. Maybe you are wise." But he could not play the part for long. "For God's sake, Vincent—you are trying to act as if you didn't understand. After all, I am talking to the man who wrote 'The Sociology of the Written Word.'"

Kramer was appealing to the best of Vincent, appealing from young Vincent Hammell caught in the dream of the great world to young Vincent Hammell seeing deep and clear, with all his wits about him, into the modern situation. He was conjuring his young friend by recalling to him his own true words. Vincent's essay with the pretentious title had appeared in *The Prairie Review* and nothing that Vincent had ever done had won Kramer's blessing so completely. And indeed it was the best thing that Vincent had ever written, the most elaborate and the most mature, and quite the freest, for it had been touched with wit, a long and rather desperate examination of the various perils which beset the young man who gives himself to the life of the mind.

Vincent had been proud of this essay and Kramer and his younger friends had quite justified his pride by their praise. But now the piece seemed youthful and priggish and Kramer's appeal to it was not effective. "I've got to get away from here," he said. He felt dull and miserable and confused. All the sprightliness that Kramer so often aroused in him was gone. He used the sentence he had earlier spoken to his mother. "I can't go on like this," he said. He made a gesture to indicate the environment as far as the mind could reach, and Kramer needed no explanation beyond this to understand that Vincent was referring to this great rich city with its busy life and its great emptiness. For Kramer himself this had become the right—or the inevitable—setting for all the things of his life, his family, his home, his work and his fears. But he was a scholar of rebellion, of the free and developing spirit, and he knew what Vincent felt.

Kramer looked at his young friend with intent shrewdness. "Vincent," he said, "if you were appointed to a full-time instructorship, would you stay?"

The question, which implied that the instructorship was actually available, was shocking to Vincent. Perhaps it was the more shocking because it was crammed full of attractions, even temptations, all the prosaic charms of a settled position, not notable but surely comfortable, and of a settled salary, not large but regular. It meant to him the giving up of all his hopes and that was its charm. He saw the gentle sad pleasure of acquiescence to the family wish. His parents could scarcely be so deceived as to be overjoyed by such a position, yet a son with two thousand dollars a year would make the difference between worry and comfort. Vincent saw stretching before him, and not with the usual horror, the long days of serviceable piety. Everything that he feared for himself and that Kramer had feared for him had a sudden strange lure.

33

But he saved himself. He thought of what was implied about Kramer by Kramer's offer. He said coldly, "I thought you didn't approve of my taking a job at the university. When I wanted one two years ago, you talked me out of it. I thought you couldn't do anything for me in the department beyond my assistantship. You've told me that often enough, and now you seem to be making me an offer."

Under this almost direct accusation of insincerity, Kramer did not flinch. "As for doing anything for you in the department," he said, "anything I do for you, Vincent, will be done at a certain cost to myself. You know what my position is. It is not good. But I am willing to put what position I have to the test. I am ready to endanger myself."

Vincent found that he was suddenly impatient of Kramer's extravagant sense of vulnerability. He had accepted it at Kramer's own estimate and it had been a kind of bond between them. Kramer and he shared the sense of danger that made heroes. But now he saw that the good Kramer, although by no means the most powerful of professors, was no more insecure in his position than anyone else. It was the insight of anger. He checked himself—he had felt anger too often that day.

"I have always," Kramer said, "I have always been opposed to an academic career for you. It is not in your temperament. I am one of those who teach, you are one of those who can *do*." And as Kramer made the old stale antithesis that had been so fresh when Bernard Shaw had made it in Kramer's boyhood, Vincent had a moment of sadness for his teacher. "But, Vincent, I am even ready to see you make a possible sacrifice of your talents by taking a regular appointment here. Maybe you even can make a future. I am ready for anything rather than see you involve yourself with Harold Outram. You say you can't go on like this. All right. Admitted. Granted. But when you go on to something different by the help of Harold Outram then—no! Anything else."

Kramer kept his eyes fixed on Vincent's face. He was very stern and direct. It seemed to Vincent that his friend had never had so much dignity as was now lent him by his passion. "Anything," Kramer said. And again, "Anything."

He went on. "Vincent, I know you do not want to become what I am. I know—" He held up his hand to check Vincent's stricken protestations. "And why should you? I'm stuck—I'm a Jew, I'm a married man, with children. I'm stuck. But leaving money out of account, *you* have every advantage. You can be something and not be corrupt. But that man, if you let him, that man will corrupt you—corrupt you to Hell."

It was nonsense. Yet whatever in Kramer was ridiculous had quite vanished. Vincent heard him almost with awe and wholly without an answer.

At that moment the bell rang for the beginning of the next hour. Kramer selected three books from the row across his desk. He piled them neatly on the folder that contained his lecture notes. He rose. When he was at the door, he smiled a wan and intelligent smile which was very charming, for his teeth were fine and white. He said, "Perhaps, Vincent I am only jealous." He smiled again, almost with a touch of saving mischievousness, and then he was gone, leaving in the air a large reverberation of meaning.

For a moment it seemed to Vincent that something had been explained. But then he found that he was not at all clear about the object of Kramer's confessed jealousy. Was it Outram that Kramer was jealous of? Was it perhaps Vincent himself? Was it conceivably Vincent in his connection with Outram? Or Outram in his connection with Vincent? He could not tell, but jealousy implied the estimate of value, of store set upon something. And as he walked to his luncheon appointment with Outram, it seemed to him that what Kramer had expressed was not an evaluation of Vincent's youthful advantages or of Outram's power. No one could be more precise in his use of language than Kramer, and he would have said envy if he had meant it. Jealousy meant that Kramer had in mind the connection that might develop between his two friends. It was love that Kramer had been thinking of rather than power, and to exist with Outram in Kramer's emotion gave Vincent a kind of parity with the man he had not yet seen. He felt an excitement which he thought of as confidence.

It stood him in good stead, this confidence, for Outram had appointed the Athletic Club as their place of meeting. He was staying at the Club, which of course quite became his position, and the Athletic Club at lunch hour was quite different from the Tennis Club of the morning. The Tennis Club was, at best, gentility—that is, status without power—and even its gentility was lately being somewhat eroded. But the Athletic Club was the power that made status. It proclaimed its nature in the largeness of all its furnishings, in the solidity of the walnut that panelled its walls and the permanence of the leather that covered its armchairs, in the very darkness of the great lobby, in the smell of the bar that was just off the lobby. Vincent felt sure that no club in New York or even London could better give the feeling of massed masculine force. One of Kramer's stories about Harold Outram had for its occasion a drink at the Harvard Club, and Kramer had been annoyed at Vincent's quick foolish cry, "What does it look like—the Harvard Club?" Yet, as of course Kramer sensibly saw, a young man with Vincent's work to do would naturally have a sociological interest in any number of things, in settings or ways of life or manners that he would not necessarily approve of. Vincent and his friends liked to think. Or these were the scientists of the great plants with their rather dry but not unfriendly looks [sic]. Had anyone at any other time said to Vincent Hammell that reality was made here, he would have loftily resisted the idea. But now he felt it to be true, and he braced himself against the fact, feeling impalpable.

He really did not know how to think about power. His mind turned to the appearance of the men about him. Here, if one saw tweeds, they were not the heavy stiff harsh tweeds that members of the university wore. And actually what one saw most were dark, softly-hanging cloths, distinguished from each other only by differences of pattern of the subtlest kind. Vincent had reason to be glad that instinct had taught him that if one must dress cheaply one did best with suits of grey flannel, with shirts of white oxford, with ties of the simplest stripe—they were far harder to find than might be supposed—and with sturdy, but not extravagantly sturdy, shoes. He despised himself for being aware of his propriety, but he could not help it. He comforted himself with the thought that such matters had not seemed trivial to Balzac and Stendhal, from whom he had learned the name of Straub, the great tailor of the Restoration, although be could not have named the tailor that made these men around him so beautifully unnoticeable.

It was a small and frivolous mind that could be aware of appearance when so much reality was all about him: he was sure of that. These men made the things and decisions that affected the lives at least of thousands, perhaps of millions. That was power, that was the creation of reality. But he could not conceive the joy of that. All that he wanted was the license to move freely and without embarrassment in the world, to be swift and simple and a little touched with glory.

chapter 6

"This room," Mr. Rykstrom said to Harold Outram, "is my last large work. A little painting I still do, mornings, before the real day begins, because if you come from my country early rising is in the blood. Yes, in the blood. But it is only a little painting on little pictures. Nothing large any more. Some day I return to my old scale. Meanwhile from my responsibilities there are many pleasures. And you too must find—"

Mr. Rykstrom left it to Harold Outram to know what he would find. He meant that Mr. Outram like Mr. Rykstrom had left the life of art for the life of administration, a sad choice but having its heroic compensations.

Harold Outram said, "A job, Mr. Rykstrom, is in any language a dirty job."

This young man was making things hard for Mr. Rykstrom. It was not Mr. Rykstrom's intention to ask very much of the Peck Foundation. He chiefly wanted to involve the Foundation in the principle of aiding Meadowfield. His eye was to the future. But something was not going as it should. Outram was the kind of American Mr. Rykstrom admired—handsome, rapid, efficient and clothed with power. With such Americans

Mr. Rykstrom got on very well. But they did not usually show such irritable, almost petulant, sensitivities as Harold Outram showed, quite as if he had a bad digestion. There had been the occasion when, in the office, going over the list of the faculty, Mr. Rykstrom had come to the name of Solocheff. "That Solocheff," he had said, shaking, his head, "that Solocheff. A man not without talent, you understand, but not our best type. A Jew as we discovered, not a Czech at all. And like all Jews, a radical in secret. You know—a little *bit* radical, the way they are. He does not really fit." That was all Mr. Rykstrom had said, yet when he looked up from the list he saw Outram openly scowling at him.

This had been the more disconcerting because, although Mr. Rykstrom was opposed to Jews on principle, the principle being their excessive tendency to abstract intellectuality, he had no feeling against Solocheff himself, who was actually not very clever. He had merely wanted to suggest to the secretary of the Peck Foundation how sound Meadowfield was. The late Mr. Peck had been known to dislike Jews.

And now there was the moment when they were standing in the great reception hall known as the Saga Room, its walls covered with Mr. Rykstrom's murals representing incidents from Scandinavian story, and Mr. Rykstrom was moved to say, "So you, an artist, deal with the millions of Frank Ewart Peck, and I, an artist, deal with the fortune of Gilbey Walter, and we deal with each other. It is funny, isn't it?" In his boyhood, Mr. Rykstrom had read in novels of people making statements through clenched teeth but he had never actually seen that phenomenon until Harold Outram answered his question by saying, "Very funny."

Mr. Rykstrom could not understand on what principle his guest was showing resistance. This handsome young man, this American type, was clearly making a reference to something within himself that was hostile. Mr. Rykstrom was used to an American division of feeling, the reference to a principle which was not the one by which the man daily acted. In most cases this had been useful to Mr. Rykstrom. It frequently took the form of a kind of generous guilt and he had come to think of it as a characteristically American emotion. It was what he counted on to swell the endowment of Meadowfield and no doubt it had even been responsible for Meadowfield's creation. A situation in which the arts were involved seemed especially to bring it into play. But Meadowfield was not having the anticipated effect upon Harold Outram.

It occurred to Mr. Rykstrom that his guest had perhaps been talking to the people at the university. But this did not seem likely and in any case Mr. Rykstrom could not take the university's rivalry with any seriousness. The City University had never recovered from the decisive defeat which Meadowfield represented. It was still not able to explain what terrible error it had made that had decided Gilbey Walter to divert to the creation of Meadowfield the huge sums once clearly destined for the university. As any member of the department of philosophy or of English literature could have explained, men can endure catastrophe if they can only give a meaning to it—and so, after ten years, it was still a lively question what was the act of president or trustees, or some dean or professor, or even some student, that had brought about Gilbey Walter's terrible change of heart. But nothing had ever been discovered to make the event understandable. One day the university believed that it had in store a great future of libraries, laboratories, gymnasiums and high salaries. The next day it knew that these things were dreams and that a strange institution to be called Meadowfield was to be a reality. Not all the wisdom of the university could make the explanation. It could only counsel a tragic acceptance. The hopes were now in the past and there was nothing to do but to remain proud, earnest and second-rate.

The university was alone in its grief. No doubt, if it had been made richer and handsomer by Gilbey Walter, the interest and affection of the city would have gone out to it. As things were, the city took its pride and pleasure in Meadowfield and probably understood it better than it would have understood even an expanded and renovated university.

On three square miles of good ground, not far from the limits of the city, Gilbey Walter had constructed his center for the artistic life of the region. Within two years he had built and staffed a school of painting, another of sculpture, another of architecture. There shortly followed a school of instrumental and vocal music, a school of musical composition. The arts of dramatic production, including opera, had a building to themselves, with four theatres, three small and one large, and many workshops. Textile design and manufacture had been provided for, as well as ceramics and glassware.

In addition to its training of professional artists and craftsmen, Meadowfield reached out to touch the city's life at many points. With great success it introduced the pleasures of community singing. It taught adults the arts of finger-painting and clay-modelling and instructed housewives in interior decoration. And although its original program had not included specifically intellectual pursuits, it had come to devote some part of its efforts to study-groups and with so much success that more and more of the city's organizations put their cultural problems into the efficient care of Meadowfield. But the chief intention of Gilbey Walter had been to establish here in the Middle West an institution which would be a home for every art. He had had it in mind to check the emigration of the young artists to the East and to Europe and to attract here the great figures from Europe and the East. The latter intention was an afterthought. If it seemed to contradict the regional premise of Walter's great enterprise, actually it was a true expression of that premise. For one thing, it was a kind of revenge, a raiding of the metropolitan centers. And then the scheme required that the great cities should confirm its defiance of them. And the men of the old centers of culture had been drawn to this mid-western American outpost. The French, it is true, were not well represented among the foreign artists who came to Meadowfield. To Gilbey Walter while he was alive and to his representatives after he was dead, this was not entirely a matter of regret. The French practice of the arts took an insufficient view of the part which national feeling plays in the creations which most truly speak to the human spirit. It was rather from the nations which had a just and exacerbated sense of national suffering and national destiny that the Meadowfield faculty was drawn. Certain Finns, Poles, Letts [sic], Croats, Czechs and Germans fitted admirably into the plan. They had a quick response to the young musicians who wished to write compositions entitled *Prairie Suite* and to the ideals of young painters who, tired of theories, wished to record the lives of what they called their own people.

Harold Outram disliked Meadowfield. He tried to keep this feeling in check. He held before his mind the genuine beauty of the buildings—Meadowfield had been in existence for no more than ten years, but its brick and stone had been so well chosen for color that its buildings seemed ageless, an effect the founder had insisted on; all the Meadowfield buildings had been designed to conform to the contours of the ground, and where the ground had been flat, contours had been wonderfully contrived, so that one felt that all these buildings, organized around the lovely little lake, were the natural and beautiful consequences of geological forces; with their long low modest lines, they seemed reluctant to rise above the earth from which they sprang. Surely these buildings, Harold Outram thought, must represent something good in the institution. It was necessary for him these days to be extremely careful. He had in his hands some part of the future of the nation—it was as simple and as important as that. He must not feel the irritation he did feel. He admired the fabric that he was shown, the glassware, the pottery. But he found that he was soon bored by them, then annoyed. He reminded himself how important it was in the life of a people that it should produce beautiful objects. Yet he could not overcome his feeling that he was being involved in something frivolous. It was surely a deficiency in himself that he was unmoved by the paintings he saw. They expressed the national life—each painting had its due amount of vigor or of serenity and sometimes its due amount of violence. There was something very cleanly about these paintings, they were hard and firm. He had made too many mistakes, he had led himself into too much suffering to be able to judge them truly. He was indifferent to the paintings but he did not dare explore his mind to justify his indifference.

"If I dislike them," he said to himself in the explicit, formulated way he had taken to using, "they must be good. Or good enough to be endowed."

For he knew that although he had made up his mind to do nothing for Meadowfield, the decision was mere childish play. There were no two ways about it—Meadowfield was a going concern, its endowment large and safe, its purposes sound and not only sound but *democratic*, its management able to handle whatever plans for expansion it proposed. After he had caused Mr. Rykstrom sufficient uneasiness, he would recommend the grant, a large one. But as they entered the Saga Room together to look at Mr. Rykstrom's murals, he gave himself the pleasure of disengaging his arm from Mr. Rykstrom's guiding hand.

When they were back in Mr. Rykstrom's beautiful blond office, Mr. Rykstrom said gently, "And now you have seen all. It is very beautiful, is it not? Very well conceived?"

And Mr. Rykstrom said, "I have given up my own art to it—I am no longer a painter, I am an administrator. But I do not regret the loss. You can understand that?"

This time Harold Outran was touched. He smiled generously to Mr. Rykstrom and said, "Yes, I can understand it." But as soon as he had said it, he knew that he did not understand it as Mr. Rykstrom wished it to be understood. If conceivably Meadowfield was being administered by an artist, the murals in the Saga Room had been painted by an administrator.

He picked up the handsome Meadowfield catalogue in its earth-brown cover. He sifted through its pages. "Now explain to me again what you mean by your 'Organizational' courses."

"Gladly," said Mr. Rykstrom with executive briskness. "You understand of course the assumptive principles on which Meadowfield was founded. The hand," and Mr. Rykstrorn held up both his strong hands, "the eye," and with one finger Mr. Rykstrom struck his temple, close to the corner of his eye, "the thorax and diaphragm," and. Mr. Rykstrom demonstratively clutched his throat and then struck his solar plexus with the flat of his palm, "the feet and legs" and Mr. Rykstrom tapped his shoes and his trouser-legs, "it is with these that we think quite as much as with the mind," and Mr. Rykstrom struck his forehead with the tips of four fingers. "Indeed, can we differentiate what we call the mind from the soma, the body, the whole organism? Yet our civilization has put all emphasis on the mind that thinks—that thinks in concepts, ideas. Too much Plato," said Mr. Rykstrorn with a smile. "We wish to put the emphasis the other way. The hand, the eye, the thorax and diaphragm, the feet and legs—we wish to bring these into play."

"And the section in between?" said Outram.

"I beg your pardon?" Mr. Rykstrom leaned politely forward.

"I said, the important section between the legs and the diaphragm." And Outram looked hard at Rykstrom. He was sorry he had started this. He did not want to pursue the matter. But he had certain privileges and he was glad that Rykstrom looked uncomfortable.

"You are Freudian?" Mr. Rykstrom asked in an objective voice.

"No. Go on—I'm sorry I interrupted."

"So then: not the intellect but the whole being. It was that conception that made Mr. Walter not give his money to the university. He was," said Mr. Rykstrom judicially, "in many ways a very deep thinker. Eccentric but deep. And so Meadowfield was conceived. But inevitably the civic duty arises. The Women's Guild wants this, the Junior League asks if we can do that. The Round Table Club wants a course. The Fellowship of Reconciliation wants some lectures. In what? In current events, in Russia, in psychology, in short-story writing. It is not our program, but you can see how we must serve the community, so we arrange courses. These we call our Organizational courses."

"I see," Outram said. He had found something of interest in the catalogue and he said, "I see you have a young man giving a course in short-story writing—Hammell, Vincent Hammell."

"Hammell?" said Rykstrom, but the name meant nothing and he reached out to take the catalogue from Outram.

"Oh yes—gives the course for the Junior League. Such people are not on our faculty—they are hired for the occasion. But wait!" and Rykstrom was struck by a recollection. "I have a letter!" and he opened a desk file. "Just yesterday it came. A lady from the Junior League class writes to say that Mr. Hammell is—what is the expression—'giving me nothing.' It is nothing to his discredit. It is a group of wealthy ladies, not junior, and every year they need a new man to teach them to be literary artists. I assure you, if they began with finger-paints they would make more progress and more satisfaction. You are interested in this young man Hammell?"

"I'm going now to have lunch with him."

"And not lunch here? I am disappointed."

"I'm sorry." Outram was disposed suddenly to be quite polite. "I have so little time and this is important."

"If you are interested in the young man—" Mr. Rykstrom indicated possibilities.

"I don't know, I've yet to meet him," Outram said in a voice intended to make the director feel venal.

"It is not to his discredit that the ladies are not satisfied. Every year they find out they are not satisfied." And Mr. Rykstrom smiled in reference to the remark Outram had made that had caused Mr. Rykstrom to ask him if he was Freudian.

"But he will lose the job?"

"The indication is yes."

The knowledge that the young man, all unknown to himself, was to be deprived of his job made him appear to Harold Outram in a new and more attractive light. As he was driven back to the city in Mr. Rykstrom's car, having first made the telephone call to warn Vincent of his lateness, he thought of the young man as being alone in the world and therefore the readier to give and receive friendship. At that time in his life Harold Outram thought often of friendship and was conscious of his need for it.

He identified Vincent Hammell almost at once. The great dark lobby of the Club had cleared and the young man was easily to be picked out. Outram took in at once the quality that he saw in Vincent's face, the handsomeness that was made not so much by the features as by the intelligence that organized them, the quality that Outram thought of as "breeding," or so he named the quality of the face that had been put there by some solicitude, no doubt parental, the appearance of someone set apart as special. What Harold Outram was not aware of was that young Hammell's face attracted him because it matched one of the several, one of the more forgivable, ideas he had of his own appearance.

At almost the same moment, Vincent became sure that this tall man entering the lobby was Harold Outram. He was struck with a poignant dismay. It was a response he often had to men of Outram's age. Old men or men who had crystallized into true middle age did not disturb him. They were of another race. But when youth still lingered, when the jaw had still a clean line and the expression still retained boyishness and good looks, he was often frightened and repelled. Nothing else gave him the same sense of life in process, the process being one of decay and disintegration. It was the loss, he felt, of the vital and moral strength. It seemed to Vincent that upon men in their thirties life had worked only to their shame. His first emotions upon sight of Harold Outram were of fear and pity.

chapter 7

The two men sat in the great bright dining-room of the Club. They had still scarcely spoken, yet it seemed that by merely leading Vincent to the dining-room, by choosing a table and ordering lunch, Harold Outram had established a connection, even an intimacy. Vincent looked back to his first impression with wonder, so vivid, so charming, so beautifully organized did Harold Outram now seem to him. Decay and disintegration were words most precisely inappropriate to his presence. By his air, in every detail of his manner, he confirmed to Vincent the promise of life that his letter had made. Outram was tall and well set up and held himself straight, especially when he walked through the dining-room, as if he were resisting the glances that might be directed his way. His close-cropped hair was light in color, but not so light as to seem less than masculine. If there was a hint of the late Greek in the full mouth and the rounded chin, this was contradicted by the solidity of the skull, the expanse of the forehead and the restless, repressed energy of the eyes.

Outram had made no apology for his lateness until they were seated and their cocktails and lunch ordered. His apology, when it came, was charged with personal meaning for Vincent. "I'm sorry I was late," he said, "I was held up at Meadowfield. That Rykstrom! What a bastard he is." To hear so great a power as Outram handle so great a power as Rykstrom made Vincent's current of life flow faster. It suddenly came to him that the still greater powers of the world, the presidents and the premiers, the marshalls and the millionaires, talked about each other in just such a way. The veil of anonymity fell away from government. He saw into its very heart. He felt like the efficient young agent or secretary of a cabinet minister, he with his clear vision and heightened pulse.

"What a reactionary bastard he is," said Outram.

Vincent had now to understand that he was secretary to a political personage of the liberal persuasion. It was a point necessary to have clear after those political wanderings of Outram's.

"Am I right?" Outram asked.

"Yes, you're right," Vincent said in a matter-of-fact tone.

"Firings?" Outram's voice was professional, precisely to the point.

"Well—forced resignations. Petty persecutions, that sort of thing."

"Friends of yours?"

"Well, yes—close acquaintances." Vincent had the sense of being brilliantly succinct.

"What's their story?"

Vincent told what he knew about Meadowfield and Rykstrom. Yet he did not speak as he would have expected to. For the first time in his life he had a relation to a reality of money and tangibilities. To himself and his friends Meadowfield was a whited sepulchre of culture and Rykstrom was a byword, a man at once sinister and ridiculous. But as he talked now he had clearly in mind the solid existence of the Meadowfield buildings, the hundreds of students and the scores of teachers who daily used them, the details of kitchens and furnaces, gardens and repairs, all the manifestations of existence that an institution makes. The power that Outram represented made him aware of Meadowfield's solid, bulking, corporate life, its existence not merely in the mind but on the earth. It was the first time that Vincent had ever been in connection with such an existence. All that he and his friends had ever owned or dealt with existed only in the mind. He found that the scandalous, sour gossip that he and his friends exchanged about Meadowfield was no longer so relevant as it had once seemed. It had to be strained through the sieve of a new sobriety and responsibility.

He thought about this later and with a little dismay. His sudden new conception of Meadowfield seemed to him a defection from the purity of his idealism. It was to be for him a measure of Outram's quality that in so brief a time in Outram's company he had learned so much about politics. For the second time that day he had occasion to be aware that his youth was over.

The conversation about Meadowfield drew to an end. Outram had the sense that they were now at the close of a prelude. Outram smiled and said, "It was kind of you to write that letter to me."

And then he added, "But also, of course, it was cruel."

The second remark, casually flung out, might have been made simply for the purpose of seeing how the young man would handle it. At any rate, the young man felt it to be in the nature of an emergency and a test. He did not handle it badly. "Yes," he said quietly, "I thought of that, but I took a chance that you would feel the other more."

At this a silence fell. They both contributed to it as if it were a conversation. Then Outram said, "Tell me—do you believe in fate? in destiny?"

Vincent that morning had made a wager with his fate on the tennis court, yet to him the question seemed a bizarre one and he looked embarrassed for his companion. He groped for an answer and, as he hesitated, Outram looked at him with an impatient glance, as if he were being excessively dull. "It will interest you," Outram said. "One evening a friend of mine, name of Philip Dyas, walked over to my house—I live in the country—and he brought with him a copy of a magazine, *The Prairie Review*. He wanted me to read an essay by a young man, name of Hammell. The next morning a letter came to me from the same young man. It sounds like fate, doesn't it?"

And then Outram said sharply, "You don't *know* Philip Dyas, do you?"

Outram's sudden question seemed to suggest that his friend Philip Dyas had been conspiring with Vincent. It was an odd enough notion to make Vincent laugh as he said, "Never heard of him." But it also made his heart beat faster. What end could Outram have supposed the conspiracy to have?

"No, of course you never have," Outram said. "So you can see why I asked you if you believed in fate?" But of course Outram had not explained anything about "fate." He had only related a coincidence. Fate surely meant that the coincidence would yield a great and presumably desirable event. The blood beat in Vincent's ears like the hooves of approaching horses. The explanation of "fate" was clearly still to come.

"It's really remarkable," Outram said. He was not referring to the coincidence, for to Vincent's astonishment he drew from his breast-pocket the very article itself, cut from *The Prairie Review* and neatly stapled into a little pamphlet. He laid it on the table as if it were a document in the case, the papers of some transaction that was in negotiation between them.

The essay was the same that Kramer had spoken of, the one pretentiously entitled "The Sociology of the Written Word." It began with the statement that in every age society provides certain means by which the young man of the lower middle class, sometimes the actually poor man, can rise to honor and power. Such a means is the law, the church, the army in time of war. Another means is the arts, of which literature calls most often to the young man of good gifts and generous ambitions, for literature seems to need not much more equipment than a firm will and a good intelligence. But for that very reason, Vincent had gone on to point out, literature is the most treacherous of all the artistic professions. The young writer has no such demonstrable seal upon his calling as the manual skill of the young painter, or the technical dexterity of the musician. He cannot be disciplined in his craft by elementary teachers, there are no masters to judge for him the proficiency of his technique at an early age, no finger exercises by which he can show his first mechanical skill. His is the art in which technique is least specific, least communicable, seems to depend largely on a condition of inner life. He dares trust no one to say where he has gone wrong. He needs a courage which amounts to arrogance, and, if he lacks this, he can become so panic-stricken that he cannot work.

Following this, Vincent had sketched the moral dilemma the young man faces. For the choice of the literary career bestows upon him a moral status which is of considerable, if ambiguous, interest to those around him. He sets himself up, by his choice, in a moral superiority, he is moved by an impulse of protest and separation. Yet at the same time that he sets himself apart, he files his application for praise and fame. Now follows, Vincent had said, a game with almost impossible rules. Moral superiority consists in being indifferent to society's demands and even hostile to them. Yet praise and fame are being sought—what else can bestow them save this rejected society itself? And if praise and fame come, is it because the writer has been morally convincing or because he has surrendered his moral integrity? In short, the rule that the solitary player establishes for himself is that he must make a goal at both ends of the field and simultaneously.

Outram leafed through the stapled pages as if refreshing his memory of them. "How old are you?" he said.

"Twenty-three."

"You know a great deal. It's the kind of situation that they set up to drive rats crazy in psychological laboratories. And you're very clever with your 'Ways.'"

He was referring to Vincent's enumeration of the ways the writer may be tempted to take through the stony land. There was what he called The Way of Tom Sawyer, in which the writer lives by his joyful presence at his own funeral—he settles for present intransigence and misunderstanding with praise and fame to come after death. The Way of the Virgin was the surrender of the dedicated talents to the wealth which is nowadays so lavishly ready for them—a youthful dedication has the effect of raising a writer's value and of stimulating the interest of money, precisely as did a fresh virginity in the old comic plays. The Way of the Pillar of Salt was the writer's choice of integrity together with sterility—he becomes a writer in name but not in deed, and he makes this choice on an historical principle which holds that creation has ceased to be possible in the modern world.

"You're a very mordant fellow," Outram said, "yes, quite a mordant fellow." There was a harsh and challenging note in his voice.

It was by way of being a kind of compliment, but Vincent's heart sank. Outram was looking at him curiously. He felt mocked and belittled. Under Outram's gaze, his high sense of life sank to extinction.

"But there is one Way that you left out," Outram was continuing, "It's an important one. The Way of the Darling. It's a new one, and it's remarkably effective. You must be very young and attractive for it, and really gifted. You must be very taut and energetic, willing to work hard, but full of deep feeling. The fire of idealism must be in your eye, the light of dedication. And if the fire is of the right kind, it is astonishing how many people will try to keep it burning there for you—and make it their own. They will love you for the youth and devotion they don't have any more. You will be their rebel—for you must be rebellious, a little rebellious, and at the right time you must rebel against unconsidered rebellion. You will be their darling. Very subtle, that one."

Suddenly Vincent felt very weary. All the sense of quick, heightened life which he had had at the beginning of the interview was gone from him. His essay had been written with a certain irony and also with a magical intention—for if you could represent the case as bad enough perhaps you could propitiate the fates. Outram was taking the essay with a literalness that was not intended. It seemed to represent for him a perfect reality. And when he had spoken of the Way of the Darling had he been accusing Vincent himself of having chosen that Way? Vincent's guilt for his deep desire made it seem terribly possible that the accusation had been made.

But perhaps not, for Outram said searchingly, "And you—do you think you will avoid all the Ways?"

Whether or not the specific accusation had been made, a wave of misery swept over Vincent. Yes, all the irony and all the magic had gone from his poor little essay. He had been dealing, after all, with facts. The man across the table was taking them as facts. Indeed, the man across the table was living proof of the reality of the facts. "No," Vincent heard himself saying, "I am quite a common type, really quite ordinary. I want to live the life, not be the thing."

It was a terrible thing to say. In his worst moments of despair he had never thought this of himself. He did not know why this idea about himself had come to him now. He did not know whether or not it was true, this admission that he was not a truly dedicated spirit. But he had suddenly had to say it. Something in Outram's presence had demanded that he say it. And not only to say it but feel it.

Outram said, "It's a great temptation to pay for the life of the writer with worry and self-torture. It's much harder to pay for it with work."

His manner was stern, it had a nearly paternal firmness of authority. This allowed Vincent to make his own next remark almost angry. "You make it sound easy," he said. "But the work—the work is to resist, to resist, and then to continue to resist." It seemed to him that he was no longer talking about himself. He said, "You talk as if it were a matter of industriousness. It is not. It is—"

And here Vincent stopped, for he did not know how to go on, so heavy was his heart, so hopeless, in the company of Harold Outram, was all possibility of living as one would. Outram had not said anything about that hopelessness, yet it was his message, it was announced, he intended it to be announced, by his whole being. It was the poetry and drama of his existence, to be heard in every tone of his voice, in the way in which he handled his cocktail glass and his knife and fork. And as poetry and drama it had a nobility and charm, it had heroism. It called to Vincent like the possibility of a voluptuous experience.

Vincent tried to say what he meant. "It is not effort and will. It is—" But still he did not know how to go on until he heard himself say, "*You* should certainly know what it is."

It was a dreadful thing to say, unforgivable. Outram's own great failure, it is true, had been taken for granted between them. It was a fact that Outram had laid on the table just as he had laid Vincent's essay. Yet even so, it was a terrible thing to say. But as the words came, Vincent knew that if they did not immediately destroy all relationship with this man, they would establish it beyond anything he might ever say or do.

He saw Outram pale under the direct blow. Then Outram raised his head and looked him full and searchingly in the face. The forms of politeness, the plane of ordinary social intercourse, had been transcended. Outram said quietly, "Yes, you are right. Who should know if *I* do not?"

Then he said, gently, solicitously, "What is it you resist?"

Vincent did not know. He had never put into words the dark and terrible moods that could descend upon him. But he found that he had the impulse now to speak sorrowfully and with dignity. Here in this great room, surrounded by the representatives of alien, unconscious power, he wanted to speak of what he felt. He said, not knowing what the words would be until he heard them, "Loneliness. The certainty that you are not connected with the past or the future. That no good can come of you. Or to you. That humanity is something that happened long ago."

"Yes!" Outram said, and the intensity with which he spoke, the full sad relief with which he sighed out that assent, astonished his companion. They sat silent as men do when they have agreed to share a common pity for a fate they have in common.

chapter 8

For both of them it was a difficult silence to come out of, so intimate was it. Vincent, despising himself for not being able to support it longer, said, "I've just been seeing an old friend of yours."

"An old friend? Who could that be?" Outram was polite, but Vincent heard in his voice a note of caution.

"Theodore Kramer."

Outram repeated the name in a grave and musing voice, seeming to let it evoke what memories it would. Vincent found himself a little surprised at this mild unshaken response. He wondered what kind of response he had expected, what kind of effect he had wanted to work upon Outram by the mention of Kramer's name.

"Old Teddy Kramer," Outram said. "Of course—he's been here at the university for a long time now. Was he a teacher of yours?"

"Yes he was," Vincent said, and some contrite loyalty led him to add, "and a very good one too."

"I'll bet he was," Outram said with great heartiness. "And how is Teddy?"

"All right," said Vincent. "All right and working hard."

"And that book—that big book on—who was it?—Wassermann was it? How is that going?"

"Sudermann—not Wassermann."

"Sudermann, of course. Is it finished yet? Teddy sends me reprints of articles from learned periodicals every now and then—studies for the book, I suppose."

The cold of shock and the warmth of great internal laughter simultaneously suffused Vincent's mind. Kramer's little treachery—was it treachery?—was so comic, so wonderfully, humanly frail that it had a kind of fragrance the reason for which he could not at the moment understand. In answer to Outram's question, he shook his head, and smiled—no, the book was not yet finished. There was an answering smile from Outram. Both smiles were grave and understanding. Between them, quite finally understood, lay the touching career of their friend, Theodore Kramer. At its bedside, filled with pity for it, Vincent Hammell and Harold Outram became increasingly aware of each other. Each of them responded to the quality of life in the other, which seemed the more vital by reason of that poor moribund career of Kramer's. They were closer together than they had been before.

"What's the matter with Teddy? Is he up to his old tricks, too conscientious, waiting for that last pointless document to be unearthed?"

"Yes, something like that. He is cursed with encyclopedism. He feels that he can know nothing without knowing everything. He has taken all knowledge for his province and he daily becomes more provincial."

Outram smiled at the young man's wit and passed it by. "Teddy has never forgiven me for what he calls *deserting*," he said. "The last time we saw each other in the East, he quite denounced me and left hating me."

Vincent said with mature assurance, "He would scarcely send you reprints of his articles if he hated you. I know he doesn't hate you."

Outram's curiosity was frank. "He talks about me then?"

"Yes, naturally he talks about you."

"We were never intimate friends," Outram said, as much gratified by the assurance that Kramer did not hate him as he had been by expressing his own belief in Kramer's animosity. "Still, we were good friends."

Then, quite changing the subject, he said, "Tell me about yourself—what do you do?"

The suddenness of the question, and its proprietary tone quite jarred Vincent and made the little list he could give seem very bleak. "I have a little job at the university," he said, "what they call an assistantship. I give a section of freshman English. Then I give the course at Meadowfield—"

"Wait," said Outram, "I can guess the rest—a little tutoring now and then for the football team, reading examination papers for the big course the Dean gives, a speech ghosted for a state senator, a little work for one of the newspapers. Am I right?"

"Well, pretty much."

"We've all done it one time or another. And I bet I'm right about the atmosphere in which you live, the clutch at the belly when you think of the passing of a year, the parents a little proud but very puzzled and always worried about the present and the future. And always the struggle to keep enough time for the book. Enough time and enough pride. I suppose there *is* a book?"

If his voice had a touch of mockery, it was of the most fraternal sort.

"Oh yes," Vincent said, using a little mockery himself. "There's a book all right."

"A novel of course."

"No, not a novel." Vincent had no impulse to explain further.

"Ah yes—your generation no longer worships the novel. In my time it was novel or nothing. We spent our days getting ready for it, looking for experience. An *honest* novel it had to be—honest was the big word. And always one novel was what we thought of. Only one, very big, enormous. Then, having laid this enormous egg, I suppose we expected to die. It had to be big and explosively honest—you'd think we were collecting dynamite grain by grain, you'd think we were constructing a bomb. We expected to blow everything to bits with our honesty."

Outram was giving way to an extravagant humor, but Vincent found it harsh and jarring. "You're a cagier generation, you live—I suppose you think—in a tougher, narrower time, you play it safer and wiser. I suppose," Outram said, "it's a critical book?"

"Yes, in a way it is," Vincent said with reserve.

"Good, good," Outram said with savage ironic approval. He doubled his fist and struck the table with it. Then he did this again. "Good," he said. "Build with the bones of the dead men and you'll be much safer. Judge the corpses and tell us how they smell. That's the right way to do it."

His silly words were uttered through clenched teeth. His face was very violent. The bitter hostility of his voice was not directed at Vincent in particular, but it took in so much that inevitably it included Vincent too.

Vincent was bewildered for himself and at the same time overcome with embarrassment for his host. He wished to look away. In Outram's outburst there was a quality of hysteria that entirely disconcerted him.

The hostility in Outram's eyes seemed to suggest that the vague wonderful opportunity which Outram represented either did not exist or was now suddenly to be withdrawn. And withdrawn it might have been if at this moment Vincent had obeyed his almost overwhelming desire to turn his glance from the fierceness of Outram's face and from the panic in it.

This he himself was later to understand and he never ceased to wonder how, out of his unformed and untried youth, he had been able to snatch the craft and courage to look full into Outram's eyes. But he did look—and not only with stubborn resistance but with sternness and even with a challenging and almost cruel curiosity.

Outram met the look full and it checked him. The whirling bitterness that had taken charge of his will met something resistant, perhaps not indestructible but at least showing an intention of not being destroyed. There was therefore no longer a temptation to destroy it. He permitted Vincent's look to engage his, he felt released from a bad necessity.

He said quietly, "What is the book about?"

Vincent held his answer, not too long, not vindictively, just an appreciable moment. Then he acknowledged the encounter over. He even allowed himself a smile of deprecation as he said, "It's about American literature."

Outram's expression of astonishment was perfectly good-natured. "All of it?" he asked, "At your age?"

"Well, perhaps eventually," Vincent said, his sense of power brought forward by the flattery of Outram's surprise. And he went on to speak of the scope of his enterprise. Outram scrutinized his face as if to learn whether the task was within his abilities.

"Let me ask you a question," Outram said.

Vincent waited for the question.

"Why are you undertaking this thing?" And as if Vincent were about to answer immediately, Outram held up a checking hand. "Oh of course, from the point of view of a career, it is perfectly understandable. You're very wise in your choice of subject. The American subject—it's in the cards. There's going to be an enormous boom—there is already. Things are bad in Europe, we're going to start looking inward, we're sick of running ourselves down when the rest of the world is such a mess. If your tone is right, you may have a great success. But I don't mean that. I mean apart from that."

There was an answer and Vincent was prepared to give it. He had given it before, to himself and others. Perhaps he had given it too often, for it was by now so well formulated that the phrases came a little too pat to suit his own ear. Yet, for all that, the answer was a sincere one—the answer that nothing in the world interested him so much as the American mind in its effort to comprehend the American complexity.

He was about to make this answer, knowing that the note of sincerity and even of passion would sound in his voice, sensing that this would move Outram and impress him. But Outram's remarks about the cleverness of his choice of a subject made him hesitate. The assurance that his project might succeed because of tendencies that Outram spoke of with a certain scorn, suggested to him how much his intellectual passion was interwoven with his vulgar will to be "successful." And as his answer, its sincerity now a little suspect, was not quick, Outram went on to define the question further.

"Are you driven to it? Is it an absolute necessity? Or are you doing it because you are a young man with ambitions and this is the way that presents itself to you? Is there, for example, nothing else that would satisfy you as well as this?"

"The question interests me for many reasons," Outram went on. "The fact is that literature is dead. The literary culture of Western Europe—it's dead, dead and done with. What is the greatest country in the world today? You know as well as I do that it's Russia. Sooner or later we will understand that Russia is our future and our hope. And Russia has produced not one single notable work of art. Oh, don't jump to what you think is the defense, don't tell me that time will produce masterpieces. I don't know what your politics are, but they don't matter in what I'm talking about—I'm talking beyond politics. In nearly twenty years, out of those millions of people, not one young man has forced his way forward with his creative talent. They groom that one composer, What's-his-name. Advertising, just advertising. He lives off Beethoven, via Brahms and he makes it look like a cultural continuity—very useful, as the real people there of course know. At the *beginning* of the revolution, there was some real work done, when you would least expect it, in the midst of a civil war, in the midst of starvation. But it's done with now. And the fact is that Russia is right. Literature—art—it was a phase of man's development and Russia is showing the way to the new phase. And you know as well as I do that the arts cannot survive. Let me put it this way—"

At this moment the waiter appeared to remove their plates and serve their coffee. Outram waited to resume his speech until the waiter was at some distance. It was as if what he had to communicate was a secret.

"Let me put it this way: that Russia has perceived before any of us that the arts, about which we are so politically sentimental, are one of the great barriers in the way of human freedom and decency."

Vincent wanted to object, but his mind was not responding to his will. It was not possible to answer a statement so extreme—it was not merely that it was wrong, but that in the extremity of its wrongness it carried him outside the borders of known discourse. If Outram had said to him, "You, Hammell, are a liar, a pimp and a traitor," he would not have been able to argue it. He could only wonder if it were true, else why should Outram have said it. He had his second political insight of the luncheon, he understood the power of the accusatory lie. He saw that it was not Outram's ideas that he had to meet. The ideas of this man whose intelligence was so beautifully stamped on his face were so foolish and shallow that it was almost as if Outram were saying aloud, desperately, "Pay no attention to my ideas—look only at the impulse behind them. Look there!"

And it was exactly the impulse behind them that Vincent knew he had to meet, the pain, the wild sense of loss and the consequent desire to destroy. And it was exactly that impulse that was too strong for him. It numbed his mind and made his will impotent. He had no response to make, neither to defend himself nor to help Outram. He had checked Outram once and saved them both. But he could not do it again. He sat silent, passive to whatever Outram might go on to say in development of his wild theme.

"But all that doesn't matter," Outram said with a dismissive and concluding sweep of his hand. "The fact is that they are dead, and putrescent. Tell me, what does the name 'Jorris Buxton' mean to you?"

chapter 9

The change of subject was bewildering and irritating. He of course knew who Buxton was. But he could see no reason why the capricious introduction of even a very adequate minor poet and novelist of thirty years before should shunt him off from the answer he must make. What Outram had been saying had a quality of conviction beyond what it should have had. It made Vincent's spirit sink down toward the despair which was all too ready for it. Outram seemed to have some wish to depress him. He was responding to that wish against his will, yet willingly. But he managed to resist. He ignored Outram's question about Buxton and said, "I think you're wrong. I think you're looking at it over too short a span of time. The human spirit does not change its needs so easily as you seem to think."

The slight tremor with which he uttered these words was really the expression of the misery which had invaded his mind. But it gave to what he said a great intensity, the color of a high conviction. To Vincent himself the words sounded insincere, but in Outram's face he saw a flicker of response, an almost childlike heed, and he perceived the ambiguity of Outram's intention. In all his twenty-three years he had not learned so much about human conduct as he was learning in this brief hour. And on this latest piece of knowledge, the awareness that Outram wanted his guest to fight his despair—or at least wanted that as much as he wanted to impose his despair—he was able to act, although Outram's dominance of face, its strength and beauty and bitterness, seemed to forbid manipulation. "No," Vincent said and shook his head fiercely, "the human spirit doesn't willingly diminish itself, even if it contracts momentarily at times."

The phrase which he had already used twice, "the human spirit," would ordinarily have disgusted him, but on this occasion he clung to it and used it again.

"Do you see so much that supports that fine idea? Christ, look around you," Outram said.

His matter was the same, but his manner had changed. He said, "We're all dead men, walking dead men. Even you, Hammell, young as you are—you're a walking dead man with the rest of us." But now it was as if he were making a genial joke, stating a comfortable absurdity.

He said very levelly and quietly, "There is only one man I've ever met whom I respect, and pretty soon he'll be really dead. I asked you about Jorris Buxton. He'll soon be eighty. For me he is the last manifestation of heroism in the human race. Men were like that once. Or maybe they were. But he is the last. But for me he also points the way to the new race. What do you know about him?"

"Well, I must confess that I didn't know he was alive—"

"That's not surprising," Outram said drily and morally. "Very few of his countrymen know that he's alive. But what do you know about him?"

"Not much, really. It seems to me that back in the 'eighties he taught Greek in a little college in New England. He published a volume of lyrics in the Greek manner. Then he seems to have given up teaching and to have travelled a good deal. There were, I think, a couple of books of travel. Then he took up painting and then he wrote three novels. The novels were never popular, though every now and then someone discovers them and writes a little essay. I read one of them quite a while ago. After the turn of the century he seems to have stopped writing and to have dropped from sight. I'm afraid that's all I know."

Outram was nodding to each of the facts of Vincent's recitation. "Yes," he said, "dropped from sight." And he sat there as if musing elegiacally, his fine eyes focussed into the distance.

"Now I'll tell you a little more," he said. "When Buxton was forty, he gave up the arts. Like that! He just gave them up. America didn't want him as a writer or a painter. Perhaps if he had been wanted he would have been better. He knew he was good, but not really of the first rank, and I suppose that that helped him make up his mind. But don't think he made his decision in a fit of pique. It was an act of free will, or as nearly an act of free will as we can imagine. At any rate, it was an act of self-understanding. He knew he had simply outgrown the arts. Outgrown them. Can you understand that? He never had to worry about money—when he was still a young man he came into a sizeable legacy. And at forty he felt that he had grown up. Do you know what he did?—evidently you don't. He became a physicist. He engaged a tutor and in a year he had learned everything that a brilliant student learns in four years of college. I asked him once if he had found it difficult and he shook his head and said that everything he had learned seemed to be there inside him ready to be unfolded. That is, he was a genius. He went to M.I.T. and his doctoral thesis is still famous. That was thirty-odd years ago. He took jobs in several of the great physical laboratories. He went to Europe and studied mathematics. A few years ago he retired to the country. He's a neighbor of mine."

Harold Outram took a cigarette and lighted it slowly. "Do you know what mathematical physics is?" he said. His voice became suddenly very quiet as if a large peace had been imposed upon him. "Do you know that there are men who with paper and pencil construct the plan of the universe down to its subtlest, most secret aspects, sitting alone, with no tools but their minds?" Out of the raptness of his voice there came a note of accusation, as if Vincent had been unconsciously persecuting the mathematical physicists of the world.

"Buxton is one of the leading mathematical physicists of the country. Of course you wouldn't know that, being a literary man. You're surprised to know he's alive. And I didn't know it myself until a year ago because I'm a kind of literary man myself, a vulgar cheapjack journalist. Or was. Did you know that?—I mean Buxton's position as a scientist?"

"No," said Vincent, consenting to admit again the admitted fact. "I didn't know it. It's a fine story."

"Fine story. It's *the* story of our time." And again there was accusation in the voice.

"I've recently come to know him. He lives near me at Essex where I have my place. Naturally I don't talk much to him—what would I have to say to a man like that? But whenever I speak to him—well, nothing in my life has ever meant so much to me. Can you understand that?"

"Yes, I think I can understand it," Vincent said in a neutral voice. But his heart was beating with presentiment. Something in Outram's manner suggested that something was still to come for which all that had been said, with its passion and confusion, was but a preparation. Outram took a long breath and put out his cigarette with delicate care. He seemed to relax as if he had at last reached level ground after an exhausting ascent. He leaned back in his chair, regarding Vincent as from a distance.

"Perhaps you can begin to see where I've been leading. Buxton, after all, can't last very long. We want his story told. He ought, I suppose, [to] tell it himself. He won't. But we've got him to promise to help a biographer. Buxton will talk, he will answer questions, he'll supply documents. What we are looking for is the man to write the book."

Vincent had the sensation of being able to reach out and touch it, so firm and certain did the great opportunity seem, so impossibly materialized out of the fantastic but passionate hope of his tennis court bet with himself. As solid and real as a hunk of mineral placed on the table, the opportunity was before him.

There it was, but it had not yet been offered and Outram had fallen silent. For a moment Vincent said nothing. Then he said, "Why don't *you* do it?"

"For Christ's sake!" said Outram. He spoke not with anger but with a kind of intense exasperation, as if some old friend had made an error about him after every chance of knowing better. He said with large kindness, "Hammell—Vincent—get this straight in your relations with me. I'm finished, I'm through. Get it straight, Vincent, so that it doesn't make trouble between us. I know what I am. I know all about myself."

"And besides," he went on, "we want to give a young man this chance."

But having gone this far, Outram still did not say what every nerve in Vincent's body wanted him to say.

"You say 'we'—'we want,'" Vincent said.

"'We' is several people, but chiefly Garda Thorne and myself. She lives near me and she has very strong feelings about Buxton too."

If the mineral had been wonderful in its solid reality, it now began to glow with light. And with a gentle and reassuring light at that. For if ever anyone stood as a negation of all the desperate denials that Harold Outram had been making, it was surely Garda Thorne with her wholly enviable career. In the perfection of everything she did, in the quiet, delicate integrity of her life, she, though a woman, stood to many young men like Vincent as an assurance that virtue was possible. And as the mineral glowed, "Do you want it?" Harold Outram said at last.

To keep his gravity, for he was in danger of smiling foolishly, Vincent carefully moved his water-tumbler from one place on the table to another. Then he was able to look up at Outram and say, "Yes."

"Good," Outram said with decision. "You'll be hearing from me about the details. I'm sure they'll be satisfactory." He put out his hand across the table and they shook hands with seriousness.

chapter 10

Nine women sat awaiting the arrival of Vincent Hammell. The room they sat in was beautiful and bright; its broad windows looked out on the little lake around which the buildings of Meadowfield were disposed. The women sat around a table of plate-glass and their nine handbags lay in an archipelago upon its great lucid surface.

Of the nine women, all were very wealthy. They made Vincent's first experience of wealth and nothing he had learned from books or even from the gradual growth of the fortune of Toss Dodge's family had prepared him for what he found. It seemed to Vincent that only in the case of one of them, Miss Anderson, the chairman of the group, had wealth been a true condition of life, shaping and marking her as nothing else could have done. She alone bore something of the imagined appearance of wealth, the serenity and disinterestedness to which wealth is supposed ideally to aspire.

Vincent supposed that either the size or the age or the nature of Miss Anderson's fortune had led her—as fortunes of a kind sometimes do—into an historical lapse, an aberration of her sense of time. For Miss Anderson, although not "old-fashioned" nor long past her youth, seemed not to inhabit quite the same present in which her friends lived. She seemed, indeed, to live in reference to certain delicate points of honor such as Edith Wharton, but few after her, would have been concerned with. It might be assumed, for example, that some high moral decision, its meaning now obscured, accounted for the unmarried state of a woman _____ [blank in original] so pleasant as Miss Anderson. It was surely to be laid to some sacrifice of herself, some service of an idea. The idea which she served would not have to be very complex or important, but still it was an idea. Perhaps this explained the "historical" impression she made, for to many people the present consists of things, while the past consists of ideas. Like the past, Miss Anderson was a failure, yet in some way she continued to exist with a gentle unsought authority which perhaps came from her friends' dim response to the power of the idea and their recognition of the magical, if limited, potency of the past.

Now and then Miss Anderson submitted to Vincent's criticism the stories she wrote. They were elaborate and literate—well written, the class called them—but they had no relation to any reality Vincent could identify. In the world of Miss Anderson's stories, servants were old and loyal, wives hid nameless diseases from their husbands or silently bore the most torturing infidelities, or found themselves hideously in the power of depraved lovers; memories played a great part, the memories of single passionate nights or of single significant phrases, and it sometimes happened that flowers or white gloves were forever cherished. When Vincent discussed these stories with Miss Anderson, he was always surprised at the small conviction with which he spoke about their lack of reality—he almost believed as he spoke to her, that there might actually be such a world beyond his strict modern knowledge.

The distinction which Miss Anderson had was perhaps but a weak one, yet it gave Vincent Hammell a standard by which he could fairly measure the inadequacy of her classmates. If she did not carry the power of her position, she at least seemed to carry its tragic consciousness. Wealth and position, Vincent felt, should appear in their proper forms and add to the variety of life. He was sure that there were proper forms both of refinement and vulgarity. But these women of the Creative Writing class made but a commonplace spectacle. Thus, the meagre taste in dress of Mrs. Stocker quite matched the meagreness of her face, which showed the irritable energy of a person whose social self-esteem is not matched by cash in the bank. Or Mrs. Territt was so very coarse in complexion, so brutally dull in manner that it was inevitable to suppose that what gentility she had was hanging by only a thread of income. Mrs. Knight was ruddy and healthy from an expensive outdoor life, but in other respects she appeared no more than merely well-off. Poor Miss Wilson's truly painful nervousness and her evasive eye quite transcended the bounds of class. But on the other hand it was even more difficult to believe in the actual status of Mrs. Broughton, Mrs. Forrester and old Mrs. Pomeroy, for wealth had marked them only in the way of parody and they were all three so "typical" that one had to suppose that they had been produced not so much by nature and circumstance as by certain artistic imaginations of rather limited range. In the East, Vincent had always felt, in cities of complex culture, wealth would surely make a better show, would impart a more firmly bottomed assurance, a more interesting arrogance.

Vincent, as he well knew, had not been a success with the group. But he knew that none of the instructors who had come before him had succeeded any better. The university had sent its best men, professors first, then young instructors and assistants, likely to be more modern. Each autumn the new man had been received with taut feminine expectancy, each spring he had been discarded, for he had not conveyed the precious, the inconceivable secret which the women had come in hopes to receive. Yet although Vincent understood that he was not successful, he always supposed that he was a little forgiven by reason of his sex and age. Actually, he was wrong to count on this feminine extenuation—his being masculine and young had made his case, if anything, even worse.

His own particular failure had no doubt begun when, upon being invited to instruct the group, organized by the Junior League, he had conjured up a vision of gently-bred ladies, all pretty and all precisely thirty years old, gracefully filling empty days and hearts with the delicate practice of an elegant art. He had not been prepared for the urgent women who were actually his pupils, nor for their really quite grim dark worship of the potency that print conferred, nor for their belief—more intense than any coterie in metropolitan garrets could have—that they were held in bondage by a great conspiracy of editors. Responding to Miss Anderson's gentleness and to her authority as chairman of the group, he had put to her the question of his progress. Using all her gentleness, yet bound by her authority, Miss Anderson had told him. She quite dissociated herself from the general feeling, perhaps dimly feeling it to be vulgar if not mistaken. "They feel, Mr. Hammell," she had said, "that you are very brilliant, but a little—*theoretical?*" A question in her voice deferred to his superior knowledge of words and gave him the right to reject this one if it in any way hurt his feelings. "What they want is something more—practical." This time there was no question, for she was sure that he could not be hurt by their desire for anything so ordinary, nor feel at fault for his inability to give it. "They think that perhaps they ought to get a literary agent from New York. What they want is 'straight dope'—contacts and the right approach." They despaired, these poor ladies, of having the secret of creation imparted to them and now they dreamed of the other secret, of the "straight dope," of contacts and the right approach. And even Miss Anderson, although she pronounced the first of their desires as if it were slang, uttered the other two quite without quotation marks, as literal and legitimate things.

Vincent carried a briefcase, an elegant piece of luggage of excellent leather and the best bronze hardware. It had been a gift from his parents who, with such gifts, useful but very fine and extravagant, kept for themselves and their son the memory and the hope of better days. Vincent laid it on the plate-glass table beneath which his own legs and the legs of his pupils were visible. Usually he was glad of the briefcase, for its elegance helped to arm his youth and poverty against the wealth of his pupils. But today he did not need its help. For the first time he felt the deep, pure pleasure, almost sensual, of freedom.

If anything could have heightened the great wonder of the lunch and its almost incredible offer, [it was] the arrival at his home that same evening of a bottle of the most extravagantly fine Scotch whiskey, elaborately wrapped, a gift from Harold Outram. The card enclosed said, "To celebrate the beginning of your enterprise—and our friendship," and the simplicity of its wording, the openness of its offer, gathered up all the aspects of Harold Outram that were charming and impressive, forming a figure that was enormously reassuring. The arrival of the whiskey in its red ribbons and with its cordial note made it both necessary and easy for Vincent to explain to his parents the nature of his good fortune and even to accept the quiet look of triumph and wise foreknowledge his mother legitimately wore. But two weeks had passed, then three, and May wore on into June and no word of confirmation or definition had come from Harold Outram, until the lunch and the offer seemed but a fantasy and only the bottle of whiskey and the card proved, like evidence in a fairytale, that the event had really taken place. But the letter had come at last with dates of arrival suggested, a check for travelling expenses and the whole financial arrangement laid out, and the thing was as real as it could be, making everything real with its own actuality. Already the Techniques of Creative Writing class seemed to him a lingering item of his past.

He opened the briefcase and took from it a thin folder of manuscripts. "Two weeks ago," he said, and waited for the class to come finally to order, "two weeks ago l asked you to write a story about some simple outdoor experience. You were to concentrate on the physical details. You remember that we discussed as models a passage from *Huckleberry Finn* and a story of Ernest Hemingway's." He picked up the folder and examined its thinness. "Some of you," he said drily, "carried out the assignment." For the fact was that very few members of the group ever wrote anything at all.

Mrs. Stocker moved in her seat to indicate a protest which Vincent understood—all this was elementary. Mrs. Stocker had once, but only once, sold a story, to a women's magazine, for a sizeable sum, and it was in part the memory of that great check that kept alight the flame of aspiration in the Techniques of Creative Writing class.

Vincent ignored Mrs. Stocker's demonstration and said, "I'd like to read one example." He took a manuscript from the folder. Only three of his pupils had attempted the assignment, two of them very dully. But he was rather proud of Mrs. Knight's little story. It was quite unpretentious, about a young wife who is left by her husband in their hunting lodge in the Canadian woods. She wakes in the night to hear a howling that can only be that of wild animals and then the creaking hinge of an of unlatched door opening and closing. She is not alone, but of her two guests one is another woman and the man is incompetent. She lies still and miserable, bearing all the sad isolation of responsibility. Her emotions are in conflict, she is afraid of the wolves but afraid to take steps to protect herself; yet more than anything is her fear of the contempt her absent husband will feel for her lack of courage. But at last she becomes bold—and finds that though indeed the door is unlatched, the howling is only that of a high wind. Her self-deception was perhaps not wholly convincing, but something in the matter of her story was indeed convincing, her desire to seem manly to her husband and the whole impulse of the story to discover safety where danger seemed to be.

Vincent read this story aloud. When he came to the end, he looked around the table, inviting comment.

"Very nice," Mrs. Broughton said. "Very nice indeed."

Mrs. Broughton had been imagined by a radical caricaturist of rather conventional fancy. Careless of verisimilitude, concerned only with the political passions he would arouse, this artist had drawn her short and pudgy, with a face of gross and foolish pride and a bridling neck that gave an air of condescension to her remarks, many of which were in their intention actually quite good-natured.

"Yes, it is quite nice," Mrs. Stocker said, suppressing as much as she could the professional condescension she felt. "Of course, it has no plot, no complication, no conflict really, but it has a kind of twist at the end, it is true to life and it has touches of realism."

"Oh, very realistic," said Mrs. Broughton.

"Well, I don't think it *is* very realistic," said Mrs. Forrester with sudden authority. As compared with the inventor of Mrs. Broughton, the imagination that had conceived Mrs. Forrester was of greater complexity—some social satirist, gifted but not profound, had projected this slim and elegant woman, no longer young but still beautiful, and had endowed her with an intensity of self-regard and a sense of *noblesse* so petulant and shoulder-shrugging, yet so easily snubbed, that poor Mrs. Forrester lived in a constant alternation of blind attack and bewildered retreat, with the result that since her beautiful girlhood scarcely anyone had felt toward her any emotion save the various degrees of contempt. "Not at all—to me it doesn't seem realistic at all. It isn't *convincing*," she said. "Now take the central problem—yes, take the central *problem*. That definitely is *not* convincing. She lies there worrying about what she should do. *Why? What for?*"—her appeal was vehement. "All that she had to do was ring for the guides and that would be *that*." Her beautiful dark eyes flashed finality.

There was a gasp from young Mrs. Knight. Her cheeks flamed. She almost rose from her chair. Her voice was choked. "It just so happens," she said with terrible scorn, "it just so happens that you couldn't ring for the guides, because in our lodge—there—are—no—guides—to—ring—for."

Mrs. Knight was defending not only her story from criticism but also her way of life from—it was relative poverty beside—Mrs. Forrester's great wealth and be-guided lodge. The group was quite with Mrs. Knight. As usual, Mrs. Forrester was put down.

Mrs. Stocker said, "Mr. Hammell, I gather that you like that story of Mrs. Knight's. And I like it too. It has a very fresh quality, definitely fresh. But the question I want to ask is whether in your opinion a story like that has a marketable value. Now you take Constance's stories—Miss Anderson's stories, Mr. Hammell. You yourself admit they have something. They're well thought out and they're well-written, they have suspense and a twist at the end. But the editors just never take them."

Miss Anderson looked up in surprise and unhappiness. Although now and then she sent her stories to market, she seemed to feel no chagrin at their refusal.

"Now why do you think that is, Mr. Hammell?" Mrs. Stocker said.

There was a silence, a degree of attention, even a note of embarrassment that suggested that Mrs. Stocker's question was pointed, that it was the outcome of expressed dissatisfaction with his methods. Miss Anderson looked detached from the matter at hand. While he considered how to answer, Mrs. Broughton broke the silence, bridling, "It's because they are refined and charming and what they want nowadays is coarse—and middle class. About miners. There was a story I read about two children who could hear each other practicing through the wall of their apartment." She tossed her head resentfully. "Who cares?"

Now Mrs. Territt spoke up and her coarse voice was injured and defensive. She said, "You all talk about selling stories. What I want to know is how to write them. That's what I come here to find out." She looked hostilely at Vincent. "All this talk about what's been done already! I came here to learn how to do it in the first place."

Three or four of the company were swayed by this utterance to confess among themselves what they had never before realized. "Yes, yes," they murmured and nodded to each other. The group was now divided between those who believed that the secret lay in learning to sell and those who believed that it lay in learning to write.

"Personally," Mrs. Territt said, and her glance at Vincent was now malevolent. "Personally that is what I give up my time to come here for. And I haven't got it—nothing." The agreement she had won had gone to her head and she was breathing hard.

Vincent said, "Mrs. Territt, one can only learn to write by writing." For the fact was that Mrs. Territt had never yet submitted a manuscript.

She bridled. "I suppose that's very smart." She used the word *smart* not in the English sense of something clean and precise or fashionable and elegant, but in the old American sense of something clever and impertinent. In the eyes of all present this declassed her.

Vincent said, "How long do you spend at your desk every day, Mrs. Territt?"

She did not answer but looked sullenly at the table before her.

"Four hours a day?" Vincent said inexorably. He could feel the solidifying interest of the group. The many handsomely shod feet seen through the top of the table looked like aquarial creatures as they shifted a little with interest.

"Three hours? Two? One solid hour every day?"

Mrs. Territt was sulking like a scolded chambermaid with an inexpressible grievance. Suddenly she flashed out, "No, why should I? When I never get any ideas?" It was a direct accusation of Vincent.

Someone snickered and no doubt the fight was won, but he went on. "How long do you spend every day trying to get ideas?"

She looked at him blankly from her raging sulks.

It was necessary to bring the matter to an end. Vincent took from his briefcase the book he had brought. It was a volume of stories by Garda Thorne. "Shall we go on?" he said quietly and impersonally. The women nodded, quite on his side against the revealed stupidity of Mrs. Territt.

Vincent began to read aloud the story he had selected. It was about two young American girls who were visiting friends in an Austrian village. They were Catholics and they were sent by their hostess to pay a call of ceremony on the priest of the village. The priest had received them charmingly, he was very polite. He was in an especially good humor because the new wine from the grapes of his own little arbor was just ready. It stood in his tin bathtub on the floor. Just as the visit began the priest was urgently sent for. He begged his young guests to remain until his return. They could not but agree, but, as his absence continued, they sat there bored and impatient and wondering how to amuse themselves until first one and then the other took off her shoes and stockings, held her skirts high and stepped into the tub. If you stopped to think of it, it was not entirely probable, but you did not stop to think of it, and it was a wonderfully funny and charming picture, the first girl standing in the wine, then the second, then both together, elegantly dressed and with their wide straw hats on, the drops of wine splashing up to their thighs, their white feet and ankles scarcely visible to themselves as they looked down into the roiled wine.

Then there was the scramble to get themselves presentable before the priest should come home, the scrubbing with inadequate handkerchiefs, the sanding of the stone floor to clean off the prints of their feet. When the priest returned they had to sit there demure, with their legs still sticky under their stockings. The priest served them glasses of the wine they had bathed in and their manners were perfect as they heard him say that never before had he known the wine to be so good.

As the story went on to its end, Vincent was sorry he had chosen it to read. The silence was becoming unusually intense. He had always admired Garda Thorne and her work was now naturally in his mind. And he had especially wanted Miss Anderson to hear the story, for he thought it might suggest to her, with its simplicity and gaiety, that there were better subjects than the artificialities she so feelingly contrived. But, as he read, he felt that it had been a cruel mistake to read this story to these women. As it went on through its narration of the flash of skirts and underskirts, of white stained thighs, the grave silence of the girls and then their giggles and the beautiful prints of their naked feet on the stone floor, it seemed to him that his own youth had been thoughtless to have chosen the story. He felt, too, like an intruder into feminine mysteries and the sweat came to his forehead. He dreaded the return of the priest and the end of the story when he would have to take his eyes from the book and look around. At last he finished. He did not look up but moodily sifted through the pages of the book. This had the histrionic effect of letting the story hang for a while in the air.

For a moment the silence continued. Then it was broken by Miss Anderson crying, "Oh that was lovely, Mr. Hammell," and "Lovely," "Lovely," "Lovely," echoed the women around the glass table, beneath whose surface there was a shifting of legs and a pulling down of skirts.

Vincent now ventured to look at their faces, which were relaxed and benign. There were little half-smiles on their mouths, directed tangentially at him. It was as if he himself had been the author of the story and as if the story had celebrated the things that were their peculiar possessions, their youth, their beauty, their femininity.

In the sunlit room, in the soft spring air, there was a moment of musing silence as the quest for the fierce and precious secret was abandoned. Despite himself, Vincent experienced a sense of power, in all his months of teaching the class, the first he had felt. Yet in the entrancement of the women, in their moment of brooding relaxation, there was something archaic and mythological, something latently dangerous. It was thus that the women of Thrace must have sat around Orpheus before they had occasion to be enraged with him. He would have liked to remind them, but it was not possible, that he had merely read aloud the story which someone else, a woman, Garda Thorne, had written.

It was old Mrs. Pomeroy who memorialized the moment. Mrs. Pomeroy was by far a gayer creation than either Mrs. Broughton or Mrs. Forrester. Perhaps she was aware of her role, perhaps she had even had the wit to invent it herself—she was the old lady of widest experience and profoundest wisdom, and it was impossible not to see her lengthy past of drawing rooms (at home and abroad) in which the brilliant and the famous were received. Silence and a twinkle were the evidences of Mrs. Pomeroy's breadth of culture. At certain literary names she would smile, as at the memory of old, intimate and special delights. But only once had she made vocal her feeling for the great past. On that occasion the name of Proust had been mentioned by Vincent and what Mrs. Pomeroy had said was, "And also Paul Bourget." She had added a knowledgeable whisper of explanation, "Psychology!" And now, as her way was, she smiled sadly and wisely as she spoke. She closed her eyes and said, "Such a story makes one truly glad there is literature. We should be so grateful."

She spoke so seldom and perhaps she was really wise—at her benediction upon literature and her admonition to gratitude everyone looked
solemn, as if, in the moving picture, they were present as Anatole France
delivered the panegyric at Zola's funeral.

"Very excellent," said Mrs. Broughton. "Very."

And now Mrs. Stocker spoke. "What I like about the story," she said,
"is that it is neither one thing nor another. I mean that it isn't highbrow
or commercial."

It was not that she wanted to bring the discussion back again to the
matter which so much interested her. No doubt she as much as anyone
else had been caught in the moment of contemplation, but in uttering
her feeling about it she used the only language she knew. And having
used that language it was now natural for her to say, "Tell me, Mr. Hammell, does this writer sell well?"

And at her question there was a little murmur of agreement to its
relevance and eyes turned to Vincent for his answer. Victory, it seemed,
was not permanent. But today he was so much at ease with himself that
he set out to win it again. He was glad to be able to speak simply and
with enthusiasm about Garda Thorne, telling how at infrequent intervals
she produced her exquisite stories, which, having made their way slowly,
were so eagerly sought after and waited for by the editors. He did not
speak of the symbolic place which she held in the minds of many people,
especially the young. At the moment he felt so in alliance with her that
he could speak about her only modestly. Nor did he find in himself any
malice as he spoke to these women of her skill and fortitude. But, for the
first time, he felt he was indeed their instructor.

And they seemed to take pleasure in what he said. Mrs. Stocker did
not press her question. Old Mrs. Pomeroy again smiled sadly and said,
"A heroine—a true heroine of literature."

"Very noble," said Mrs. Broughton briskly. "Very."

When the class was over, Miss Anderson stayed behind the others.
She was never quite at ease with Vincent, partly because he did not have
the advantages of her own class and this made her feel guilty, partly because he had other advantages and these she feared. The events of the
afternoon had made Vincent a more lively figure in her imagination than
he had ever been before. She admired, even while she disliked, the way
he had handled the disagreeable incident with Mrs. Territt. And the reading of Garda Thorne's story had put him in a new and slightly disturbing
character which, if Miss Anderson had examined it, would have seemed
to her not dissimilar from that of her physician. She was moved by ad-

miration and pity for him, she wished in some way to reward and placate him because he was not to be invited to teach the class next year.

"I wonder," she said, "if I might borrow the book."

Vincent understood the friendliness of the request. Miss Anderson often read the books he mentioned, but naturally she bought them.

"Oh, she's so good-looking," Miss Anderson said, for on the back of the book-jacket was a photograph of Garda Thorne. "That's rare, isn't it? A good woman writer who's so good-looking? Aren't they all supposed to be plain, like George Eliot?" Vincent knew that to the gentle Miss Anderson it was a matter for unhappiness that she was already seeing him as the dispensed-with teacher of the group. But he was armored in youth and armed with opportunity. He was in alliance with reality and drama. In all this great dull city of his childhood and youth there was now no opinion that could harm him.

He smiled politely in response to Miss Anderson's naughtiness about the appearance of women writers. "I expect I'll be meeting her soon," he said.

"You will?" she said almost incredulously. "Oh lucky you," she said. "How did you get the chance?"

As well as a wish to announce his independence there was a friendly impulse toward Miss Anderson that made him tell her about his great fortune. She took it in slowly, it was all outside her experience. The name of Harold Outram made it clearer to her, for she sat on the board of Meadowfield and she knew something of Outram's function. Her understanding of Vincent's fortune presented itself to her as a vision of a bright organized company of young males, moving forward, well accoutred, to positions that had been prepared for them. The young men moved in light, they shone with freedom, they glittered with the power of their poverty, they gleamed with the great strength of never having had mothers of high cultivation, nor three years of schooling at Lausanne, nor long visits in England and France, nor long talks on Botticelli with Professor Montani.

"Oh, that's wonderful," she said. She said it fervently because her envy, sharp as if she had been struck with one of the weapons the young men carried, was so truly unwanted. In an instant this Mr. Hammell, a young man on the point of being dispensed with, had been transformed into a member of the bright advancing band from which she was forever excluded.

"Oh I am so glad for you," she said, and she took his hand and held it.

Her intensity surprised Vincent. It was not inappropriate to this great event, but it was strange coming from the gentle Miss Anderson whom he would perhaps never see again. And the advice she gave him as she stood there holding his hand, as if at some ceremonial of rank, was also surprising, again not because it did not fit the occasion but because it was Miss Anderson who gave it. "I hope," she said, "oh I hope you can remember to be fierce."

chapter 11

On the great day of his departure Vincent woke early. He woke without gaping or stretching. To wake in this way was a matter of pride with him. It seemed to him a measurable adventure in love or adventure [*sic*]. Rising, he went to the mirror to examine his face. He saw that its contours were fined down by what his mother called "the intellectual look." She insisted that she could always tell when he had been working well. "It gives you the intellectual look," she said, "and then you're almost handsome." He thought she was right. Usually he did not approve of his face, but when he had been working with concentration he could see in it the attractive appearance of true disinterestedness. Today he had the look, but it came not from work but from his elation at the adventure before him and of the feeling of mastery it gave him.

He sang as he went to the bathroom and from the kitchen his mother called up to him, "You'll cry before dinner if you sing before breakfast." He answered her by lifting his voice defiantly. He continued to hum the song—it was Leporello's—as he stood before the mirror brushing his thick dark hair.

Mrs. Hammell's eyes that day were keen and weary. It was a hard day for her, and Vincent felt a pang at the thought of his departure. Not for a long time had he felt so alert for his mother or so confirmed in his loyalty. He had long dreamed of being free of his home, but now that the fulfillment of the dream was at hand, he thought of the pleasures and the rightness of living close to his roots, warmly in touch with his family and his past. For a moment his adventure seemed cold and astringent.

Mrs. Hammell poured her son's coffee and said, "Have you packed? You haven't shaved."

"I'll pack before I go down to say good-bye to father and I'll shave after I come back."

She reached her hand across the table and took his. In the manner of that gesture there was a great and frightening triumph for him, for she seemed to be claiming his hand with no more than the legitimate love of person for person which includes within itself the knowledge that the tie, however strong it may be, can possibly be broken. And there was this knowledge in her voice as she said, "Vincent, I don't care what you say, I'm going to the train with you."

He had not wanted her at the train, for he wished to depart manly and alone as befitted the occasion. But her voice, as she made the demand, so rang with her awareness that he had the right and the power to refuse her, that he was glad to relent.

The avenue down which Vincent walked was shabby. In a few years it would surely become sordid, but now it still held the memory of days when it was substantial, even fashionable. The new generation of the well-to-do lived in ample new suburbs and could scarcely imagine that these close-set heavy houses had ever represented comfort and standing. Manilla Boulevard had become a street of apartments and rented rooms, and, lately, of improvised stores, little hat and dress shops in which business was conducted with a confidential air. It was becoming too a street of specialists in certain technical services to the body, masseurs, podiatrists, electrolysis experts, beauty operators, and undertakers. A few lawyers combined home and office and declared their existence by signs which represented them as Counsellors at Law.[1]

Yet the Boulevard still had its trees and its small lawns. Among its houses were some that kept a strict respectability of trim hedges and flower borders and a few of the very oldest families of the city stubborn-

---

[1] This description also appears in chapter 4.

ly held their seats. The freshness of the morning air, the trees, the few houses that still resisted degradation, but most of all his near sense of departure, allowed Vincent to find a kind of beauty in American things not usually loved and now he was being rewarded by being able to find a valuable pathos in what he was leaving.

When he reached his father's place, his father greeted him with an air of general benevolence which somehow seemed to ignore the fact of his son's departure. Mr. Hammell said, "Good morning, my boy. I know you will appreciate this."

He held his old blue Everyman Spinoza at a conscientious distance from his eyes and read, "He who understands himself and his emotions loves God, and the more so the more he understands himself and his emotions!"

He lowered the book and looked mildly at Vincent. "Do you think that is true, son?"

It was not his father's habit to discuss philosophy with him and this seemed an odd occasion on which to begin. But Vincent undertook to answer as well as he could. "It isn't a question of true or not, father," he said. "It is true in its place, I suppose."

"You always want to put things in their place, my boy," Mr. Hammell said, his face suffused with sorrow for himself. "There are some things that can't be put in their place so easily."

Vincent made his answer respectful. "I only meant that some of the statements that Spinoza makes are true in their context. For instance, what he means by God isn't what most people mean by God."

"It is what I mean by God," Mr. Hammell said.

Vincent doubted this but did not reply. A year ago he would have argued, though not so fiercely as the year before that, and both of them would have become bitter. But he had learned how the pleasure of quarreling with his father always subsided into flat sickness with himself. And certainly now there was no necessity for him to quarrel. But at his silence, Mr. Hammell's face flushed and bloated with anger and he said, "That's what I mean by God—and by God, I'm no fool either."

"All right, father," Vincent said quietly and then was ashamed that he had been able to say it quietly.

"You stand there and talk as if Spinoza wasn't one of the greatest philosophers the world has ever known. You and your modern ideas, you and your crazy ideas, your crazy communist ideas."

Vincent said, "You know I'm not a communist, father." But there was no escape. To stand there all reasonable against his father's petulance, to wait out the tantrum with paternal forbearance, would leave him as drained as if he had spoken in rage.

He said, "Father, I came to say good-bye. I'm leaving today."

"I know," said Mr. Hammell. Then he said, "Son, we don't get on the way we used to."

By the tone of his voice it seemed that the past he meant was but a year or two before, but actually, as Vincent knew, he meant a time when Vincent was a boy of five and there had existed a great community between father and son.

"You used to understand your father. You don't understand him any more. Some day, son, he must have a talk with you." Mr. Hammell seemed to get a gratification from talking about himself as if he were someone else. "There are things you don't understand about him, things he could tell you that would open your eyes."

"I know, father," Vincent said.

He knew what his father meant—the rights of the long quarrel with his wife, the humiliations inflicted by her family, the deep hidden justice of all his actions. But more than any of these he meant at this moment the sacrifice of his talents which he believed he had made for Vincent, the curtailment of his possibilities, the surrender of his powers to the family's safety. For like many another young American, Vincent was the son not only of hope but of despair.

"You don't know, my son, you *don't* know," Mr. Hammell said. He was standing behind his counter and his voice rang with the desperation—no less terrible because he was consciously trying to express it—of a man who has no wife, no son, no work, no memories and no hope save that which made him cling, more than most men, to life and the regard of others.

And the word which he seemed most to rely on, the word "son," had no other effect upon the person it signified and to whom it was addressed than to make him wince internally as at some lapse of taste, as indeed it was. Vincent thought of the Pullman car he would soon inhabit. He thought that distance translates itself into time and that when he had arrived in the East, his father would be many years behind him. And he thought of the object of his journey, of Jorris Buxton, in his great old house, living with his knowledge of the universe, mighty with years, wisdom and power.

"Father, let it go for now," he said. "Please, father," he said. "I've come to say good-bye. Please let's not quarrel. After all, I'm going away."

Mr. Hammell smiled secretly, sadly and distantly. "Yes. I suppose you're doing what you think is right. But it's a terrible blow to me. It's a betrayal, son, I need you here."

A kind of panic came over Vincent, so completely was his father oblivious of him. In his father's mind there stood some abstract notion of the son he had planned to have, but the actual son who stood before him had no reality save as he denied the function of that other son of his father's mind. "But father, this is my work, my—" he was about to say "life" but he heard the panic in his own voice and with a great effort he said nothing more. He could not bring himself to make claims for his life in that voice. He said in the manner of routine, "Soon, father, I'll probably be able to help you."

"I'm sure you will, my son," his father said piously. "I know you have every intention of so doing. You are bound to succeed. Tell me, are these people you can trust?"

"Which people?" Vincent asked. Mr. Hammell never knew directly about Vincent's affairs and was always in an exasperating confusion about them.

"These people who have engaged you to take care of the old man— are they trustworthy?"

Vincent stared. "Father, you haven't understood. I'm not going to take care of an old man. How could you think that? I'm going to write a biography of a famous person. Jorris Buxton is a great man." Then because neither for his father's sake nor his own could he bear to let his father's appalling misconception remain, he said, "It's as if I were going to write the biography of Spinoza while he was still alive."

"He's an old man. I know how it is. You'll have to look after him."

Mr. Hammell's blind insistence made Vincent's heart contract. He suddenly saw his father as an old man—illegitimately old before his time, for Mr. Hammell was but in his sixties, but old and saying so, and asking for help beyond anything financial. A sudden deep jealousy had made him quarrelsome and wrongheaded. He had become a child to whose family another child had been born. He had chosen to be an old man and now his son was preferring another old man to him.

There was nothing to say or do but what was false and formal. Vincent said, "I'll be home on a visit soon. I'll write often. Take care of yourself." And he held out his hand.

Mr. Hammell did not take his son's hand. He came out from behind his counter and laid his arms around Vincent and put his head softly on his son's shoulder. A kind of shudder went through Vincent, but he put his arms about his father's slight back and patted him several times, awkwardly and reluctantly yet still with the intention of giving comfort.

chapter 12

When the taxi stopped at the Outram house Vincent said with more emphasis than he intended, "Is *this* it?" The driver, thinking that his own good sense was being questioned, replied, "Well, sure it is." But what Vincent meant was that the simplicity of the house quite startled him. With the reality before him, he could not now recall the house his imagination had shaped, but certainly it was not this low, long ramble of a place, so fresh, so weather-beaten, so honest.

And when he had been installed in the drawing-room while a grizzled housemaid went in search of Harold Outram, his surprise grew. And with his surprise, his disappointment grew. Was it for no more than this that Harold Outram had exchanged his great young talent? For as Vincent Hammell looked about the room, everything was precisely as he himself would have wanted it.

He had naturally never put to himself the question of what a perfect drawing-room should look like. But now that he saw this room, he felt that it perfectly expressed his own taste. Everything in it pointed to ease and simplicity, nothing to richness. There was, indeed, even a kind of shabbiness to be observed in the room. He looked for the expected luxury and could not find it, not knowing that he was in its very midst. He was naïve enough to think that luxury must appear as vulgarity. He could not know what made the effect which called forth his admiration—how much of chintz and how much of dull, glowing wood, how much spruceness and how much casualness, how much thought and how much calculated dependence on accident. He believed that money was only for the striking and the *chic*, for what was intended to overpower the beholder. He did not know how expensive was the modesty of some simple fabric or the intellect that inhered in a cherrywood lowboy. He did not know that mind could give to mere objects the validity of great uttered ideas and that people could so train themselves that they could endure to have only these right ideas about them, to sit in or eat from or to be the content of their casual regard. Now he only saw that everything here was to his own stern young taste. Indeed, the note of exculpating shabbiness was so perfectly struck that the room seemed almost within his own financial reach, or at least not forever outside his own financial possibility. It was therefore below the right status of Harold Outram.

But within a few minutes he understood the room and the whole Outram establishment rather better. The maid came back to say that Mr. Outram was not to be found but that Mrs. Outram was at the pool with the children. She opened the door that led from the drawing-room to the little flagged terrace and pointed down the lawn.

The woman who stood at the edge of the pool was sturdy and well shaped. Her thighs were full but her legs were delicate, and she had a ripe bosom and pretty rounded arms. Her damp hair hung to her shoulders. She was talking to the bobbing heads of two children in the swimming pool and to make her point more forcibly—she wanted them to get out of the water—she crouched down in the beautiful classic attitude, the knuckles of one hand touching the ground beside her lower knee, her other arm resting lightly upon the upper knee. The children, laughing and protesting, climbed out of the pool on either side of her. To Vincent Hammell on the terrace, the picture they made was a very charming one, the mother so richly formed, the children so slight and coltish, all three of them with their tanned skins gleaming with wet. He felt that now he had a true sense of Harold Outram's life. Not that the breadth of the lawn seemed magnificent to him, or the swimming pool a luxury more unattainable than the drawing-room, but that mother and children here in this setting seemed costly quite beyond his reach. He felt a pang of youth and inadequacy at the scene. If anyone at that moment had asked him,

"Is this what you want?" he would have said no. Yet he felt debarred from something, he felt suddenly poor, young and untried.

Mrs. Outram slipped on a short light robe and advanced to meet the guest. The children, a boy of ten and a girl of six, walked by her side.

"You're Mr. Hammell," she said. "Harold is around somewhere."

She held out a damp hand. Vincent took it but he felt a little at a loss. She added no word of welcome or of greeting to which he could reply, and he had nothing to say once he had agreed to his identity. Yet he was not uncomfortable.

Theodore Kramer had represented Harold Outram's wife as a small-minded woman who lived for pleasure and prestige. But Vincent's first glimpse of her made that estimate impossible. She too much resembled a Maillol bronze, she was a warm and almost majestic mother. Yet now, as he stood close to her, he had an impression which confirmed neither Kramer's opinion nor his own delighted first judgment. At near view she seemed puzzled and embarrassed and rather deprecating, more at a loss than he himself was. What chiefly came to him was her shy awkwardness which relieved him.

"I suppose you'd like a swim," she said in an oddly discouraged voice that seemed to suggest that his taking a swim could only be a weariness to him and a nuisance to everyone. "Or maybe you'd like a drink. Kiddy,"—she addressed the little boy—"run and tell Emma to bring something to drink."

"Highballs?" the child asked.

"Highballs, anything. Yes: highballs," his mother answered. As if in bewilderment at the strange ways of childish precocity, she turned to Vincent, lifted her eyebrows high and shrugged. The gesture struck Vincent as commonplace and provincial.

There were chairs and there was a table with a large gay sunshade over it and May Outram invited her guest to sit down. She seated herself with a little comic groan.

"The girl who takes care of the children is away and I'm all in," she said.

There was very little of the lovely Demeter-impression left, yet Vincent found himself being pleased by his hostess. He found it hard to understand what part she played in the life of her husband.

"So you're the new biographer," Mrs. Outram said. And then she added brightly and with pleasure, "The new *Boswell*."

"The new one?—have there been others?" Vincent saw a long line of biographical employees who had not given satisfaction.

"Oh no, you're the first. I just meant that you're the biographer and you're new." She made a gesture as if to throw away the conversation that had become so troublesome.

She was remarkably pretty and her face glowed with a tumbled hoydenish friendliness. She vigorously fluffed out her damp hair, piled it up on her head and carelessly pinned it there, making a charming coiffure that accentuated the bucolic quality of her face. Vincent was conscious of the innocence of the nape of her neck and also of the smoothness of her thighs and the rise of her breasts, for, as she lifted her arms to adjust her hair, her little robe fell open. Her movements were not quite graceful, they were even a little awkward in a reassuring way.

It was clear that Mrs. Outram was not the rapacious woman of Theodore Kramer's strict imagination. Neither was she, Vincent had to conclude with regret, the grave Greek personage of his first glance. He decided that she was not very clever but that she had treasures of warm sensuality to give. Vincent had read of such women. He admired Harold Outram for the wisdom of his choice of a wife and he himself felt the wiser for giving this admiration. This new world was still all unshaped in his mind, it made him feel a little lost and light-headed, and he was glad that, from the shifting uncertainties that attend the arrival at a strange place, one clear conclusion had so quickly emerged.

He said, "Do you see much of Mr. Buxton?" for it was necessary to say something.

"Oh yes, we do," Mrs. Outram said, "as much as anyone does."

"What is he like? Will I find him difficult?"

"Difficult? No, he's sweet. Well—difficult. Yes, I suppose he can be difficult. He can be tough. He knows what he likes, and what he likes, he likes."

It was not exactly illuminating.

"You mean he's crotchety?"

"Crotchety?" She considered the idea solemnly and then repelled it with energy. "No. Wherever did you get such a notion? You mean because he's old? Oh, get any such idea out of your head. He's not old that way. My God, no! There's none of that kind of thing about him. My God! The one thing about Mr. Buxton is that he's a *man*."

In the midst of this speech something caught her attention and although she went on in her petulantly passionate way, she became more and more abstracted from Vincent and from what she was saying. It was her husband and someone else, a woman, coming out of the clumps of woods beyond the lawn, and she rose and waved to them. Her rising and lifting her arm coincided with her statement about Buxton's being "a man," so that when she made this affirmation she was standing at full stretch, as if marking her utterance. The posture was beautiful, but she had quite lost interest in what she was saying.

Harold Outram, seeing Vincent, took his companion's arm to hurry her along. She was slight and compact and she walked with a bright nervousness that kept her light skirt in more than usual motion. Even at the distance there was something engaging about her, as there should have been, for when Outram had warmly shaken Vincent's hand, he said, "I know you'll forgive me for not being here when you came if I tell you that I went to bring Miss Thorne to see you." He said, "Garda, this is Vincent Hammell," and at her name so casually spoken, Vincent perceived the charming face of Garda Thorne materializing out of the vague resemblance to her picture. He began to understand—it came over him like a vertigo—what kind of world he had entered. And it was a world so much fuller of little prizes than he had ever imagined, for just as he was about to try some speech that could only have sounded foolish, Garda Thorne had her hand in his and was saying, "I've been wanting so long to meet you, Mr. Hammell, ever since Harold told me about you. He says you are so clever and such a good critic. I don't know, myself. I avoid such things."

Her very voice suggested the reason for the avoidance—it breathed intuition and a respectful distaste for the critical intellect. She might have been speaking of bear-hunting, so surely was the critical intellect consigned to masculinity. The voice was a true voice, not the acquired passport of a class. Miss Thorne was dainty, the liberal gray of her dark hair was but a humorous comment on her years, and she looked at the young man with blue eyes that made him the very center of her notice, and her notice the very center of the world.

And now the grizzled maid brought out a tray and they had highballs at the white table under the shade of the big parasol and the great elms. May Outram cried, "Good God! take off your coat!" and Garda Thorne said, "And your necktie—and your necktie too." And when he had taken off both jacket and tie, Harold Outram smiled to him and said with approval, "Now you look as if you had come to stay."

They were all ever so kind to him and he sat there in [a] sort of brilliant haze, though he did not show in his face what he felt. The scene itself was beautiful—the afternoon light was soft, the pool shimmered under the blue sky, the tree under which they sat rustled in a gentle breeze, there were beds of bright flowers, and beyond a hedge he saw the young corn stalks of a large truck garden. Every cliché of felicity was here, down to the tinkle of ice in the glasses. All his companions were handsome. He ceased to feel either the protection or the disadvantages of his own age. The four seemed of equal age together and it seemed to Vincent to be a sign of the provincial, of the vulgar and poor in spirit, to mark the differences in years. The setting sun was on his left and the thought came to him that to his right, where there stretched a long bright haze, was the east and the ocean he had never yet seen.

chapter 13

In a little while May Outram left them. Shortly after, her husband announced that he was going for a swim. It was not an invitation to the other two. Vincent and Garda Thorne were left alone at the little white table.

Garda Thorne said, "Shall we have another drink, Mr. Hammell?" And then, holding the whiskey bottle poised just at the rim of his glass, she said, "Do you mind if I immediately call you Vincent?"

It occurred to him that Harold Outram had left them alone together for a purpose.

"I'd be honored," was the reply that came from him.

She lifted the bottle brusquely and let the whiskey fall into the glass.

"Honored is not precisely the word I should have wanted you to choose." She said it with manifest dryness.

He could feel the blush suffusing him. But she went on, "And you must please call me Garda immediately." She poured whiskey into her own glass.

"I'm making these stipulations, Vincent, for a quite specific reason," she said.

She put ice into each of the glasses, then soda. She stirred his drink and handed it to him. She was pacing this little colloquy as precisely as if she were composing it in a story. There was nothing for him to say or do. He could only await the next development with a sense of its ultimate importance. But at least he had now a clue to the will that shaped Garda Thorne's career.

She said, "The reason is that we must be friends from the start."

She raised her glass to her mouth and looked at him over the rim. Then, having taken a sip, she said, "*Must* be, Vincent."

This, clearly, was intrigue.

"You are," said Garda Thorne, "the biographer of Jorris Buxton."

It was as if he had been sitting at a table at the Café de la Paix and a stranger had come up to him and said, "You are the bearer of important dispatches to the Archduke of Merovingia." He replied, "Well?" with as much cool reserve, as much question in his voice as he would have used in responding to the Merovingian statement.

"Well, aren't you?" Garda Thorne said tartly.

"Oh, yes, of course," he said in some confusion.

She accepted his admission. "That is why we must be friends from the start. For there's nobody who can be of more use to you than I can."

She paused, and the Merovingian tone recurred as she went on to say with considerable emphasis, "And you can be of great help to me."

He managed to sound the secret-agent's note by saying, "In what way?"

For a moment she considered. "Let me put the fact simply," she said, "and then you will be able to understand how I can help you, how we can help each other."

She opened her handbag, took out a cigarette case, opened the cigarette case, took out a cigarette and lighted it. So elaborate a preparation seemed justified by the statement she now made. "I was once Jorris Buxton's mistress," she said.

It was a statement of obvious weight, but it did not impede the light rapidity with which she now spoke. "What an old-fashioned word. Is it ever used any more? Do I have to explain that I don't mean a casual affair, a matter of weeks or months? I mean we were lovers in every full sense of that word. And over a period of years. There were long separations. I don't mean that anything went wrong between us. There were reasons why we had to be apart. I speak of these intervals because they were the occasion for his letters."

She had been gazing beyond Vincent's shoulder as she talked but now she looked him squarely in the face. "There are a great many letters. I am very fond of letters, they are my favorite reading, I read volumes of them, and there aren't any to equal the ones of Jorris Buxton. They are wonderful in themselves, and to a biographer they should be invaluable. I should say, indeed, essential."

By now Vincent should have thought of something to say, but he was too absorbed watching Garda Thorne move skillfully toward her goal of stipulation which he now knew must be coming. Besides, he was making arithmetical calculations in his head.

"Buxton is nearly eighty," Garda Thorne said, as if she could perceive the digits moving inconclusively about in his head, "and you want to know when this happened. If I told you twenty-five years ago, would that satisfy you? Ah, it's sweet of you to look bewildered. I was eighteen—no, nineteen: —oh damn, I was twenty."

She smiled, charmingly shy and guilty at the little evasion she confessed. Then she added, and it startled Vincent, "And a very tasty little thing I must have been."

She said it with a kind of bitter relish and it shocked Vincent Hammell. Of the two girls in her story who had taken off their shoes and stockings and lifted their skirts to step into the tub of wine, Garda Thorne herself was surely one. He had always been charmed and a little aroused by that scene of gay young girlhood, but somehow he had never supposed that the femininity it suggested, sexually delightful as it was, would ever develop into actual sexuality. Garda Thorne's recollection of herself as a fresh young girl who had pleased the sensual appetite of a great man even hinted that the girls had not been, as he had always assumed, necessarily virginal when they had stepped into the wine-tub.

Vincent had still not said a word through all his companion's great rush of talk and now he decided that his best maneuvre was to continue his silence.

"Buxton's life could be written without these letters," Garda Thorne went on, "and it would still be, as they say, a monumental life. But it would not be at all the life that could be written by the man who had the letters to work with. I am going to let you use these letters, Vincent."

He said, the Merovingian tone coming in again, "But on a condition?"

"Yes, on a condition. But I think not a hard or a disagreeable condition. The condition is only this—that you use them as my friend."

This had every appearance of dishonesty and she knew he thought so.

"It doesn't sound well the way I put it. But it isn't the way it sounds. When I give you the letters I'll give them to you outright, with no strings except the ones that tie them up. And I'll give you every one of them. Not to keep, of course. Of course not to keep, but you can read every one of them and you can copy them—that's the way they do, isn't it, copy them?"

"Yes, or photograph them. The best way is to photograph them."

"Well, you can photograph every one. And you can use them as much or as little as you please."

"But then what do you mean," he said, and there was an edge of impatience to his voice—astonishing that he should be speaking so to Garda Thorne!—"What do you mean by my using them as your friend?"

With some elaborateness she looked at the tip of her cigarette. "I mean specific things by that," she said, "and some of them are simple and some are not. You see, Vincent—oh, I don't have to tell you—no woman could ever be ashamed of having been Jorris Buxton's mistress, or anything but proud of it. You see, it's the first thing about myself that I've told you. Not that I make a practice of telling people, but under the circumstances—. And it's known, of course, it's not a secret. And I *want* it known—eventually, ultimately—as one of *the* things about myself. It's something *of* myself, and so I cherish it and I'm proud of it. Oh, I'm a vulgar woman, a beastly vulgar woman—I have a sort of fame of my own, but it's a little, little fame, and I *am* vulgar, don't for a moment suppose, Vincent Hammell, that I don't want to go down in history as the love of Jorris Buxton's life."

She said it delightfully. She wanted a toy and she so legitimately wanted it, and she so clearly had not a touch of vulgarity about her.

"But there are considerations," she went on. "We none of us know how long Buxton can live. Oh, he's robust enough, but it must be touch and go now. There are chances that he might not live through the writing of your book, which will surely be a matter of a couple of years. That is why you're here now and you should have been here earlier. Harold delayed too long making arrangements. The book won't come out until he's dead, and it's brutal to say but that can't be *very* long. But that's not the point. I'm getting confused, you see. I don't know precisely what I want, I want two contradictory things. What I want for history I don't want for now. I don't want to see myself fixed and crystallized as Buxton's mistress. It's all right for when I'm dead or old. It's not a reputation I want mixed up now with my writing reputation. To be part of history at my age—no. And then I just might, of course, just marry again. Do you know the story of the Duc d'Orsay who married the Countess Guiccioli? He used to introduce her as 'My wife, formerly the mistress of Lord Byron.' Only in French it's worse, 'Ancienne maîtresse de Lord Byron.' That's not the sort of thing—"

She ended decisively. "So you see!" she said.

He did not see, and yet he did. But he had no chance to report on his degree of enlightenment, for she immediately went on. "And then from Buxton's own point of view there are considerations. When I stumbled about my age a few minutes ago, you surely thought I was lying like any woman, protecting her age. I said 'eighteen,' then 'nineteen,' then 'twenty,' not for my sake but for Buxton's sake. Because if you judge it in cold numbers, I suppose it doesn't make an entirely pretty picture by the usual notions—a man of fifty-five and a girl of seventeen, for that is what I really was. He could have been her father—almost, possibly, her grandfather: that's what they would say. Ah, but we have such silly pictures of young girls. I was quite a match for any man, even a clever man, or a remarkable one like Buxton. More of a match then, it seems to me now, than I was later. I gave myself generously but I gave myself very wisely. Oh yes, there is a kind of wisdom in that first hot rush of adventurous feeling. I didn't know then of his greatness—none of us knew, but I sensed it, sensed something. Every good thing in my life came from that, as I know now. Oh indeed it was anything but a vulgar seduction. And somehow the truth of that must be kept, even if it means concealing meaningless facts."

Suddenly the torrent ceased and she sat perfectly still. Vincent remained silent. A great deal of life had just swept by and it awed him. Almost for the first time he had a sense of his undertaking as a biographer, a life-writer.

"I think I have a notion of what you mean," he said. "But of course you haven't yet been very specific about your conditions."

"Well, conditions—" she murmured. "But it's exactly that I don't want to set conditions."

She was being evasive and feminine and difficult. He saw that he must respond in a masculine way—he demanded definiteness. It was only later that he understood that it was he, not she, who had insisted on conditions. "We have to be clear about it," he said. "I must know precisely what you have in mind."

"Well then," she said reluctantly, "the first thing is that my name mustn't appear. But no mystery must be made of the person to whom the letters are addressed. You mustn't melodramatize the reason why the person is anonymous. That of course is just a matter for your literary skill to handle. It's a matter of tone, and surely you can manage to do it delicately."

She paused and waited for his assent.

"I think there ought to be no difficulty about that," he said.

She hurried on. "Then there is the matter of my letters to Buxton. He has them, and it's possible that he will show them if you ask. Now in regard to those letters—"

He had not been looking at her, he was looking down at his drink on the table. When she suddenly broke off her speech it was part of what he believed was his diplomatic reserve not to lift his eyes. So he did not see her face, and he only heard the cry she uttered, the great "Oh" which began as a wail and finished as a sob.

The cry struck him cold to the heart. Her quick hand covered her mouth and she closed her eyes. He saw her for a moment as she sat there with her clenched eyes and her stopped mouth. When she uncovered her face again it was almost composed. It was even stern, forbidding pity. But the cry in all its horrid coarseness hung in the air, heard still by both of them.

It was a graceless cry from an unaccepting spirit, and it was animal, awkward, gross. As Garda Thorne sat here now, there was every mark of mind upon her. Mind shone from her wonderful blue eyes, it informed the curve of her cheek, it was in the very tendons of her fine brown hands. But the cry came from behind mind, from the incommunicable privacy of flesh, at the sight of youth irrecoverably gone and death wholly real. For that, as Vincent knew, was what Garda had seen, and the tone and timbre of her cry shocked him. In literature he knew and loved the idea of death as the element that carries and volatilizes the savor of life, like the alcohol in wine. But it was not in reality the way it was in literature. Some day Garda Thorne's mind would take hold of this sudden horrifying vision of hers, this coarse, feral cry, and write a story around it. The story she would write, the story of a woman perceiving death as a reality, would be bound to issue in a mood of high, chastened acceptance. Death, in that story, would be quite overcome and refined by art. There is no art that can encompass the panic fear of flesh, and the mind recognizes what the flesh feels only to betray it. But Vincent had heard the pain of the flesh itself and it was the negation of all the conciliations that literature had ever made. It was too terrible to be kept in memory.

Garda Thorne said, "We will talk about this again, Vincent—when I'm less likely to act like a fool."

He had nothing to answer.

It was Harold Outram who interrupted the silence they shared. Whoever would have come up at that moment would have been intrusive and at a disadvantage, but what Outram said was, "Have you two been chatting?"

Garda Thorne's eyes were as furious as her voice. She said, "Yes, Harold, chatting—and isn't it sweet of us?"

Outram flushed up and stood there looking hurt and haughty. When he spoke again, it was to Vincent. "I thought I'd have a surprise for you to-night—Buxton agreed to come to dinner. But at the last minute he's had to call it off. But I've arranged for you to go over to-morrow morning."

"Oh but of course, that's much the better way, Harold," Garda cried. "It's right that Vincent should see him first alone."

Outram took the high ground. "I'm sorry, Garda, if I've acted without due sensibility," he said.

"Sensibility—pooh. What a word. Make me another drink and ask me to dinner," she said, perfectly indifferent to his irony.

chapter 14

But the next morning did not, after all, bring the meeting with Buxton.

Vincent was sitting at breakfast with the Outrams when the message came. It had been a rather silent meal. Vincent instructed himself that in his long visit there would of course be many occasions of family silence which he must not find uncomfortable. But the telephone rang and when Harold Outram came back from answering it, he had news which seemed to be worth talking about. Apparently it was not so much that he had been told that Jorris Buxton wished to postpone his appointment with Mr. Hammell as that his information had been conveyed by someone named Claudine Post.

At this name May Outram's eyebrows went up very high and she [said] with a grievance, "Really now!—that Claudine Post."

"Nasty, possessive bitch," Outram said. "She ought to be hanged, she ought to be burned."

Someone named Claudine Post could apparently assert a claim upon Jorris Buxton which had the power of enraging Outram. Such a person was clearly of importance to Buxton's biographer and Vincent sat alert for the enlightenment Outram would give him. But Outram, after his outburst, only stirred his coffee with a fierce and silent abstraction and all that May Outram had to add was another exasperated "Really." Vincent was on the point of asking for the explanation that seemed his due when Garda Thorne came into the dining-room and brought the table to attention.

"Dear Claudine!" she said when she received the news. "Dear, *dear* Claudine! She was perfectly bound to make some little demonstration for the occasion. Have they told you about Claudine Post, Vincent? Your arrival is of course the occasion. Have you told him, Harold?"

"He'll learn fast enough," Outram said drily.

"He should be told. You should know that Claudine Post is a witch, Vincent, our local witch."

"Bitch," said Outram in stubborn correction, although he himself had only a moment before prescribed a witch's punishment.

"All witches are bitches," Garda said, "but not all bitches are witches." She laughed with pleasure at the sound of her own logical proposition. "This bitch, Vincent, is an enchantress. Not that she is enchanting, but she knows how to enchant. She has enchanted your subject, Vincent— poor Buxton is under her spell. Or should I say 'in her power'—for she is a dragon, Vincent, a perfect dragon, and you will have to deal with her as such. And she has a little attendant sprite, a familiar spirit, a little ancillary devil—"

May Outram said, "Oh, now Perdy isn't so bad."

"Bad? I never said she was bad. Enchanted too—dragonned—dragonned—what is the verb for what happens when a dragon has you? Poor darling—poor damsel, poor damnèd damosel."

Under the little spate of words May Outram sank back.

"What was the name?" said Vincent. "'Perdy'?"

"Yes, Perdy—pretty Perdy," said Garda. "From Perdita," she explained. Her respect for the beautiful Shakespearean name made her speak with sudden gravity. "Poor lost Perdita!"

That Claudine Post was a bitch, a witch and a dragon, that Perdy was Perdita, this was all the explanation that Vincent got, for now the telephone rang again. Outram came back from answering it and said, "That was Buxton himself. He says he will come to dinner tonight." He grinned, boyishly triumphant at the reversal.

"Oh good!" Garda cried. "The darling has made a stand. I'll bet there was a scene, a perfect rumpus. Oh good for him."

She rose from the table as if her emotion were very great, and she strode rapidly up and down the room. Her comic manner had left her, but her manner of exultation was not so very different. Vincent was struck with how alive and finely shaped was the body that expressed her high spirit, how lithe and alert was her step. When she tossed back a lock of hair that had fallen over her clear forehead, he remembered that a month or two ago he himself had found two or three anomalous gray hairs in his own dark head.

"Oh that dreadful, dreadful woman," Garda said. "He must get rid of her, he must. What an atmosphere for him to live in now, so late."

She turned suddenly to Vincent and pointed a finger straight at him. "It is you who are going to have all the trouble with her. Watch out! You must be crafty and you must be strong!"

Then, having come to use the Outrams' telephone, for she had none of her own, she turned abruptly and left to do her errand.

Garda's pointed finger and passionate tone as well as her very explicit words gave Vincent a stake in the situation which was now perfectly clear. Even so, he could not bring himself to ask a question about it. Harold Outram seemed to have some intention of not informing him of what seemed so relevant to his situation, and this hurt and confused him. But Outram said, "Of course Garda's right—you'll have to know about this business."

He broke off and took counsel with himself. "I wanted you to find out for yourself, without preparation and prejudice. And even now I wonder if that wouldn't be the best way. I still think that the less you know about it the better. I mean for your sake, for the sake of the job. You already know, at any rate, that there *is* a Claudine Post and that we, Garda and I, have a strong feeling about her and about her relations with Buxton. And you can guess that in our opinion she can make trouble for the job we want done. In a way I'm sorry you know even that much. It would really be best if you could start with no knowledge at all, if your mind were perfectly free from all feelings about the matter. As a matter of fact, I'm going to say nothing more to you about it, after all. I suggest that you try to forget all about our feelings—even assume that our feelings are mistaken and prejudiced. You be perfectly objective and meet Mrs. Post as if she were simply a respectable lady of the town, which she is. You know how around any great man little factions are likely to form. Set down our feelings to that and you remain quite above the battle. And so, if you don't mind, I'm going to give you no more information for a while."

And Outram ended with a smile to his young friend, a frank smile that made him seem very young himself. Vincent could not but respond. Nevertheless, he felt that this was an occasion for anger, and a speech that would begin, "Look here!" presented itself to him. It was not Outram's place, he felt, to manipulate the degree of his knowledge or ignorance, to contrive for him a state of innocence which should have some advantage in a situation which Outram saw but which Vincent knew nothing of.

But he did not say "Look here!" or anything else. For he suddenly saw that this occasion for anger was but part of a much larger occasion. He had wondered before, but only with delight and self-congratulation, why he, so young and inexperienced, had been invited to an undertaking which would have gratified a much older and much more established man. But the vanity of his youth had not allowed the question to be a real one. But it was real now. And an answer, an all too likely answer, was beginning to appear. The answer seemed to be that Outram—and Garda Thorne—had chosen him not merely for what talent they saw in him, perhaps not for his talent at all, but exactly for his youth and inexperience.

"Crafty," Garda Thorne had said, and "strong"—but what craft and strength could they expect of him at twenty-three when they themselves, surely crafty and strong enough in their maturity, gave every sign of being baffled by a situation which they could not explain to him? He had thought that in his conversation of yesterday with Garda Thorne he had comported himself with firmness and clarity and a right sense of his own position. Yet as he looked back at it now it seemed to him that Garda had been acting with a motive that all her frankness had not disclosed, that she had involved him in some commitment the terms for which she had not really stipulated. And this new view of that conversation supported the idea that his youth and inexperience had not been elements to be overlooked for the sake of his talent. They had been the very parts of his equipment that had determined his invitation. He had been chosen not for his strength but for his very weakness, for his usefulness as an instrument rather than for his power as a mind. As he thought of this possibility he felt a childlike ache of having been fooled and betrayed. The disintegrating, the almost tearful sense of wrong was more immediate than any possible anger.

When Outram said, "Will you have some more coffee?" and May Outram immediately said, "Take another blueberry muffin," he accepted both offers and let the matter slide in cream, sugar, butter and jam. He postponed his anger until he could better consider its justice.

chapter 15

He did not consider its justice that day. It was Saturday. One could feel it in the air. It was a day for tennis, for swimming, for lying in the shade watching the children at play. The two men played tennis. May Outram murmured vaguely at their madness, the heat being what it was, while Garda Thorne mocked Harold Outram's infrequent errors—he was a remarkably good player—in a tone which led Vincent to wonder whether it was merely as friends that these two knew each other. And so in sport, felicity and the sensation of heightened life which Garda Thorne gave him, in speculation about the true realities of this new existence, Vincent quite neglected to consider his anger and the justice of it.

If anything else were needed to make him neglect that unwanted task, the evening brought the approach of the dinner party with its large compliment to him. It was to be quite his own occasion. The three guests, he learned, had been invited before his arrival for the particular purpose of meeting him, and now the addition of Buxton himself was making it more than ever the young man's event.

Garda and Vincent sat alone together at the edge of the pool. Their feet dangled side by side in the water. She moved her toes, watching the strong articulation of the big tendon of the thumb-toe. In an emulation that was aware of its childishness, Vincent wiggled his own toes. With the same awareness, she replied to his response, then he answered hers again. In their play there was a primitive intimacy. Like children, they were pretending to abdicate all their personality to these feet of theirs. They sat and gravely watched the play of these self-willed and beautiful animals that, in their far-off aquatic life, had the same mind and habits and were distinguished from each other only by the sexual difference of size.

To Vincent, the odd nervous grace of Garda's body as he had seen it in motion all day made it impossible that her years added up to the sum they really made. The sum was a barrier, but over the barrier he had a glimpse of the truth that her high spirit and charming legs were as quick and gay as when in girlhood she had stepped into the tub of wine. Her feet were as white and delicate, as curved in the instep and as brilliantly flexible in the toes as her art had ever suggested. Garda's eyes turned from watching their four feet at play and looked at him, smiling and happy. It was impossible to suppose that they had seen, only yesterday, the horrid vision which had made her cry out in his presence. Now she was kicking her feet up and down in the water, almost hiding them in the white churn she made, and her eyes, darker now, almost gray, were full of peace and gratitude. Their gaze was gentle, expectant, almost passive. He was frightened and said, "Who are those people who are coming to dinner?"

"Find out for yourself!" Garda said, with no more brusqueness than she had a right to.

She saw the shadow cross his face. With how many starts and stops, with what a superabundance of doubts and false imaginings and searches for hidden significances, with how many attempts to master its own inchoateness would this young mind of his move toward such an idea as her mind had just so simply conceived. In clearness and distinctness, in muscularity and stamina, his mind was far behind his body. He would never expect of his mind the stamina he would demand of his body, he would allow it to succumb all too easily to hardship and he would even think of his quick surrenders as coming from a virtue which he would call sensitivity.

She put out her hand to touch his in apology for her brusqueness.

"I mean," she said, "that I know them so very well that I'd give you only a rather weary picture of them. They are nice people—there is Philip Dyas who is headmaster of the school here, and there are the Hollowells who are so very rich."

For a moment they sat silent. Then Vincent said, "Which way is your house?"

She did not point. She was sitting with her hands on the smooth coping of the pool, resting her weight on them, her body leaning forward and her shoulders high, and at his question she turned her head slowly and looked at him again. "Over there," she said with a small inadequate movement of her head backward. "Through that little piece of woods." Her high voice, usually turbulent with overtones and echoes, was flat and still. Her eyes were again grave, wholly without their usual brilliant challenge, as receptive as the pool itself. And as Vincent looked into them, he knew the meaning of the question which he thought he had asked idly. His heart beat wildly. He could not at that moment have spoken and his next communication would have had to have been made by touch, but in dismay Garda cried, "Oh, Jorris is here. He's come too soon," and Vincent saw across the lawn, on the terrace, the figure of a man. Evan at the distance the paleness of his face was notable. It was not so much the absence of color but almost a glow of colorlessness, a phosphorescence against his black jacket. Garda scrambled to her feet and began to gather up her belongings, a bag, a swimming-cap, a cigarette case, a pair of bright sandals.

The man, after having waved to Garda and received a negligent wave in reply, had gone back into the house.

"That isn't—?" said Vincent in dismay, for at the distance the pale man might have been of almost any age, and his appearance was ignoble.

"That's Brooks Barrett—he's brought Jorris. Oh, what a nuisance."

Her paraphernalia all collected, Garda suddenly put them all down again and looked about her almost distractedly. She saw what she wanted and slipped into the robe that May Outram had left lying on a chair by the pool. She was tying it close about her when the door to the terrace opened and Brooks Barrett came out in company with Jorris Buxton.

"Come!" said Garda and took Vincent decisively by the arm. "Come and have your introduction."

The two men were walking to meet them, Buxton moving, as it seemed, with a far more vigorous step than his younger companion. But it was not the old man's vigor that gave Vincent his quick sense of relief. It was that Buxton wore a beard. It was the best kind of beard that a man can wear, it was short and firm and jutted a little forward. It gave a base to the head and did not mask the face. It suggested fortitude and the possibility of just anger.

The beard was the first fact about Buxton that Buxton's biographer had acquired for himself. No one had happened to mention to him that Jorris Buxton wore a beard. Out of the haze of other people's attitudes this immediate fact emerged with a happy, bristly reality.

And now that he had Buxton's beard to hold on to, he understood that he had been shrinking, all unconsciously, from the sight of the aged face, imagining it to be shrunken and wizened. But the beard was all alive, it was the great classic symbol of strong age, of masculine power not abdicated.

Buxton was not a tall man, but he was satisfyingly bulky, he filled his jacket of light gray flannel. There was no need of Garda's introduction, for when the two little parties met midway on the lawn, Buxton said at once, "Hammell, I'm glad to see you."

The hand with which he grasped Vincent's was warm, strong and pleasantly calloused. But it was not only the sentiment nor the friendly hand that gave Vincent his pleasure. It was the form of address, the use of the simple surname preserved by Buxton from a past in which manners were less intimate and more masculine. What had once been the accepted form of address among men, had come, among Americans, to seem cold and even unkind. Any company was quick to reduce itself to the anonymity of the given name. If Vincent had an impulse to be abashed at being dressed only in swimming trunks on this notable occasion, his impulse did not complete itself—at the sound of Buxton speaking his family name, he felt adequate in his naked youthfulness. He thought dimly that some day, if he were lucky and virtuous, he himself might be bearded and gray-flannelled and give to a young man, as yet far from being born, the same sense of established and continuing life that he was feeling now.

Brooks Barrett hovered over the meeting, a sad presence in a black alpaca coat. He acted as if he had a function. With one hand he sponsored Vincent to Buxton, with the other hand he indicated Buxton to Vincent. He used the vague ghosts of gestures that people make in introducing guests at a large party. There was a great appreciation of the event shining in his face.

"Is it—is it *Doctor* Hammell?" Brooks Barrett said in a delicate whisper of huge tact.

"No," Vincent replied, and stared in astonishment. "No, it is not."

The haughtiness of his own voice almost shocked him. This man invited condescension. His eyes were so ready to perceive offense, his lips to smile it away. And the whole long, spare body seemed prepared at an instant's notice to hunch into the smallest possible space. He made a gesture to Vincent as of one man of the world to another, indicating that it was well known how vain and empty academic titles were.

Garda Thorne said, "Jorris, you'll want to talk with Vincent Hammell—I'll run along and dress and see you later at dinner."

Buxton looked at her with a large paternal mildness and said, "Yes, do, my dear."

But she did not go. She wished to be released from this confrontation of the old man and the young man which bracketed her life so much too completely. Yet she could not leave. She stood there silent and ambiguous, touchingly at a loss. In the gentle abstraction in which Buxton seemed to move, he could scarcely have perceived her difficulty, yet it was he who extricated her. He took her arm and walked away over the lawn with her in the direction of her own little house.

Brooks Barrett waited for a moment after their backs were turned and then said to Vincent in eager explanation, "I asked if it was Doctor Hammell because I seem to have heard of a university connection. Not that I consider that the doctorate is any guarantee of scholarship."

And he offered Vincent the additional placation of a disdainful sniff in the direction of the doctorate. Even the whites of his eyes and the darkness of his lips were toned to the strange pallor of his face. "I do not know," he said, "if my position has been explained to you. I stand in the position of—that is to say, I am Dr. Buxton's assistant."

There was nothing of the scientist about this man. He suggested the back-office of a counting house in the English nineteenth century, or some small religious conventicle. He appeared to enshrine every outworn gentility. Yet if he was Buxton's assistant, his foolish manner must be merely an eccentricity which cloaked his intellect.

"I want you to know, Mr. Hammell," he said, "that I consider it a privilege to meet you. And I want you to know that you can rely on Brooks Barrett, you can rely on him for any help he can give, of any kind." He seemed to get pleasure from speaking of himself in the third person, as if he were someone else.

Reaching beyond the impossible manner of the man Brooks Barrett, Vincent addressed himself to the scientist. "Thank you," he said, "it's kind of you. Perhaps you can be especially helpful to me. You see, I know so very little about science."

Whatever sense of Barrett's inferiority Vincent had at first now vanished as he abased himself in his confession of scientific ignorance and experienced the somewhat complacent guilt of the literary man. He felt relieved that Barrett was now established on a better basis.

Barrett said, "How I wish I could. But alas."

"Alas?" said Vincent.

"Yes. Alas. I am entirely ignorant of the subject. Indeed, I am more like you, more the literary type."

"But you said—didn't you say that you were Mr. Buxton's assistant?"

"Yes. That is to say, I assist him. But in small matters. Oh, in the larger aspects of his life I have no part. I suppose 'secretary' would be more accurate. That is to say, I help with his correspondence—and in a general way I look after him. In that sense of the word, an assistant. He is an old man—I assist him."

And then, as if he were not sure that be had sufficiently persuaded Vincent of the truth and cleared himself of any appearance of false pretence, he said, "But not in the larger aspects."

He went on. "But my help can be given in other ways, I am glad to say. Or I should say, 'sorry to say.'"

He spoke lower and faster and drew closer to Vincent as Buxton, walking toward them, came nearer. "There are other ways than science," he said. Then he said in a piercing and significant whisper, "Human relations!"

"Thank you," Vincent said in confusion. "Thank you very much." There was nothing else for him to say and he was glad to give his attention to Buxton who by now had completed his slow, sturdy return over the lawn.

chapter 16

The old man lowered himself slowly into a lawn chair and with a gesture he invited Vincent to sit opposite him. There was a third chair and Brooks Barrett eyed it. His body was in a hover, signalling that he could as well go as stay, as well stay as go. But it was clear that the direction of his shambling, strong will was all toward staying.

"Sit down," Buxton said to him, and Barrett fairly pounced upon the third chair. He leaned back to be inconspicuous, but he sat alert to be a witness. A flush of cruel impulse rose in Vincent against this dreadful man. That he should be included in the company substantially lessened the value of the occasion. It was thoughtless of Buxton, even unkind.

Buxton took the old man's privilege of delayed speech and looked long at Vincent. He said what he had said before, "I am very glad to see you, Hammell." Then he said in a deliberate way, "Hammell, you are my biographer and your job, as you know, is to learn to understand me." His voice had a gruff texture, a good timbre, and it expressed very well the irony that was in Buxton's intention at the idea of his being "understood." Vincent smiled.

"So your first act of understanding," Buxton went on, "ought to be what it means to a man to meet his biographer face to face." His smile to Vincent was very winning, so direct was its intention of friendliness. But his eyes did not smile. They were living a life of their own.

"Hammell," Buxton said, "in a man's life there are very few people who are unique, who perform functions that are not repeated. A man can have several wives, many mistresses ..."

He paused, seeking further examples of multiplicity.

"Numerous children, friends, relatives," he said.

"But—" and now with his left hand he counted off on the fingers of his right hand the instances of uniqueness. He began with the thumb. "Only one father," he said.

Then the forefinger: "Only one mother."

He held the third finger and considered it. "Many physicians but only one obstetrician," he said.

"Then only one undertaker." This was the fourth finger and he paused over it. "I suppose there might be more than one—they no doubt work in crews." But he shrugged off this modification and took hold of the little finger. "And then there is you, Hammell, the life-and-letters man, the proto-biographer, the official one, the only one I shall ever set eyes on. Do you understand why you frighten me, Hammell?"

If it was a little garrulous or a shade too insistent, it was nevertheless most engaging. Vincent smiled as Buxton meant him to. Brooks Barrett squirmed with delight at the speech. He looked at Vincent to see if its full value was apparent.

As the white beard wagged with the words Buxton was speaking, Buxton's eyes were involved in some other activity. Under the heavy brows, the eyes lived with the life of the contemplating mind. There was nothing abstracted about Buxton's manner as he made friends with Vincent. The fact that his eyes were engaged in some other order of activity did not make his words seem insincere or like a social "effort" or a mere politeness. Vincent thought that it was as if the connection being made by the friendly words was supplying the vital energy for the eyes and the mind. For the eyes showed, or so Vincent felt, a life beyond the words that Buxton was speaking. And, far more than the words, it was the eyes that were giving Vincent his strange new sense of well-being.

Vincent had read of the kind of life the eyes were living. On more than one examination paper he had repeated what Aristotle said, that true happiness consists of the intellectual activity of the soul. Like many things that are confidently stated on examination papers, this had little meaning for Vincent, as it can scarcely have for a very young man. But now he knew its meaning, for he could see it.

And seeing it, he could correct the description of it as given by the authority on the matter. For the philosopher had remarked that intellectual activity transcended in the human scale even the activity of morality. But what Vincent saw was that from this movement of intellect came something very like morality itself. For why had Buxton invited Brooks Barrett to remain as an intrusive third at this interview? Not because he had the wish to be good to this poor servant of his. It was simply because the contemplating mind had gone beyond the awareness of Brooks Barrett's striking repulsiveness. Vincent Hammell, all aware and too aware of human differences, could immediately see and judge the man's weakness and servility. But the contemplating mind was not aware of the existence of these qualities. It was not that Buxton forgave Barrett, it was simply that he saw no fault to forgive.

Nor had he seen the fault in Vincent himself that made him want privacy and the undisputed possession of the old man. Barrett was worthy to be present. Vincent was not so unworthy as to wish Barrett to be away. So it appeared to Buxton.

It could of course be said that the contemplating mind had been in error. For Brooks Barrett was, in point of fact, a pretty sad specimen. And in point of fact Vincent Hammell had actually wished him away. But Vincent, looking at Barrett now, seeing the intensity of his concentration upon his master's face, felt suddenly that this was reason enough for Barrett's being here. By wanting to be here, he deserved to be here. In this acceptance of Barrett's presence by Vincent there was no kindness or moral choice. It was simply that it suddenly seemed to him that there was no reason to fight for the possession of Jorris Buxton. Possession, indeed, was impossible. For it seemed to Vincent in that strange moment of perception, that the mind of Buxton contained them both and brought them to a strange equality.

Later, with a notebook before him—for it seemed necessary to record this first experience of Buxton, not only for itself but to give point to the more striking experience that followed it—Vincent tried to give words to the emotion he had felt. It was, he could say, the emotion of pure disinterestedness, the emotion of contemplation. It was like being drunk with sobriety itself. He had had it before, but never without the stimulus of music or Shakespeare. Vincent made use of the word "pure" because that word best suggested the sensation of crystalline, translucent being that he had felt. He eventually hit upon another word, "peace," remarking that what was probably meant by that word was a perfect poise of the energies without the alloy of personality. He reminded himself that the ancient philosophers, when they spoke so passionately to recommend death, probably had these conditions in mind. They obviously could not mean non-existence. They must have meant an existence in this perfect equilibrium of the impulses and powers, with no element of that greed which they identified as the personality. This condition of being was sometimes permitted by life, but life was always presenting demands that brought the experience to an end. Hence, Vincent supposed, the recommendation of death.

There was a considerable difference between what Vincent wrote in his notebook about his first meeting with Buxton and what he later wrote to Kramer. The notebook was open on his table as Vincent wrote the letter and naturally a few phrases from the first account did reach his friend. But what he had written for his own eyes alone, or for what was much the same thing, the eyes of posterity, seemed both too private and too pompous to communicate to Kramer. And so Kramer received a description of Vincent's feelings which was certainly not without its truth but which certainly did not convey the truth in its fullness as Vincent felt it. "I felt for him," Vincent wrote, "that he stood like a denial of every vulgar modern assumption, like a rock of refuge from every contemporary cheapness."

In writing so he could not help knowing that he was trying to reassure Kramer that his student still thought of the important things. And his affection moved him to bring Kramer into the scene. "You would find him, as I do, the negation of everything you have ever fought against." It was only at the moment of writing that he felt Kramer had anything at all to do with the situation. If there was a kind of generous insincerity in bringing in Kramer at all, there was the same insincerity in reducing the matter to considerations of "vulgarity."

For all its pompousness, the notebook account was the truer one. Still, the account which he wrote for Kramer was not untrue. One could, if one wished to, think of the old man in that way. Outram thought of him so. And Kramer would most easily comprehend him from such language. Yet the impulse to bring in Kramer did have its illuminating outcome. Vincent, in his generous insincerity, sought in his mind for ways of continuing the connection between Kramer and Buxton, and he found it in a recollection of his sophomore year. "Do you remember," his letter continued, "in that Wordsworth poem about the leech-gatherer of which you are so fond, how the very old man beside the stream seems to be a rock, a great boulder, and then the rock begins to seem like a great beast from the sea? A kind of metaphor within a metaphor? Well, in some odd way Buxton reminded me of that. And do you remember how what the old man says to the poet gets rid of the depression and fear he experiences?—really an excellent description of the neurotic state. I understand how that could happen now and that it wasn't any particular thing that the old man said that cheered poor Wm. up, but just his existence in wonderful everlastingness." That was truer, that came very close to the truth. The reduction of the incident that Vincent had made to bring it into the range of Kramer's temperament led him to see it in a new fullness of meaning.

But neither the notebook nor the letter recorded the end of the meeting. Suddenly up the driveway that led to the garage a girl appeared on a bicycle. She cycled halfway up the drive and then, seeing the group on the lawn, she dismounted, leaned her bicycle against a tree and walked toward them, or, rather, as it turned out, toward Buxton. The suddenness of her being there was the notable thing. Another person's coming might have seemed more gradual. But she was immediately all there. And this sense of her being on the scene all at once gave Vincent no chance to ask the young man's question of whether or not she was a pretty girl. Yet the definiteness and concreteness of her appearance was certainly not mystical essence. Whatever it was, it expressed itself as a physical fact. There was, for example, the definiteness of her breasts under the jersey she wore. Vincent took note of that with a young man's tallying eye. It was not sexual directness that made him do that but rather an impulse of self-protection. The girl's appearance seemed sudden to him because his response to her was so sudden, so wholly in advance of consciousness and judgment. Exactly because it was the wholeness of her appearance that had its effect, he tried to protect himself by taking note of her breasts, an act of insensitivity, even of vulgarity. For the same reason he looked to see if she was pretty. As she came nearer, he saw that the question had no meaning for him. This frightened him.

The girl had eyes only for Buxton, and Buxton was very glad to see her. He held out two hands glowingly and she placed hers in his. Vincent noticed the color of her voice before that of her hair. Both were dark. "It's so nice to see you," she said to the old man, and Vincent heard the true timbre of gladness in her voice. They were smiling at each other as they held hands and the affection shone from one face to the other. Suddenly, on the perception of this free sunny interchange, Vincent felt bleak at his heart. He had, he felt, never given, never seen given, and could never give what was now going from one to the other.

He had risen and stood there silent and supernumerary. Brooks Barrett had risen too and was smiling benevolently on the meeting. Barrett cleared his throat officiously as if about to take over the social necessities of the moment. He inclined his body and began to make a gesture of indication. But Buxton released one of the girl's hands so that she could face Vincent and he said, "Marry, this is Vincent Hammell." He said it with a kind of enthusiasm for both the names, as if he were surprising each of them with the gift of the other and calling attention, with a naïve benevolence, to the youth and charm they each had. He was quietly but wonderfully aware of them.

Vincent said, "How do you do," and hated himself for the lifted, remote intonation he heard, the affectation of accent. Barrett murmured, filling out the informality of Buxton's introduction, "Miss Cathcart, Miss Marion Cathcart." And Miss Cathcart looked at Vincent and said with a coolness that was as great as his own and much more calculated, "How do you do." It seemed to him that she was looking at him with a moral curiosity and he resented it. He passionately noticed that not possibly could she be called pretty, and that he did not like her voice. All the fierceness of his claim on life presented itself to him at that moment, under that curious gaze, as guilt. Had he been a Jew meeting another Jew where another Jew was not expected, or a homosexual person introduced to another of his kind, he could not have felt more the anger of guilt than he did upon meeting this person who matched his youth with her own and made him conscious of the fierceness of the claims that his youth made upon life.

This, then, was the "Marry" he had heard of from the children. In the face of the authority they seemed to attribute to her, their "Marry does it this way," their "Marry says we mustn't," he had still supposed that "the girl who takes care of the children" was a high school girl of the neighborhood. He had no expectation of a person who would look at him with so arrogant an assumption of moral competence.

May Outram came over the lawn to them and at her approach Barrett receded a little into the background, abdicated any claim he had to being of the company. "Marry," she called from a distance, "I'm so glad you're back." And she said, "It's been such a trial to have you gone. You've met Vincent Hammell? Vincent, you've met Marry Cathcart? She went away by herself for a few days to cool off. She and Harold had a tiff. Oh, more than that—quite a blow-up. Wasn't it? It was about you, Vincent Hammell, you made all the trouble. Are you cooled off, Marry? You look cooled off inside but hurry and get dressed dear and look lovely. You too

Vincent, both of you do hurry. And Marry, tell Emma you're here so she'll set another place for you. Do hurry."

They were both young enough to be ignorant of how to evade her commands and so together they walked toward the house. Something had to be said. Vincent did not lack the courage to ask the question, but he could not find the words that would not belittle the situation between them. He could not say, "Did you really quarrel about me? Why?" And so they walked on together across the broad lawn, silent until Marry said, "I'm sorry she said that," and turned dark miserable eyes toward him. "Of course it wasn't really *you*." He saw that the miserableness in her eyes was not for herself at being put into an awkward position, it was for him. Rather impersonally for him, however—there was much reserve in her look. It was open to Vincent to be obtuse and to ask the cause of the quarrel. But he knew as clearly as if he had been present at the "blow-up" why this girl had quarreled with Harold Outram about him.

"I know it wasn't," he said, "I know what it was."

She stood and faced him. "You do?" she said, and the surprise robbed her of the moral competence that made Vincent so stiff against her. "You do? Did they tell you?"

"No," he said. "They've told me nothing. Or," and he now faced her, "very nearly nothing."

She dropped her eyes. His speculations of the morning had been correct. But now that they were proved, they did not affect him with the sense of betrayal and dissolution he had had when he had first thought of them. He felt that he had simply discovered the conditions of his work. He did not like this girl, who was the kind of person who needed bicycle trips to cool off her anger, but he wanted to reassure her.

"It was generous of you," he said, "but I wouldn't worry—"

In his new clarity he said it too lightly and loftily, and she undertook to shatter his vanity. "Worry?" she said. "I'm afraid you take it too personally." And they parted as sternly as they had met.

chapter 17

Between Philip Dyas and the Hollowells there was a joke. Or rather, there was a matter which now, on this occasion, had all the appearance of a joke. At another time and in another setting it might have had a different meaning. The joke was that the Hollowells, or more particularly Linda Hollowell, wished to buy the school of which Philip Dyas was head master.

"He is so stubborn, Mr. Hammell," Linda Hollowell said after the joke had established itself for the newcomer. "He knows my heart is set on it and he will not even give it a thought. He refuses me point blank, absolutely. Don't you, Philip?"

"Oh, point blank. Absolutely," Philip Dyas answered. He was a thick set man and not tall. His hair was rather thin and his face was round. It was not a fleshy face yet it gave the impression that fleshy faces sometimes do give, of there being an inner face, the essential one, within the outer one. This face was sad and even in some lights rather stern. But when Dyas smiled in friendliness or amusement, the mouth was tender and the meditative eyes were heartily responsive. Vincent liked him from the moment of his warm greeting and firm handclasp. He had never given much thought to the man who had had so important a part in his destiny by bringing him to the attention of Harold Outram, but now that he had met Dyas he felt proud that so impressive a person should have had so personal a hand in his life.

Dyas's reply to Linda Hollowell made it quite clear that he too took the matter as a joke. Yet Vincent had the impression that when it came to jokes, Philip Dyas would have taken part in some other joke with more pleasure. There was just a trace of sourness in his amusement.

Linda Hollowell shook her head in reproof at Philip Dyas. "Stubborn," she said.

Mrs. Hollowell was not beautiful and she was not constructed on a scale large enough to let her be called handsome. Nor was she pretty. But she was remarkably good looking. The mere femininity of her appearance was modified by the signs of intelligence and virtue. These gave the effect of a boyish plainness, although the modelling of her face, with its strong delicate cheekbones, was firmer than any boy's could be. Vincent found the interesting contradiction of her face repeated in her name. He knew that in Spanish Linda means pretty, yet it seemed to him that no name in sound or appearance could be cooler or more modest, even ascetic. And so the play of contradictions went on. Her eyes were so dark and fine and yet they were almost blank with earnestness. Her unrouged mouth was tenderly shaped, but compressed in thought. Her body was well made, yet it seemed to hold itself to a mere adequacy of female grace. Vincent found her stiffness and even her quaint didacticism attractive.

Through the early part of the dinner Linda Hollowell had been silent. The table was so well appointed, the silver gleamed so perfectly in the candlelight, the whole occasion of Vincent's first dinner-party was going off with such an air that Vincent found it easy to imagine that there could be such an abstraction as a "perfect dinner guest" and that Linda Hollowell was it. He had at first identified her only as the young wife of a wealthy man, better dressed—he became aware of that quite soon—more carefully turned out than the other women. She had an air of fully and consciously listening to whoever was speaking, turning her whole attention on and even calling attention to her attention in a wonderfully "social" way. But as dinner went on, scraps of information made him modify this picture. Linda Hollowell had been to Russia and to Spain. There were plans for a publishing house. There were committees. She was a young woman of active and useful life. And the desire she expressed for Philip Dyas's school, though of course a joke, was not entirely a joke.

"I find it odd—" Vincent said, and felt the quality of his new life, for at this rather ponderous opening, everyone turned to listen to him. "I find it odd, the idea of anyone *buying* a school."

Philip Dyas lifted his head and looked at him and Garda Thorne at the other end of the table leaned out to see him and to smile at him.

"But why should it be odder, Mr. Hammell, to buy a school than to own one?" It was Arthur Hollowell's question. It was asked with a humble neutrality. Hollowell waited respectfully for Vincent to answer. Vincent's impression of Hollowell had been obscured by his knowledge that Hollowell was "so rich" and he always supposed wealth to be brutal. The intellectual humility of all this money rather confused him. His answer did not come very firmly. "I don't know—somehow a school—I suppose because it has a life of its own." And he felt himself blushing.

"True," Arthur Hollowell said and his agreement was charged with the most respectful enthusiasm. "True. A school is, as you say, a living organism, an organic entity, having its own development and its own laws of development, having its own integrity. And in an ideal society, your point would be not only ideally and theoretically right but practically right. But in our society,"—and although he said "our," he said it with a little movement of his head and an inflection of his voice that seemed to throw Society into the possession of everyone at the table except himself: only out of politeness did he consent to share the ownership of the messy property of our Society. "In our society with its morality of profit and loss, we have to recognize that things are for sale. It is a dreadful fact, of course. It seems to deny the moral potentiality of the human race. But it is the fact with which we have to live. We can't, after all—can we?—escape the necessities of our historical period. Individually we can do nothing about it. We must act within the pattern of culture if we are going to affect [*sic*] any change in that pattern. We can scarcely be effective if we escape from the realities into a morality of saintly perfectionisticism."

This was indeed a kind of rich man that Vincent had never imagined. As he spoke the veil of crude wealth that had obscured him fell away and for the first time Vincent saw his human appearance and was surprised by it. He saw that Hollowell was a young man and that his [blank half-line in original]

And this strange rich man went on. "We have to recognize the fact and work with it—that in our culture even spiritual values are for sale, like everything else. Even living organisms, as you so well point out, Mr. Hammell."

It came to Vincent that he had only said that a school has a life of its own. He had said nothing about a living organism or an organic entity, or laws of development.

"And so," Hollowell went on, "although the state should certainly have the control of all education, in our culture it is still possible to buy a school."

And Arthur Hollowell shrugged and smiled—at whatever cost to his own feeling he accepted the way of the world.

"As things now are, Mr. Hammell," he concluded, "There is a monthly periodical devoted to the interests of head masters in which quite as a matter of course, schools are advertised for sale. So much is it the accepted fact."

At this he retired from the conversation. He had entered it with no personal interest, but only with the intention of bringing his objective intelligence to the aid of clarity. Having finished, he smiled boyishly first to Dyas then to Vincent. And although Vincent was not quite satisfied, he felt that he had encountered an irrefutable logic. And perhaps everybody felt that. All the table was silent for a moment, perhaps contemplating the visions of the future, the outspread view of Society, or hearing the wings of the various moralities that Hollowell had sent aloft.

"Philip would be a fool to sell."

As Garda said it, the visions of the future and of society rolled up and the large gray wings of the various moralities ceased to beat. It was Garda's contribution to the joke to make her manner as tough as if she were at what she imagined a haggle of big-business must be like. "But if he does sell it to you, he ought to charge you a pretty penny for the spirit and value he's put into that place. Taking that run-down, ramshackle seedy affair and making it what it is now. If you want the measure of what he's done, just remember that he's made *me* admire a *school*."

She let them look at her, the ordinarily implacable enemy of elementary and secondary education, now making that one significant exemption from her hostility.

"Is that what you call the good-will of a concern?" she said and she looked at Hollowell with such aggressive shrewdness that one could almost see the big cigar of the _____ [blank in original; haggler?] in her mouth. "How much do you think that's worth, Arthur?" And she added, "Huh?"

Hollowell smiled in patient recognition of Garda's well-known and delightful extravagance. He said with mild forbearance, with the air of being in the conversation only in the interests of clear thought, "Garda, you talk as if Linda were trying to put something over on Philip. For one thing, price is no object, as Philip knows. And Philip isn't, you know, being forced to sell."

Before this mature reasonableness, Garda's bright childish bubble of indignation collapsed. But she recovered. She skillfully borrowed from Hollowell his own reasonable manner. "No, really," she said with gravity. "It makes me a little angry with you and Linda. The school was made by Philip. It's not his property, it's—it's his work. He doesn't own it, he lives it. And now just because Linda wants a school, she wants Philip's because it's near her home. No, really. I think it's wrong Linda, I think it's wrong."

Linda had been let out of the dispute by her husband's impersonal entrance into it, but now she had to come back. She said, "Really, Garda"—it seemed that *really* was the word that marked dispute on the high level of this company—"really it is not right of you to make it sound like some mere whim of mine. You make it sound like something frivolous—and insufficiently motivated. And you make it sound as if we were trying to make Philip do something against his will. We're just asking him. He's not forced to sell to us."

"Oh!" Garda cried with great impatience. She made a gesture with her hands to brush away certain cobwebs that had been allowed to stay too long. "Forced! Forced! You know perfectly well that he may well be forced. You know very well that he's still putting money into the school and isn't making any."

At this there was a silence in which the Hollowells seemed more deeply plunged than anyone else. Philip Dyas sat with his forefinger along his cheek, intelligent and imperturbable. Harold Outram seemed full of unuttered laughter, Marion Cathcart had seemed very remote from the whole conversation but now Vincent saw that she was very intensely aware of something. Dr. Buxton was looking at Garda with gentle and friendly curiosity.

Garda's gaze went wildly about the table to estimate the havoc she had wrought and to find help. She had, as even a stranger could see, carried the matter beyond a joke by suggesting that the Hollowells were capable of using money not merely as a means of exchange, a lubrication of the gears of life, but as a force. Like any guilty person, she covered one desperate act by committing another. "Well, I don't know what Harold's damned Foundation is for if not to help just such things as Philip's school."

And she turned to Outram with a flash of blue fire from her eyes that had the intention of illuminating the problem of his duty.

Outram smiled to her in a mocking, friendly way, unharmed by her anger, but May Outram opened her mouth and eyes in shocked surprise.

It was a great tension that these friends had worked up among themselves, actually a quarrel. Yet in a way it was not like any quarrel that Vincent had ever known. He remembered that in a book by a famous revolutionist he had read that it was foolish to suppose that when the State eventually withers away in the ultimate society, there will be none of the conflict which now makes life interesting but bad. The badness would go, but the interest would stay. In the ultimate society there would be the most passionate differences of opinion—people would glowingly debate such matters as a new aqueduct or bridge or work of art or philosophical idea, and even parties would be formed on the ground of these differences. These interests would be all the more intense because everyone concerned would be disinterested, with nothing personal to gain. There would be none of the desire for personal gain that now makes life hideous. All the purer desires would be that much freer.

There seemed to be present now at the dinner table some vague incomplete intimation of that future. It may have been that Vincent simply did not know the full meaning and force of all that was said. His own exploration of the tone of things was that the quarrel was taking place in Buxton's presence. Buxton had not yet said a word, but in the purview of his glance the "quarrel" was taking place without the tone of quarrels. Whatever the quarrel might have been in another atmosphere, in the climate of Buxton's presence it had almost a nobility.

Still, the table had fallen silent. Vincent would have liked to come to Garda's help, but he did not presume to. Whatever the Cathcart girl felt, she too obviously had to remain silent. Dyas could say nothing. Suddenly Garda turned to Buxton and cried in a passionate wail, "Jorris, am I wrong?"

The old man had his wineglass in his hand. It was surely with a sense of his drama that he sipped the wine and wiped his mustache before he answered. He said, "I don't know, Garda, whether you're right, but you're by no means wrong."

It could not be taken as an equivocal answer. Buxton's eyes, as he delivered it, swept the table, took in the Hollowells, first Linda, then Arthur, took in Philip Dyas sitting with his finger along his chin, took in Harold Outram and settled on Garda. His voice was very immediate and personal, as if he saw every implication of what had been said. And when he had given his judgment, the matter ended and the joke, or the quarrel, did not go on. Garda, who might have been expected to triumph brightly over her beaten opponents—it would not have been beyond her to have called out a crowing "See?"—sat quiet and almost humble. As for the others, they gave no sign of having been rebuked. They all sat together in a gentle silence. It was as if they had agreed to have out this disagreement under certain ideal conditions. It had been had out and now it seemed done with. It might almost have been started, Vincent thought, in order to draw from the old man this moment of judgment, for surely they must feel what he felt, a sense of deliverance so sudden and so sensual as to make him feel foolish. He had always thought it a failure in Greek tragedy when the god appeared high up on the tower to settle the disputes and resolve the action, thought it a failure in drama, but now he knew what dramatic possibilities there lay in the sudden voice that stilled the bickering of drama with irrefutable judgment. Back and forth went the dialogue and dialectic of passion and then came the voice, still and sure, and all eyes went up to where it came from and all voices were quiet. At that moment Vincent remembered his father in his little optometrical shop. For the first time in his life he felt that he was some man's son.

Dinner came to an end with the end of the dispute. The party went out to sit on the lawn with disagreement quite over.

The light of the long August day was at last failing. There was a large band of darkness in the eastern sky. Had the air been as usual this would have seemed no more than the massed approach of night. But there was a vibrancy in the air, a strangeness in the light, a succession of delicate little puffs of wind that turned back the undersides of the leaves and these things gave to the weighty formation of clouds its bright character of the portent of a storm.

chapter 18

As each man of the party came out of the house, he looked up and around and sniffed. There was a high thin purity of fragrance in the air. Buxton made the gesture that all the other men made, the quick, calculating sniff and the look around the horizon. It touched Vincent oddly to see it, this primitive responsiveness to weather, this taking it into account.

Hollowell, about to light his pipe, paused with the match cupped in his hand over the bowl. This seemed to give him a nautical authority of weather wisdom when he surveyed the heavens and said, "Storm coming."

It was a long way off. But it was certainly coming and already it drew everyone together in exhilaration. The little sudden puffs of wind were almost chilly. At the very height of summer there was the hint of autumn and even of winter. This reminder of time to come was a sensation shared among them all. It was almost an adventure shared. Consequently no one had to be very witty or acute to win response from the others. In the lightly tossing leaves over their heads there was an urgency, a kind of wildness. In the east they could now hear the rumble of thunder. It was far off but it was unusually decisive in tone. They could see the infrequent flicker of distant lightning. As the glow in the west diminished, they became more aware of the lights within the house behind them.

Garda Thorne, more than the others, was responsive to the charge in the air. She strolled with Hollowell over the lawn, back and forth. She had taken his arm and was actually doing what Vincent had read about but never seen, she was "leaning" on it. She looked up at the sky and called to the others, "It's going to be a regular tempest." Then, as if by an obvious transition, she said, "You can't imagine how lovely you look, all of you together."

Vincent could well imagine that they did. Certainly he had never known before how existence could shine with the quality of a moment forever caught on canvas. What Garda was seeing was something that might forever exist under the name of After Dinner At The Outrams and in the catalogue there would be the explanatory note, "The bearded figure is the American scientist Buxton. The young man at his left ..." Perhaps they all had some sense of the notable moment they were sharing. But of them all surely only Garda, with her bitter consciousness of time on the move, and he himself, recently escaped from dullness, could truly know how beautiful the moment was. He himself could feel that it was worth having lived a life of dullness, almost of sordidness, to be now able to taste so fully what life could really be. Could really be, not in imagination or in thought, but in reality.

It was no doubt inevitable that at this moment he should think of his past life, seeing his mother in their dining-room, almost smelling the odor of past meals which, in certain homes, is the palpable atmosphere of past quarrels. Yet as his mind moved toward his mother in a tenderness of guilt, he knew that it was not right of him to feel any guilt toward her. For this moment was the unconscious goal of all her plans for him. It was for this that she had bred and reared him—that he should have achieved a place amid comfort and elegance and among the powerful and easy people of the earth. No, it was not to her that any sacrifice of guilt was due. Yet he found some guilt necessary in this moment of felicity and it was to Kramer that he paid it. The memory of that friend and teacher with his pervasive suspicion of elegance, with his preoccupation with things of the mind, his perpetual sense of resistance to "temptation," came to Vincent now, and at his own bidding. And with it came the thought of "integrity" and his unhappy speculations of the morning. At the very height of his pleasure, he destroyed it, thinking miserably of the reason for his being here.

The storm was coming nearer and it brought Brooks Barrett. In his solicitude for Buxton he had arrived early. He was not early enough to get Buxton safely home. The wind had heightened and then there were a few warning drops of rain that sent the party into the house. They were barely inside when the rain came with a huger downpour than most of them had ever seen. The thunder, however, was still in the distance, as if a greater violence were being kept in reserve, but it was already very loud and almost perfectly continuous.

"At this rate it can't last long," said Hollowell in a competent voice. He said it chiefly to Barrett, who was in great anxiety, but anyone in the room was free to derive comfort from his assurance.

But the storm was not to be so easily exorcised. May Outram said with surprising quaintness, "Its fury is increasing." The old phrase was appropriate. There was really a kind of animus expending itself, a kind of will at work in the downward rush of water. It pounded on the roof and made the hollow house roar.

The children woke and cried out and Marion Cathcart leaped from her chair and sped upstairs to them. In a little while she returned with the children, who came down the stairs before her, wrapped in their bathrobes, beaming smugly at the coziness they saw awaiting and to the cries of welcome they received. But May Outram said, "Oh Marry do you think you should have?"

"Why, yes," Marion answered, and although she said it lightly and as if under correction, it seemed to settle the matter for May Outram.

The children, who looked, with their long robes and their bright embarrassed faces, like illustrations in the books they read, went up to Buxton and stood at his knee. The grizzled maid brought a tray of glasses and bottles and everyone sat about in a sociable way with a drink in hand. But the event whose anticipation had recently been drawing them together and that had, as it were, reached its climax with the arrival of the children, now seemed to have lost its charm. It even seemed to isolate them from each other. No one, of course, anticipated danger. But there seemed nothing to say.

At first Garda seemed to enjoy the tempest. It was she who called it by that name. "Why, it's a perfect tempest!" she said. And for a while she prowled about the beautiful cozy room with her light step and her glass in her hand. But as the storm lasted, she became subdued. She put down her glass and carried a footstool to where Buxton sat in a great wing chair. She sat at his feet and her face was troubled. Buxton laid his hand for a moment on her shoulder and to Vincent it seemed that the old man's hand moved heavily and he was startled to see that there was trouble in the aged face.

When the thunder broke, it was with a truly terrifying intensity. So complex were its sounds, so strange and various were its modulations that they made the effect of an articulate and meaningful utterance. The grizzled maid came in and spoke to May Outram in a low voice. "Of course!" May said in a flutter of good-natured solicitude. "Of course—tell them to come right in here." But the two young housemaids on whose behalf the permission had been sought would not come "right in here." All they wanted was as much security as they asked for and they sat in the lighted dining-room, as close as they could get to the doorway. They looked foolish and declassed and secretly pleased with themselves and very intimate among themselves.

What made conversation hard was waiting for the storm to abate. Everyone's meteorological knowledge agreed with Hollowell's—a storm's brevity was in proportion to its intensity. But this rule of thumb did not hold for this occasion. There were no signs of the storm's end. And impatience began to develop and the indignity of being imposed on and trapped.

This was most apparent in Brooks Barrett. His responsibility for Buxton gave him license to fidget openly. He paced the floor. From time to time he looked at a large pocket watch. He stared accusingly out of the window to examine the wild night. It was no longer a time for smiles and manners but for wrinkled brows and set lips. So serious was the situation that he ventured to regard the company with a manner of complaint. He seemed to be indicting not only the elements but also these false friends who conspired to keep his master—surely that was the right word—from his proper bed at his proper hour.

At last Barrett could stand it no longer. He entered into consultation with the Outrams and it was arranged that Buxton was to stay the night. It was Vincent's room that he was to have and Vincent was to sleep on the living room sofa. At this solicitude Buxton showed neither pleasure nor annoyance. When the room was ready for him, he said goodnight with a beautiful smile. Then he thought of something and trudged to where the housemaids were sitting in the doorway. They looked surprised and they blushed, and then, as he spoke to them, they giggled and rose uncertainly and, as he turned away, they sat down again, looking suddenly very charming in the flustered animation that had struck their faces.

Vincent was standing as Buxton passed them. He said, "Good night, sir," and Buxton said, "Good night, Hammell. We'll begin our grim business in the morning," and he sturdily climbed the stairs, Barrett at his heels.

For a while Buxton's being benighted here in the house relaxed the awkwardness of the group. The two children felt that it was an adventurous happening with an assured and attractive future—"Will he be here in the morning when I wake up?" Paul asked. For a little while there was the feeling that had prevailed when the storm had been approaching. But when the thunder lost a little of its force, the rain lost none, and now there was a high wind rising in power every moment. The imagination of the maids seemed limited to fear of the thunder. When that had diminished, they rose with the air of having accomplished a task or a social duty and shyly vanished. But to the fancies of the educated people, the wind was suggestive beyond the thunder and the rain. The thunder might be anger but the rain was spite. Thunder suggested a ceiling of heaven from which the bolts might be discharged, but the wind came from the illimitable unimaginable distances. They were really so affected by it that when Brooks Barrett appeared at the head of the stairs and surveyed the room and then silently descended, they all looked at him with frightened eyes. His ghastliness, although they were all familiar with it, now seemed strange, as if he had just been stricken white.

Barrett descended halfway down the stairs and there he stood, heraldic, with an arm outstretched to Vincent and a finger beckoning. Vincent looked quickly around behind him to see to whom the signal had really been made. But there was no one behind him. It was he who was being called.

He went wondering up the stairs to Barrett, and when he had come level, he felt a strong grip on his upper arm as Barrett put his head close and said in a loud whisper, "He wants you." Conscious of the watching puzzled eyes below, he was gently impelled up the stairs in Barrett's grip. He felt that this strange servant had been so grandly deputized that he did not resent this needless intimacy of touch.

chapter 19

It was not until they had reached the door of the bedroom that Vincent was able to ask a question.

"What is it?" he said.

Barrett's hand was on the knob. He kept it there as he looked into Vincent's face. "He's afraid," he said. "He's frightened in the storm."

This made nonsense. But Barrett's saying it frightened Vincent. Or, rather, it left a great vacancy into which fear might rush at will. If there was any reason for fear it was this Barrett himself who stood there with his look of a man upon whom jail has done its expected work. Yet Vincent knew that Barrett was telling the simple truth. He made a gesture to Barrett to open the door. He made it from a desperate impulse to face whatever it was that he shrank from. Yet in its curtness, it had the appearance of authority and Barrett's response to it was a kind of obedience.

Vincent had spent but a single night in the bedroom. Yet it was already somewhat his own, with his typewriter and his few books, and his hairbrushes on the dresser. It seemed strange that Buxton should be inhabiting it. Every light in the room was on, the overhead cluster, the bedlamp, the writing table. Buxton lay in the bed. He was clad in fresh blue pajamas. The neat overlap of the sheet was pulled almost to his beard. His eyes were closed, and when Vincent saw that his hands were clasped he knew that they were not clasped in prayer, but to keep the current of life flowing continuously as possible.

The emotion that Vincent felt upon seeing him was like the most intense social embarrassment. He would have liked to go away, but could not. He would have liked to advance. But he could not do that either—not until the old man opened his eyes and, turning his head slightly, looked at him with a glance that seemed to express, though faintly, wearily, a welcome and a hope. This gave Vincent the power to seat himself on the edge of the bed and do what he knew he must do—touch one of the clasped hands and urge it to relax its grip on the other hand. It was the fierce grip of Buxton's hand on his own that informed Vincent of the fear, the panic fear.

Here in this upper room the wind seemed worse than in the rooms below. One could hear up here what one could not distinguish below, the noise of the resistance of the great trees. The curtains were drawn and one could not see their movement, but one could hear it, the wild personal noise of organic matter. Buxton's white beard twitched with the effort of a smile. "Just stay," he breathed, "Just stay. Just stay," he said, and continued to whisper it like an incantation. And as the wind rose, the terror came into his eyes and Vincent felt the convulsive clutch of his hand.

Vincent thought, "He is going to die. This is death." But he did not believe that. It was a thought that expressed a deficiency of imagination. He was willing that deficiency. It was not hard to think of the extremity of death. But it was very difficult, it was terrifying, to think of other extremes. Death was well-known and it was not incompatible with the wonderful peace of the contemplating mind. Even the death-terror might be thought of as the tragic end of all mind. But Vincent knew that Buxton was not really dying. The unaccountable terror was not an end, but a contradiction. It contradicted, among other things, that wonderful peace of the "contemplating mind" that Vincent had so gratefully and proudly discovered that afternoon. It was not dying that Buxton was in terror of. He was simply in terror and he was in nothing else.

Barrett stood against the wall at the far end of the room. He held his hands behind him, between him and the wall. A faithful messenger, he had brought the one he had been sent for. Now as he watched the old man and the young man, he had the air of being outside and properly outside whatever was happening.

Vincent saw that it was the wind that started the waves of terror that overwhelmed Buxton. It was a child's fear. Vincent was quick to mock to himself, as any modern young man would be, the awe that he had been betrayed into feeling, a few hours before, at the power of the contemplating mind. But as he sat uncomfortably on the bed, his hand growing cramped in the old man's fierce grip, the impulse to save himself by self-mockery quite left him. He found that he [saw] it as a point of pride that he had been selected by Buxton as the comforter of his agony. "He wants *you*," Barrett had said. The comforter of his agony and, so far as biology would permit, its partaker. For the waves of the old man's terror lapped at the edges of his own mind. Later he was to learn, objectively, as we say, to learn it as a scientific fact, that with certain physiological conditions of the very old there is the experience of night terrors of the most extreme kind. But he himself, in the flush of his youth, could, if he wished, see an enormous vision of empty life. The analogy of Manilla Boulevard on a wet night, of vacant bright February days, of the gentility, worn and weary, of his parents' dining-room, or [the] prison of his own room on a Sunday night when life seemed to have sunk back into a half-lit nothingness from which it would never recover—these were the things by which he knew the enormous vision of emptiness, of the illimitable terror of vacuity.

Yet at twenty-three biology stands strong. And it was remarkable how the point of pride came to reinforce it. And the point of pride gave rise to the point of honor. For Vincent, grimly proud of his having been the one chosen to try to stand between Buxton and his terror, knew that it must be a point of honor with him not to relate to anyone what he was now witnessing.

He could not explain this decision of secrecy. He did not know if he made it for Buxton's sake. He did not know if he made it for the sake of the company in the drawing-room below. He only knew that when he went downstairs he would not answer truthfully the questions they would ask about what had transpired above.

By the time Barrett came from his self-consigned place against the wall and tapped him on the shoulder, he was extraordinarily calm. He followed Barrett's glance and saw that Buxton had fallen asleep and was now breathing with relative quietness.

Barrett nodded and Vincent nodded in reply. As gently and gradually as possible, he withdrew his hand from the relaxed grip and stood up. Buxton did not move in his sleep.

On tiptoes, Barrett went to the door and held it open for Vincent. He indicated by signs that he would spend the night here in the armchair. The wind was still wild, although it was now beginning to abate.

As Vincent reached the door by slow stealthy steps, Barrett scrutinized his face intently. Vincent submitted to the strange examination. He was very tired. He had never felt such a fatigue before. Barrett poked a finger violently downward, indicating the company below. He laid the finger over his lips and shook his head backward and forward in negation. He was enjoining silence, the very silence that Vincent had resolved to keep. Vincent closed his eyes wearily to indicate both comprehension and assent. And as he made that sparse gesture, which he had never made before, it seemed to him the gesture of a man much older than he actually was.

As he went down the stairs, he had to face the lifted heads and questioning eyes of all the waiting company. He was the bearer of tidings which they all wanted to hear. And they had a right to hear while he had no right to withhold what he knew. As he saw the expectant faces he had for a tumultuous moment the happy busy feeling of someone who is about to impart what everyone wishes to learn.

He was a young man who thought much of fame, power and success in life. To him this was a brilliant company, wonderfully worth impressing. The demand of its expectation was very compelling. He felt not only a great impulse but a great opportunity, to take on the tragic standing that would make him their peer. And not only their peer, but even their superior, telling them what they did not know, forcing their minds to a new conception of their admired man.

How he ever descended those stairs in silence, with his sad knowledge hot and bursting within him, he never knew. Harold Outram came forward and said, "Was anything the matter?" And Vincent shook his head indifferently and answered, "No, nothing's the matter."

He was able to say it so casually that Outram's question seemed fussy and foolish. It seemed to be at once established that nothing could be more natural than that Buxton, sleepless for some reason, should want to chat with the man who was to be his biographer.

It was not until he had told his lie that Vincent saw that he had retaliated upon Harold Outram for having that morning refused to tell him about Claudine Post. He had let fade his intention of considering the justice of his anger at Outram. He had let go by the whole question of why he, so immature and inexperienced, had been chosen as Buxton's biographer. And when the question presented itself to him again, it did not arouse in him that dissolving sense of the morning, of having been used and betrayed. It was remarkable how much stiffening his lie and his secret knowledge had put into him. There was no need to be angry, no need to be "hurt." There was suddenly no need to consider himself at all.

chapter 20

The really old Essex, the Essex that the tourist will go out of his route to see, consists chiefly of Wentworth Street. This is a short broad thoroughfare overarched by wine-glass elms of large growth. On Wentworth Street are situated the eleven houses that give Essex a kind of fame.

It is of course true that the very oldest of these houses, the Wentworth House, is almost entirely a restoration. But no secret is made of this. The studied character of the grim, solid, almost fortified structure is quite simply admitted by its being used as a museum. The other houses date from a later time, from after the violence of the Indian Wars which had destroyed the original Wentworth House and other houses like it. And there is even enough of the original Wentworth House still left to justify the 1670 marker, for its stone chimney is still standing and, although the original door is now kept inside the house as an item in the collection of historical objects, it bears not only an explanatory placard but also the scars and holes of the arrows and bullets which had been directed against it when it was actually used as a door.

The tourist who pays his twenty-five cents for admission to the Wentworth House experiences the morality that inheres in pewter and wood, in iron and copper and dark flawed glass. He sees the many utensils that pertain to fire, the flint-pistol and the bellows, the kettle and the trivet, the spit-jack, tongs, warming-pan and grog poker, and he remembers the cold hardships of a vanished, handmade world. The collection of weapons, the Indians' and the colonists', puts him in mind of the old life of daily mortal danger. Here, as in any such New England museum, hardship seems to go hand in hand with innocence. He reads the framed legal instruments on the walls and concludes from the quaintness of their language that the intention of their makers in regard to the transactions described was of an almost childlike intention.

And if the tourist is of a certain age, he is sure to be stirred by memories not only of national but of personal youth. For here, all about him, is the matter of his earliest picture-books and classrooms, suggesting the turkeys and blunderbusses and tall hats which he had cut out of paper with blunt-nosed scissors and colored with crayons of black and orange. And this is the paraphernalia of his boyish play, of his own knowledge of snow and then of snug warmth, of simple weapons, spears and bows and the gun that is lethal upon a loud shout of Bang, of forts and fires, chase and ambush and hand-to-hand fighting.

The other treasures of the street cannot speak to the visitor quite so intimately. Yet they will surely reach him in their own way, for the quiet thoughtful shapes of the old Essex houses are very eloquent. These fine doorways could have allowed the entrance and exit only of gravely happy people, or of people saddened only by meaningful sorrow. Thus the American will dream for an hour his modern dream of a past life that moved with the order, economy and significance of a narrative. Thus he makes his American Mont St. Michel, his white and wooden Chartres.

Wentworth Street begins with the restored Wentworth House, which, in its fortified seventeenth-century strength, is so very different from the houses of the later time, and it ends with the old church and what is left of the Common. What is now but a single street once constituted the whole of the town.

The tourist, unless he is of a satirical mind, will have no interest in the many new residential streets of Essex. For on these streets the houses are not white but tan or yellow or green. They are not beautiful in their proportions but likely to be hunched and high-shouldered. Their flower-beds are often outlined in brick or in large clam shells and their lawns are sometimes decorated with whimsical jigsaw representations of cockatoos, scotties and mickey-mice.

But somewhere between the charmed perfection of Wentworth Street and this sad negation of it, there is an intermediate architecture which is beginning to win an interest for itself. This is the part of town that was built in the forty years after the Civil War. It includes the flamboyant houses constructed of the brick that is part of Essex's industry and most of the public buildings, which are structures heavy with native stone and foreign porticoes. After having seemed ridiculous for some two decades, these buildings are now beginning to be thought of as having a certain interest and dignity. Sensitive people who once would have felt a kind of indignation with the conscious imposingness of their style, now regard them with wry respect. Even the W.P.A. guide-book of the state, which is written with so severe a feeling for the chastely simple that it is inclined to speak slightingly of the elaborate detail of the Federal period, admits that a certain moderate pleasure is to be derived from the confident affluence that these buildings show. There are few forms contrived by the human mind which, once they have been emptied of their immediate intention, do not have a measure of peace and nobility. The bedeviled tourist who, twenty-five years before, would have hated these post-Civil War buildings as the visible signs of the corruption of life that was at the root of his own uncertainties, can now think of them as the monuments of a more successful attempt at security than that of his own time. It is therefore not impossible to suppose that the ugly houses with their mickey-mice may one day come to seem, to a yet later tourist, the signs of a vanished peace.

As for the chief business street of the town, it has the rather huddled ugliness of so many American main streets, an ugliness that is pleasant and comfortable because of its large typicality. This same chain grocery store, this pair of competing hardware stores, this rather sad delicatessen kept by a rather sad Jew whose brother-in-law, more learned and political than he, is the proprietor of one of the three stationery and cigar stores, the several drugstores, the small dark easy bars, all of them are repeated by the reassuring thousands.

chapter 21

Philip Dyas's study was a large room in one of the finest of the Wentworth Street houses. It was lined with books and it was fitted for work and comfort. It was a room that Vincent Hammell would have understood although he had not yet seen it. Indeed, it offered itself to the comprehension of almost any man, with its great trestle table, its leather chairs, its appearance of disarray which would have misled only a woman, for it was only a working disarray and actually everything was in the most shipshape order. It was filled with light. This afternoon the light was gray. The Outram children on the lawn wore their sweaters and rubbers against the damp chill of the August day. Paul who was ten and Elizabeth who was five [six in chapter 11] industriously filled a bushel basket with the little green scrub apples that had fallen from the old almost sterile trees. Their young dachshund walked from one to the other, puzzled by their activity. They treated him with an enlightened impatience as if he were a child who was interfering with their serious business.

Within the house, Philip Dyas and Marion Cathcart watched the children at their work. They stood at either side of the window, watching silently for some minutes. Perhaps they were feeling the intimacy that comes to two people who look out of a window together. Dyas turned away suddenly. "Let me make you a drink," he said, "it's chilly. Or perhaps we should have a small fire."

The girl, left alone at the window, turned from it slowly and almost reluctantly. "Thank you, no," she said. "I can't stay. I promised the children they could feed the Hinson pigs with the apples. Do you think it's all right for the pigs to eat the apples?"

"I don't know," Dyas said. "I suppose it is. I'm sorry you can't stay. Vincent Hammell is dropping in. Do you find you like him?"

She shrugged and said "Oh—," letting her voice trail into the wide tolerance of indifference.

"I do. I like him, that young hero."

Her face became severe. Her head went up and her chin went forward. "What have you got against him?" she said sharply.

Dyas was genuinely surprised. "Why, nothing against him. I just said I *liked* him."

"Then why were you so ironical about him?"

His surprise was still real. "Ironical?" he said. Then understanding broke on him. "Because I called him a hero? But I meant it." And now he was indeed ironical in the look he turned on her. "You can't see what I mean, can you?"

Her impatience was great. "No, I can't," she said. "I suppose he's a perfectly nice boy, but when you use such language—"

He condescended from his years. "You look at it with the eyes of twenty-two, Marry. They see a lot but they don't see everything. The boy's a hero because—because every minute of his life he's looking for his destiny. Have you ever read that essay of his, the one I gave Harold?"

She said with dry disapproval, "Yes, I did read it and I didn't like it a bit. So damned self-conscious."

"Yes, of course it's self-conscious. I suppose its tone is very foolish, very young. But you know, Marry, it's a great deal harder to be a hero gracefully than to be a heroine." And he made a little bow in her direction.

"I'm no heroine!" she said very passionately.

"Oh, but you are!" He was teasing her a little, but his voice was also serious and tender, full of admiration and speculation.

"Oh, that's just—*language*." Her impatience was real and vehement and it was so strong that it made her flounce up out of the depths of the armchair. Her eyes flashed. She was really angry, as if she had been insulted or maliciously scared. Her attitude of resistance and defiance had great charm. Dyas looked at her with amusement and admiration. But suddenly she seemed to become unhappy and defenseless, quite miserable, not at all like a heroine but like a girl who might break into tears.

Dyas lowered his gaze. "I meant," he said in a quiet, reasonable voice from which all the banter has gone, "I meant only that Hammell is waiting for things to happen to him, the right things, the things that will match him. That's really all I meant by heroism. Perhaps it's too big a word. And I meant that you were waiting for the things that will match you."

"That won't be hard!" she said, loftily disdainful of herself.

"Why Marry—very hard."

Her anger and miserableness had gone. She said, "Don't talk to me like an uncle."

His smile was boyish and flattered. "I'm about old enough to be," he said. She waved this aside peremptorily, with the lost embarrassment the very young feel when their elders speak of their middle age and test the unreality of the fact by speaking openly of it.

Dyas said quietly, not to be denied. "Very hard, Marry—as you well know. You'll need to be matched, among other things, by a hero."

She gave a little pouf of laughter. "You *are* an uncle! You're uncle-ing me—"

"Avuncularizing, you mean."

She accepted it. "Avuncularizing me toward your young Hammell. Do you like him that much?"

She was flirting and had fallen into the unconsciousness of flirtation and so she was shocked by the simplicity of his anger as he said, "Don't be a fool, Marion!"

She recoiled under the fierceness of the anger. His face was flushed and hostile. But at the sight of her stricken eyes and trembling mouth he said reasonably, "No, that's a hero only potentially, Marry. He's too young, his events are too far off. Besides..."

"Well, could we change the subject?"

"Yes. But if Hammell's a hero at all, he's—I'm afraid—a tragic hero."

For two people who were fond and respectful of each other, they got angry easily. Marion's voice was charged with the deepest annoyance as she said, "Philip Dyas, you can talk such nonsense. If you like someone, why don't you leave him alone? I don't know him yet, but he seems nice enough, but so terribly on the make, so anxious to be a *success*." She threw out the word with boundless contempt. It seemed to check Dyas. He did not answer, and she pressed her advantage. "Yes, really, I think, a little vulgar. And letting himself be so thoroughly *used*."

Dyas rose and paced meditatively up and down, his hands in his pockets. "As to his being used," he announced, as if he were going to take up one point at a time. "As to his being used, as you put it—well, that's only as you put it. I know about your quarrel with Harold of course. And I really don't know which of the two of you was the more foolish. I'm sure that in every way you made the nicer picture, if I can judge from the way you look when you get angry with me—you clench your fists and your wrists curl up and you take your stand with your feet apart and your shoulders back—"

Under this love-making, for it was that, and under the quite relentless irony that cloaked and expressed it, she looked confused and childish, not at all capable now of the posture of anger that Dyas was describing.

Dyas went on. "And morally too, you were bound to make a nicer picture than Harold. That wasn't hard. You had the advantage the young always have, and especially when they are defending the young. But I don't quite know just what you are defending. You heard Harold and Garda decide that what was wanted for Buxton's biography was a young man. First let me remind you that this was openly talked about, in front of you. If there were anything to be ashamed of or hide, if there was an element of conspiracy, as I gather you think, we would scarcely have spoken of our intentions in front of you. You weren't present at any of the conversations in which I took a part, but you knew there were such conversations, you knew perfectly well that I was in agreement with the others. And yet that seems to have made no difference to you. No one is being used, I assure you. It's seldom that a young man gets the chance that Vincent Hammell is getting. If we wanted someone young and able to take suggestion, it's because we know as you don't, if you'll forgive my saying so, what the necessities of the whole situation are."

He was hard on her, but she could not miss the compliment that lay in his speaking out to her so straight, throwing his moral weight against hers without any worry that she would be unable to bear it. He went on to take up the next point. "Now about his being 'on the make.' Of course he's on the make. But if I said it another way, if I said he was 'seeking his fortune,' would that make it different? I know the signs of the foundling son of the king—the young man who has the giants to deal with, who is going to do *deeds*. The young man whose innocence is his talisman. I know—I used to be one myself."

She said with stout loyalty, "You still are. You still are, a good deal more than your Vincent."

His smile was enchanting. "No, Marry, I'm not. But since you insist on it for me, I must take it that you like the role."

"Yes, of course I like it. I like it very much." Then she said, "You still are. You and Dr. Buxton, too."

"Marry, you're a literal girl—"

"Yes I am."

"—and you don't have the vaguest notion of what I'm talking about. In the sense that I mean, Buxton is obviously not a hero at all. And never was. He's not the foundling son of a king and never was. He's the king himself and always was. Having discovered his kingdom, he simply walked into it. As for me—"

"There's the school," she said primly. "That's an achievement."

"Oh, of course it is," he said with gentle impatience. "But achievement has nothing to do with it. You refuse to understand what I'm talking about. I'm not in the least sure that Hammell will achieve anything at all. You're the one who's being vulgar now—you with your notions of achievement. It's only one's sense that he is demanding that something happen to him. And that something may turn out to be tragic."

She was in the armchair again and at this she sat up straight. "You use that word a great deal," she said.

"What word?"

"Tragic. You use it as if it were the best thing you could say about anything."

He looked confused for a moment, for a deep belief had been brought to light in a very casual way. Brought to light casually—and questioned rather firmly by a person whose years and sex made the questioning difficult. He said, "Yes, I think it is the best thing you could say about anything. And perhaps when you're my age you will think the same. You'll know as I do that the belief in

[two blank lines in original]

She listened to him attentively, not looking at him, looking down into her lap where her hands were folded softly together. When he had finished, she looked at him, full but not searchingly, as if the whole personal explanation of this opinion of his would come of itself to the surface and be apparent without any probing of hers.

But nothing did appear. She shook her head gently but stubbornly. "I don't see it," she said. "It sounds very noble but I don't see it." This ended the matter. But she was only just leaving when Vincent Hammell arrived and she disconcerted him as he entered by the intense curiosity of her glance.

chapter 22

As for Vincent, he met Marion's look with a look of equal curiosity. He too had ground for wondering if the person who now confronted him was quite the person he had at first supposed.

He has awakened early that morning at the sound of splashing in the pool and when he went to the window he saw Marion Cathcart. The first thing that surprised him was that she did not swim well. She did, indeed, seem concerned to swim better, for she had thrown a rubber float into the water and clung to it, face down, while she practiced the leg-flutter of the crawl. She found it impossible to keep her leg to the prescribed stiffness—despite all her concentration, it bent at the knee. Now and then she looked back at the heels which the bending of the knees was throwing so much too high out of the water. Two or three times she reached back with one hand to try to touch one knee or the other to remind it to keep the line of the leg unbroken. After a short while, in fatigue or discouragement, she climbed out of the pool and sat on the coping to rest. And Vincent observed that when she entered the water again, she used the steps and did not plunge or dive in.

He did not leave the window all the time she was in the pool or at it. He felt that he was spying. But he felt that the espionage was justified because it was disclosing a fraud. It was one thing to be judged by a girl whose competence he was bound to admit on the evidence of every aspect of her manner and appearance. It was quite another thing to be judged by this girl who handled herself so awkwardly in the water. Marion Cathcart, the quiet girl with the clear forehead, was not an easy housemate. It was not entirely comfortable to have to meet her level eyes across the table at meal after meal. She looked out at the world with her still, judging gaze in which, as Vincent knew, he himself did not stand very favorably. He could not resent this—he himself judged the world pretty severely and knew that there were reasons why he should be severely judged.

But now, as Vincent watched Marion Cathcart's almost timid entry into the pool, he felt not only that she had no right to judge him but that she was even compromising the youth they shared. Garda Thorne, who was perhaps twice Marion's age, swam with the same precision that marked her tennis. He remembered now he had never before, in his four days here, seen the girl in the pool, no doubt because she was ashamed of her swimming and got up before the rest of the household to practice in this guilty secrecy.

He continued to observe her as she stood on the lawn toweling herself. It was only a little past seven of the already beclouded morning. The sun was not high and it shone weakly, and in that unardent light the girl had a strange and solitary existence. She stood there alone on the lawn and bent over to dry her legs and thighs and then she dried her arms and shoulders and then her neck and back hair, rubbing slowly, meditatively, inattentively. Her bathing suit was black and close-fitting. Another eye than Vincent's might have found that its remarkable scantness was very happily justified, but Vincent was aware of no particular grace or charm. Indeed, quite to the contrary. He would formerly have said that Marion Cathcart was a quick graceful person and tall. But now she seemed rather short than tall. He had the sense that her feet seemed to press almost heavily into the grass, they bore her weight almost inelegantly. There was a certain resemblance to May Outram as he had first seen her, except that the Cathcart girl suggested to him no ideas of fine crouching bronze statues. She was only irritating in her awkwardness and vulnerability.

Well, he was glad. He had been taken in by Marion Cathcart and now he saw through the pretense. He looked forward to meeting her, armed with this new knowledge of her. In his establishment in this new place, the last barrier had gone down. By now the feverishness which had marked all his vision and estimate of the first two days had almost entirely passed. Like a foreigner in a new land, he had observed everything, noted everything, found meaning in everything. Like any foreigner, observation and understanding were his means of defense against his alien position. Things had more significance than reality. But now proportion was asserting itself. May Outram's silences did not disturb him. He had learned what to take and what to discount in Harold Outram's violence. The children had begun to accept him as one of the household. He was on easy terms with the dachshund Wolfgang. Between himself and Garda Thorne he felt a special bond. After two sets of tennis with Hollowell, winning one and losing the other, he was no longer in confusion about great wealth. He had chatted with Philip Dyas in a way that made him feel that he was on the road to friendship with that admirable man. After two visits to Buxton, he was coming to be rather wonderfully at ease with this great subject of his. And perhaps the last indication that he was seeing things in their true normal light was that Brooks Barrett no longer seemed to have some strange knowledge from beneath the earth but was quite ordinarily the servant everybody else took him for. Within four days Vincent Hammell was no longer a strange and lonely young man in a world full of secrets and legendary dangers. Only Marion Cathcart had remained, not exactly a danger, but quite clearly a hostile element.

But no longer. She had succeeded, right up to this revealing moment, in keeping alive in him his sense of being alien. But now he could feel that if anyone was the stranger, it was this very Marion. She had the precedence of him here, for this was her second summer with the Outram children. Yet for all her precedence in time, she had not yet been able to come as close as himself, with only four days, to this world of clear decisiveness. He was impatient to meet her now, armed as he was with this new advantage over her. He was eager to recoup his position with her and he shaved and dressed with a sense of combative exhilaration.

But she did not appear at breakfast. And almost as if she were aware of his new knowledge and was avoiding it, she lunched early with the children. Vincent found himself frustrated and annoyed. He looked forward to dinner.

He had no expectation of finding her at Philip Dyas's and when he entered the study and saw her there, the surprise of her presence took him aback. She gave him that quick straight glance of hers and he met it, but he did not know that it was not a glance of judgment but of curiosity.

It put him on the defensive, where he had not expected to be. He tried to see her in the light of the morning's revelation. But somehow the new knowledge did not operate. It did not, when it came to the test, apply at all. She stood there with her brow as broad and calm as he had believed it to be, her eyes just as level and competent as he had at first thought. She stood trim and taut, really as elegant and weightless on her feet as any woman could want, or any man could want for her.

For a moment their glances clashed. But there was, after all, no actual quarrel between them, and no cause for one. After all, they were housemates, and Philip Dyas was beginning to emanate amusement. So each of them said "Hello" politely but as sparingly as possible.

Marion was on the point of leaving, but she lingered. It was not out of any inclination but only because a woman knows that she makes too much drama by breaking off her visit to a man immediately upon the appearance of another visitor. But Vincent thought of her as intrusive, as spoiling his anticipated visit to Dyas.

Dyas could not help seeing that his young visitors were in a difficulty with each other. He thought that the young woman could take care of herself more easily than the young man, for it was to Vincent that he spoke. "You've come from Buxton's, haven't you? You've begun work already."

"Yes, I have," Vincent said, and felt Marry's intrusion more than ever. He would have liked to speak of Buxton to Dyas. But he remembered the greeting between Buxton and Marion Cathcart and he felt constrained in her presence. Besides, with his quick responsiveness to surroundings, he was too much absorbed by this new room to answer with concentration. He believed that to let his eye wander so observantly about would be a little rude or at least a little raw. But the room was delightful to him, corresponding much more to something in himself, with its ascetic air, than had the Outrams' happy drawing-room. This was really his own room at home grown to maturity and authority. And suddenly he saw an object which so pleased him that he had to go up to it to examine it, quite forgetting any question of manners.

It stood on a low bookcase and it was a thing to be examined closely, a model of a whaleboat, something under a foot in length and made with amazing precision. "This is wonderful," Vincent said, looking back across the room to Dyas. And it really was wonderful. The boat rested in two curved uprights. It was constructed of pegged planks, and the planks and the gunwale and the ribs were in the most precise proportion to those of a real boat. It did not have the dwarfed and shrunken and subtly tortured look of most miniature things—it was the imitated thing itself and then something more, it had a reality added rather than subtracted by its size. Within the boat lay all the instruments for an encounter with a whale. There were three harpoons, one of them with its line attached to the rope which lay precisely coiled in its barrel. The line of the boat was all strength and speed, the boat was ready at any moment to move forward out of its cradle. Vincent found his fingers itching for it, expressing some unidentifiable impulse that came from some unrecognized depth—he had never before had so disinterested an impulse toward anything. Beside this perfectly useless simulacrum of an efficient useful thing, art itself seemed utilitarian, making its comment on life, offering explanations and solutions. This boat seemed relevant to nothing. It simply invited his fingers and his love.

"You like it?" said Philip Dyas. He had come up and was standing beside Vincent.

"I don't think I've ever liked anything so much," Vincent answered and his voice expressed very nearly all that he felt, quite matching the eagerness of Dyas's question.

Marion Cathcart left at that moment. She was standing near the door and she simply stepped out through it and the two men looked up at her step and saw that she was gone.

"I'm glad you like it," Dyas said. "I saw it one day in the window of an antique shop in New York. I was in a black mood, one of those finally desperate moods that one gets into—"

He could not have known the charm that his words had for Vincent, the literal charm that fortified his spirit at the knowledge that others than himself could know despair. Dyas sat there so solid, but that solidity had its possibility of melting no less than his own. Vincent had noted before this the subtlety of Dyas's heavy face, but now he saw its possibility of torture. It was far from being tortured now, however. It was all alive with interest, friendliness and vitality.

"—and suddenly I saw this—this thing. I must have stood in front of that window for half an hour, longer than I've ever stood before a picture. It never occurred to me that I could buy it. I started at last to leave but I had to come back after having gone only a little distance. Then I realized that I could, after all, buy it. And I did, on the spot. It cost much more than I should have spent, it was terribly expensive."

"Yes, I should think so. Do you know when it was made?" Vincent said.

"It was made by a whaling man, certainly, but I never think of its being made. It's odd—I really don't like to think of that. It must have been made over many voyages or maybe when the man had left the sea, but it's strange, I never think of his hands at work on it. It looks, does it not, like the very *idea* of a boat?"

This expressed very well what Vincent had felt and he said, "Yes, I know just what you mean."

"I suppose it's some kind of fetish for me. I don't quite know why. It isn't as if I had any feeling for whaling, or greatly admired *Moby-Dick*, but there seems ..."

He shrugged, giving up any attempt to explain or to know the reason for his feeling.

"It looks," Vincent said, "so frail and yet so tough. As if one could be safe in it."

"Yes—safe or saved. Perhaps any boat means salvation. But it's quite lovely, isn't it? Pick it up if you like."

Vincent hesitated. It was, oddly, not a thing to be handled, yet he did want to hold it. He carefully lifted it out of its cradle. He could feel the tough resilience of the wood. "What kind of wood is it?" he asked.

"They told me teak—the same kind of wood they made the big boats of."

As Vincent held the boat, Dyas lifted out one of the oars and held it up for Vincent to see. He put it back and took out the barrel with its coiled rope and the harpoon that was so wonderfully warped by its leader to the heavier line. When they had examined these and when Dyas had made Vincent examine the precision with which the planks were fitted, he put back the boat's equipment and Vincent laid the boat gently on its cradle. The two of them stood back to look together at this object again.

chapter 23

At about ten o'clock in the morning, Vincent would present himself at Buxton's house on Wentworth Street. Barrett answered his ring and in the dim vestibule the "assistant" glowed with his phosphorescent pallor and his eyes gleamed with a genteel conspiratorial awareness. Vincent could not rid himself of the feeling that every morning Barrett was about to whisper, "Have you brought it?" and that one morning he would find himself answering, "Hush—yes, here it is." But Barrett never asked the question.

On some mornings Barrett bore word that Buxton wished to see Vincent when he came, but most often the order of the day was that Vincent would go directly to the small room on the second floor that had been set aside for him. There he would work over the papers which, in cardboard files, filled two old mahogany bookcases.

It was an enormous accumulation. Buxton had long ago acquired the habit of preserving papers. He explained to Vincent, in apology for the vast clutter, that he had acquired the feeling that all documents were precious from having worked two summers with a professor of his on certain ancient papyri. "Such rubbish," he said. "It would amaze you, the triviality of the evidence on which the ancient civilizations are reconstructed." The young Buxton had played with the fancy that a dance-card or a dinner invitation might be preserved by chance for the delight of scholars a millennium hence. "I used to think about some Alexandrian who owed another Alexandrian for a consignment of sheep's grease and I thought how wonderful it was, how lucky they were, to have their names known now, Sosostris and Climenes or Laon and Diacones." Vincent knew well enough how the rest of the fancy went—how the young student would exist as a fact and a puzzle in the mind of some scholar of the inconceivable future. If you had luck, the mind of the scholar who held the dance-card or the dinner invitation would not condescend to you [who] were dead and blown away but would be unhappy because it would never know the tunes to which you had danced or the taste of the food you had eaten. The fancy had formed a fixed habit for Buxton and he had thrown into a cardboard file every conceivably documentary scrap he received. When the file had filled, another had succeeded it and after that another, and as the years passed, the rate of accumulation increased. Among the ranged files in the bookcase there were eventually some that were tight with the correspondence of only a single year. But the last fifteen years were contained in far fewer than fifteen files. Indeed to hold the letters of the last six years, a single file sufficed. Once this was understood, a single glance could give the rate of Buxton's life.

Vincent was to prowl at will through the mass of paper that had thus accumulated, doing what the biographical scholar calls "spade work." And no biographer could have wanted a wider or a richer field to work or one whose soil the spade cut more easily. Vincent had always despised the academic men for whom "documents" were the crown of existence. But now that he himself had a fine chaos of documents to manipulate, he understood the particular delight such work could give. Out of this "material," this primal matter, upon which no more than a rough chronological order was as yet imposed, it was for him to draw the organization and meaning that were there, waiting for him. And this was but the beginning, for to every letter that was contained in the cardboard files there was presumably an answering letter from Buxton himself. These letters would have to be found and read. The world concentrated here on Buxton, addressing itself to Buxton, making him the center of the world. But Buxton had also addressed himself to the world. From whatever person and place a letter had come, to that person and that place a letter had also gone. The size of the task he had so lightly undertaken would have appalled Vincent had he not been so deeply stirred by the adventure of this large creation. It was, for example, a growing excitement to him to observe how Buxton, as the recipient of all this various correspondence, imposed a unity upon the multiplicity. Different as each writer was, the act of writing to Buxton, the idea of Buxton in each writer's mind, gave each letter something in common with all the other letters, so that one could learn almost as much, Vincent began to think, from the letters Buxton had received as from those he had sent.

To master the chaos of paper, Vincent found that he had to be extraordinarily systematic. He disliked notes and indexes, but they were indispensable. He divided Buxton's life into five periods—there was Childhood and there was Youth; there were what he called the Humanistic Years; there were the Years of Science; and there were the Essex Years. He found that he had unconsciously made a distinction between the years of science and the Essex years. He did not know what Buxton did with his mornings, but he rather thought that it was not scientific work that occupied those hours.

With the "periods" laid out, Vincent began to go through the correspondence year by year, making notes on it on stiff white cards. "Series of letters from a high school friend, dealing chiefly with B's religious doubts," a card would read, and then would follow a notation of the date of each of the group of letters. On a separate card each letter was abstracted and its significant sentences copied out. From these cards Vincent would make a summary, trying to complete a single subject each day. Lunch would be brought to him on a tray by Barrett and after lunch he would continue a little longer with his work, and then spend the late afternoon with Buxton. He would bring his abstract to Buxton, who sat in his big wicker chair on the lawn or in the cool parlor, listening while his life was recalled to him. Of many incidents and people Buxton had no active memory. Had he been writing his own life, he would perhaps never have thought to include certain important matters at all. But he had only to be reminded of these events to shine with the intensity of his recollection.

"There was," Vincent might say, "a friend of yours in high school, named Leslie Miller—" And Buxton's eyes would begin to sparkle as wickedly and merrily as if he could still tease Leslie Miller. "Damn!" he said. "I haven't thought of Leslie for forty years. And we were as close as two male creatures could be. We used to hunt squirrels back of the town, and God how we talked! There was nothing we didn't talk about. We broke off some time in college—didn't we?"

"No, it was later than that. It was the year after your graduation." The ironic affection of Buxton's voice made Leslie Miller as alive and near to

Vincent as if he were Toss Dodge. Leslie was presumably long in his believer's grave, but for the moment he strode through the room—Vincent saw him as taller and rangier than Buxton—with his small-bore rifle over his shoulder and his earnest face, literal in belief, imaginative in desire. And with him there came the tinge and scent of the autumn hunting.

"Is there something about Darwin in the letters?" Buxton asked. He was always eagerly curious about the past, but he never wanted to read the documents themselves or hold them in his hands. Once, when Vincent volunteered to get some early letters to show him, he forbade it almost angrily.

"Yes, there's a good deal about Darwin. You seem to have had a considerable difference over religion. There's one letter—do you recall?—in which he breaks off communication with you. He says he can no longer know you except as his adversary."

"But that isn't really the last letter, is it? I'll bet there are more letters after that. Isn't that so?—aren't there more after that?" And Buxton chuckled.

"Yes, there are."

"I was sure," Buxton said with satisfaction. "He was a dear fellow, Leslie was, but he really had a turnip for a head. He liked to be stubborn and I liked to make him do what I wanted. If he said he would never communicate with me again, I would have undertaken to make him communicate with me again. He became an Episcopalian minister. In Ohio, I think. You know, it wasn't really a difference of opinion that broke us up. I wasn't really interested in religion then, not one way or the other. But something developed between us that made me feel that if he was for religion then I was against it. I used to think it was a kind of teasing, but it was rather more than that." And he looked at his biographer with a kind of pained candor. "I think I was rather cruel to him." And a moment later he said, "I like Dyas, but it's the way I am with him when he talks religion."

"Does Mr. Dyas talk religion?" It was surprising.

"Oh well, you know—not *religion*," Buxton said, "but he rather wants me to say there's nothing rationally inconsistent about the idea of God. Eddington's kind of thing. He's read Eddington—knew him, I think, at Cambridge. And at the same time that Hollowell girl, Linda Hollowell, she keeps after me to assure her that there is ground for a perfect, absolute determinism. I can't imagine why she should want it."

Vincent found it incongruous, even a little disappointing, that he should pick up from Buxton this kind of information about his new environment. But the old man had a great impulse toward the present and Vincent had to accustom himself to the idea that this was no mere monument of the past. It was on his response to the present that Buxton's memory of the past moved. He was greatly aware of the little circle that had formed around him. He took no account of the place he held in its center, but he took great account of its existence and quality. Vincent had to correct the striking revealing first impression he had of the man, so old and wise that the details of human quality did not exist for him. In whatever way Buxton judged what he saw, he certainly saw a great deal.

There were many other respects in which Vincent had to modify his first mythical notion of Buxton. There was, for example, the necessity of adjusting himself to the sexual note that now and then appeared in the conversation. Quite early in his work Vincent came across a letter from what must surely have been a young girl. He noted, with an archaeologist's interest, how early had been the origin of the square, back-sloping, affected handwriting of the contemporary college girl. The words of the letter were so cryptic as to be clearly erotic. They breathed reference to some great moment that had been shared, though it was impossible to tell of what kind the moment had been. The letter was undated, but it had been deposited with other letters of Buxton's twenty-eighth year. This letter Vincent read aloud to Buxton, in a dry voice, feeling shy at the first intrusion of privacy. At the name of the writer, Buxton's eyes lighted up and stayed alight through the reading of the letter. And his biographer's first impression was that this was the light of reminiscent lust. It was an appalling thought. And yet the young man had to see at once that his conclusion had been hasty, conventional and wrong. The light in Buxton's eyes was rather that of fine intelligence, as if Buxton had seen a wonderful relation between ideas. Buxton said, referring to the writer of the cryptic letter, "She was a fine bunch."

"I beg your pardon?" Vincent said, all his sensibilities retreating once more as his perception of intelligence seemed denied.

"Bunch—a fine bunch of a girl." And Buxton made a gesture, inconclusive but plastic, as of gathering, or as of holding, a nosegay of flowers. Vincent's shy, priggish retreat from the sexual awareness of an old man was wholly checked. There was in Buxton's manner so responsive a sense of the fragrance and fragility of the bunch. All of a sudden the word, which may have been the slang of Buxton's youth, seemed lovely.

The little incident of the "bunch" was the occasion for Vincent to begin his private notebook on Buxton. The notebook was a large one, bound in cardboard covers, mottled black and white, like the notebook in which Vincent tried to put down his observations on things in general, but larger. It was to be, this new notebook, the repository for all the comments and incidents relating to Buxton that Vincent wished to record for himself. Some of these entries might eventually find their way into the biography, but the chief purpose of the notebook was to record what might have no place in a public work. It might, for example, be possible and even necessary to mention in the biography that Buxton at twenty-eight had had a brief love affair with a young woman identifiable only by a rather sweet and foolish nickname, but it might be quite another thing, worth hesitating over, to say in print that some fifty years later her lover had referred to her as a "fine bunch."

One day Buxton used the same word about Marion Cathcart. "That Marry," he said abruptly, "she's a fine bunch of a girl for the right man."

Vincent heard himself replying crisply, "No doubt." At last the beautiful innocence had broken down into the senile lubricity he had feared for it. But there was Buxton looking at him very firmly and with a kind of disapproving curiosity. There was no fantasy in the old man's expression, and Vincent, hearing the words reverberating in his mind, understood that there had been no fantasy in the voice, just a simple statement of reality. Marry was a fine bunch of a girl exactly as little Paul Outram was a remarkably intelligent boy or as Arthur Hollowell was a very rich man. "You don't think so?" said Buxton with an almost haughty surprise.

"Oh yes, she's very attractive." And Buxton grunted with the satisfaction of a logical man who has driven back underground a piece of nonsense that had dared to raise its head.

It was Buxton's relation with his father that, in the first few weeks, taught Vincent most about the old man. There were letters from the elder Buxton, written while his son was away at college, and in this instance, there were Buxton's replies to most of the letters, preserved from among his father's papers. Quarrels had taken place in these letters, especially one notable disagreement at the time Buxton had chosen his scholarly career. But the quarrels, including this one, were always compounded and they even seemed to Vincent to be the incandescence of the strange charge that flowed between the father and the son.

The elder Buxton—incredible to think he had been born a round century ago!—had apparently been a man of only moderate education. But he wrote with the literacy and feeling for style that had been a national trait in his youth, and now and then his letters yielded a remarkable sentence. On one occasion he wrote to his son, "Your mother believes that your Aunt Thyrza's loss and pain are having a purifying effect. It comforts her to think so, and so I say nothing, but I have never known loss and pain to work anything but harm. I fear those persons who have suffered and it is my belief that strength of character is given to us to prevent our being corrupted by pain." He could say this kind of thing, but usually the letters were commonplace. What made them remarkable to Vincent was a quality that seemed to have nothing to do with intellect. There had been no intimacy between the two Buxtons. There had been no expression of affection. But as Vincent went through the correspondence, he began to be aware of a certain willingness on the part of the father, a willingness for the son to have the quality he did have. There was no eagerness for the son to have any particular quality at all. And there was no reluctance. There was just this simple willingness. The letters of the elder Buxton communicated to Vincent the sense of a man who was content with himself, who had enough of himself and was willing that his son should have enough of *him*self. It was as if he had presented his son not only with life, but with a specific life, the life of a man, with the right to enjoy and the right to be mistaken. It was part of the nature of the gift that, having made it, he should be unaware of it—what he had given, he had given, and it was as little for him to try to nourish it as to try to check it. But he was not unresponsive to it—Vincent was sure of that from the gravity and directness of his letters to his son.

In his own way, the father had been impressive. He looked impressive enough from his photographs, a dark man, mustached, thick-haired, heavy-browed. Looking at the old photographs, Vincent had the sense of a deep change in culture since the time they had been taken. In all these pictures the men bulked solid and plastic. They were so very much there before the camera, so clear in the many shades of black. They confronted the camera, aware of it, almost defying it. There was no catching them unaware or unconscious. They were, indeed, not "caught" by the camera at all. They did not pretend that the camera had intruded, stealthily and without permission, on their privacy, on their delicate reluctance to be portrayed, coming upon them in a moment of rest and meditation. One saw them precisely in the moment of having their picture taken, of putting themselves on record, and they posed and projected their images to the lens and the plate, standing up to the occasion and to the searching eye. They were not by any means passive to the camera. And the slow lens and the slow plate required stiffness, a genuine being there, not for a split second but for a continuous time. There were none of the soft grays of modern portrait photographs which had surely been evolved, as Vincent came to think, for the sake of women. Certainly in the old photographs the women were not at as much advantage as the men.

To this general rule Buxton's mother was an exception. There was no photograph of her taken after her thirty-second year, and she had died a few years later. Vincent was a little disconcerted by the visual image of the mother of the aged Buxton as a perpetually young woman, like some nymph or goddess of Greek story, who, while the lines deepen in her son's face, and his hair greys and his muscles slacken, remains as fresh and rosy as when she had conceived him. Mrs. Buxton held a mystery for Vincent. She was bound to have, for he was trying to find the source of Buxton's quality and it was inevitable that he should seek it in the parents. What Mrs. Buxton had, Vincent found difficult to understand. For in her appearance there was the gentleness, even the submissiveness, which the poets of an earlier day had loved to remark on in women. Yet it was strange, the gentleness and submissiveness did not suggest weakness. On the contrary, Vincent found, as he looked at the representations of that face, that there was an expectation here, even a demand, a kind of force that he had never before imagined. He was curiously excited by these pictures and he took them out again and again to look at them. He did not understand their attraction for him until he remembered that he had gone back in just this way to certain pictures in his boyhood because they had contained some sexual information or some sexual charm. In these photographs there was, he saw, a sexual fact of a high, complex kind. A convention about the last century kept him from understanding the fact, but he saw it at last and believed that in these photographs he was seeing an intensity of womanhood such as he had never seen and never imagined, grave, silent and profound.

chapter 24

Vincent had nearly forgotten the existence of the woman about whom Outram and May and Garda had shown such violent feelings, the woman about whom, as Harold Outram had put it, he was to find out for himself. He was seated one day with Buxton and the interview was just drawing to its close when Brooks Barrett entered the room and said to Buxton, "You have visitors, sir." He said it with an air of firmly-expressed disapproval. It was a disapproval that seemed to have its history—he seemed to know that Buxton would understand it. He added, "Mrs. Post and Miss Perdy." And over these names, as he uttered them, there played his uncompromising genteel reserve.

Buxton said with some irritation, "Well, show them in! Show them in!"

But they were already in. At the door there appeared first a figure of giant size, then one of fairy slightness, the one all darkness of complexion and eyebrows, the other almost startlingly blond. The first figure hesitated with a certain archness. "*May* we come in?" said Mrs. Post. "We are bad, we are interrupting, we shouldn't—but then we've never met Mr. Hammell, and we've been wanting to for ever so long."

"Mrs. Post, Mr. Hammell," said Barrett promptly. "Miss Aiken, Mr. Hammell." But he was quite without his usual pleasure in the social forms. The introduction was almost wrung from him.

Vincent had risen at the sound of Mrs. Post's arch voice. He bowed. He saw that there was nothing gigantic about Mrs. Post. She was really not much taller than many women are. But she bulked large beside the girl and there was a degree of force in her bearing as she stood there smiling that suggested the gigantic. As for the girl, she would naturally be accompanied by giants, or dwarfs, or elves, or witches, for she looked as if she had stepped from the illustrations of a book of fairy tales. She was amazingly slim, she wore a bright green dress, she had a large red mouth in a tiny face which was made the smaller, which seemed almost crushed, by a massive coif of blond curls. Two large eyes looked out from under the startling pile of her hair and two little apple-like breasts lifted the green dress. The great eyes were turned to Vincent when Barrett made the introduction, but what they signified, or whether they signified anything at all, or whether the little breasts were anything more than the expectable details in the representation of the princess who had felt the pea through the thirty mattresses, or of any well-known picture-book princess, Vincent could not tell. But upon seeing her, his heart quickened with astonishment and excitement, for he was seeing here in reality the pictured fantasy of his early boyhood.

But the quickening was stilled almost as soon as begun. The vagueness and insubstantiality that had once charmed his dreams now chilled him when he saw it in a literal actuality. Still, she made a very charming figure as she stood there with her sweet, inconclusive smile, leaning a little forward, standing almost on tiptoe.

To Mrs. Post Buxton said cordially, "Do sit down, Claudine," and to the girl he said, "How do you do, Perdita?" and to her he gravely held out his large dry hand into which she placed her little bright one. She did not actually drop a courtesy, but her attitude suggested that she was on the point of doing so. Buxton regarded her with a quiet tolerant pleasure,

"How are you getting on, my dear?" he said.

Perdita turned her head to look at Claudine Post. "Dr. Buxton means with your lessons, dear," said Mrs. Post. "Perdy has a lovely voice, Mr. Hammell, and Dr. Buxton has—"

Buxton lifted his hand in imperious admonition, but Mrs. Post was not to be checked. She shook a finger at Buxton and said, "No, no, I'll not have you disclaiming it. No indeed. If Mr. Hammell is your biographer, then you can hide nothing from him. Mr. Hammell should especially know it, he of all people should know it." And she made a gay and affectionate gesture of flouting Buxton's wish to deprecate himself. Now she became perfectly and defiantly explicit. "Mr. Hammell—Dr. Buxton has arranged for Perdy to have singing lessons. And her teacher has great hopes of her. No, I'll not have it hidden. Nor will Perdy. Will you, dear?"

There had of course been affection in Buxton's effort to keep Mrs. Post from disclosing his kindness. But he did give up the effort very easily as Mrs. Post refused to permit it, and he seemed visibly to relax into geniality under her praise. And when Perdy responded to Mrs. Post's question by giving Buxton a timid little smile and shaking her ringlet-massed head, the old man quite glowed with the gentle satisfaction of his benevolence.

Now that Vincent had the opportunity of finding out about Claudine Post for himself, there was nothing about her that he liked. Neither in appearance nor in manner was there anything to approve of, from her jutting nose and too-quick eye to her voice which was both loud and consciously polite, a demonstrative voice which seemed to evoke an unseen listener to whom the demonstration was being made over the heads of whomever else might be present. Yet whatever his judgment of Mrs. Post might be, Vincent found that there was some unnameable charm to which he responded. When, after this first meeting, she began to force the acquaintanceship, to insist that he come to tea at her house, sometimes sending Perdy to fetch him at Buxton's when his work was done, sometimes herself waylaying him as he passed, he became increasingly aware of this charm. He used that word of her, not in the usual metaphoric sense, but literally. She was not delightful—she had a charm, in the sense of a magic which had no connection with anything visibly hers, with any observable grace or interest. It was, as it were, something concealed under her dress, like the battery of a hearing-aid or a religious medal, or an amulet. It was a power, and Vincent understood what Garda Thorne had meant when she spoke of Claudine Post as an enchantress. For Vincent found that if he looked at her dark face or her body clothed in dark fabrics which always seemed to have been worn a little too long, he was on the whole repelled; but when she began to talk to him the charm asserted itself. The charm of flattery has nothing to do either with the grace of the flatterer or with the truth of what is said, but only with the intention of the flatterer, and Vincent found that in some way he was flattered by Claudine Post. When he was with her he found that he was relaxed and gratified. When she centered him in the conversation and directed all her energy of attention upon him, he could not resist the feelings that came. They puzzled him, these feelings, because mingled with the glow of pleasure was some element of almost physical fear.

His dislike of Claudine Post soon became a settled thing with him. Yet the force of that charm was always able to reach him. Part of the charm, perhaps, was the presence of young Perdita Aiken. Perdita had no attraction for Vincent, although, whenever he saw her he found a curious thin pleasure in her story-book beauty, but whenever the two women were together, Claudine Post's charm was the surer and more potent. And Vincent, aware of the girl's odd dependence on the older woman, wondered whether the awareness of the bawds in the old plays of lechery was merely a comic awareness, whether the old woman who provided the occasion for the sexual act in which she did not participate did not in some way contribute perversely to its enjoyment, for hers was the task of serving the masculinity of her customers, of bringing it to consciousness, of reassuring it.

"Perhaps, darling," said Mrs. Post, "you'd sing for Dr. Buxton now."

Perdita smiled and rose without any protest or hanging back.

"*Canterbury Bells?*" she asked. It was the first time she had spoken.

"No, dear," Mrs. Post said, as if Perdita should have known a great deal better than that, "Not *Canterbury Bells.*" The tone was as to an intelligent child. For the first time Vincent made specific calculation of Perdita's age. She was surely eighteen.

"*Voi che s'appete?*" Perdita asked. But she pronounced "voi" as if it were French.

"Not 'vwa,' dear—*voi* as in boy." Mrs. Post's voice was kind.

Perdita made a pretty little gesture of impatience with herself, snapping her fingers and ducking her head.

Mrs. Post arose and went to the piano. With a somewhat too large air of preparation, she stripped off a sizable onyx ring and a wedding ring and laid them down. How the sheet of music had got into Perdita's hands was impossible to say, but she stood there holding it and no doubt Mrs. Post had brought it for the purpose of putting it there. Mrs. Post sat at the piano in a masterly way. Her back was to Buxton and Vincent and Perdita, but before striking the first notes she turned and said, "This is an aria from Mozart's opera, *The Marriage of Figaro.* Cherubino sings it to the Countess in her apartment. Cherubino is a charming boy, but the part is always sung by a soprano, a girl."

Buxton said drily, "Thank you, Claudine. You are quite right, as I know—I have heard seven Cherubinos and, as you say, they were all sopranos and females."

Vincent had never heard Buxton use irony. Its effect upon Mrs. Post was startling. She rose from the piano seat. "Oh you mustn't—!" she cried. "I was explaining only for Perdita. She has never heard the opera. I wanted to help her visualize the part." A deep dark flush overspread her face and neck and that part of her chest that was exposed by the V of her dress. "Please don't misunderstand," she said. "You mustn't. If I didn't know your feeling for Mozart, would I have chosen this for Perdy?"

Buxton waved away the fault and the explanation, grandly, kindly. But it had been clear that his vanity had been touched. Mrs. Post stood there deeply troubled. She would have gone on with her apology, but Buxton's hand had turned into a gesture that was a command to leave off. She turned back to the piano and Perdy came and stood beside her.

The piano sounded the few opening notes and Perdy began to sing her *Voi che s'appete*. Vincent had always thought the song a strange one, for it begins in a falsetto and even in an affected manner—it is an interpolated song, intended to have the manner of a performance, and it had even occurred to Vincent that it was intended by Mozart as a parody on a certain mincing style of his day. But the song moves beyond that style to an intensity of feeling that is almost martial, so deep-throated and affirmative does it become. Perdy's voice was reed-like, thin, sweet and wholly without flow. She sang the opening bars with a pedantic precision, nodding her head to each of the clearly marked phrases. Mrs. Post's head nodded to keep time for her. The first few bars suited the strange unreal innocence of Perdita and the gauche little pedantry with which she nodded them out was most beguiling. But this same manner, which might almost have been an inspired one for the beginning of the song, continued through to its end and what had been beguiling became absurd and pathetic. The song was utterly beyond the child's powers of voice. But she went most courageously on to the end, borne up by the piano and carried along by Mrs. Post's nodding head. The piano and the voice sounded their last notes together and the silence of absurdity filled the room.

Or did it? For Mrs. Post said to Perdita, "Sweet, dearest," and turned to Buxton for his appreciation. And Buxton said, "Perdita, my dear, that was very charming." He got up and went to the girl. The sheet of music was still trembling in her hands. "Your hands are cold," he said. "Does it frighten you to sing?"

She shook her head. "No, not really frighten," she said.

"Doesn't she have a lovely voice, Mr. Hammell?" said Mrs. Post.

Vincent gave his answer to Perdy herself. "I enjoyed it very much," he said. "It was so nice." He felt very kind and mature, the girl was so strangely young. For the first time she looked at him with a personal recognition, a bashful, small responsiveness. He smiled to her and felt no less paternal than Buxton. But part of his paternal feeling arose from his pity for the perfect hopelessness of that thin, foolish voice of hers. He did not know whether Buxton had the same reason for tenderness or whether an old man, even one who had heard seven Cherubinos, had lost the ability to tell a good voice from a bad, or any interest in discriminating, and found his pleasure in the mere sight of the singing girl. And certainly Perdita, standing in her green dress, with the sheet of music in her hand, and her large tender mouth articulating the Italian words, was, in a way, in her way, a pretty and touching sight. And the two of them, Buxton in his achieved oaklike age, Perdy in her odd, excessive youth, their hands meeting, all of Buxton's warmth flowing toward this ungrown, unrealized child, made for Vincent a moment of the strangest intensity, the more intense because he could attach no significance to it, could not understand what generalization could be drawn from it about youth, age, about life and death—could not, because Buxton stood in the perfection of his existence and Perdita in the odd inadequacy of hers. The intensity of the moment seemed to become the greater when Claudine Post stood beside Perdita and put her arm about the girl's shoulder. "It was lovely, wasn't it?" she said.

"Yes, lovely," Buxton said.

The grouping was close and intimate. As if aware of it, Mrs. Post said with a large inclusive benignity, "I'm so glad you liked it, Mr. Hammell," and leaned her head sideways, mild and tender.

Vincent left. On the lawn outside Brooks Barrett stood lean as a rake and leaning on one. Barrett made a few tidying passes with the rake and Vincent had already walked down the path and was on the road before Barrett spoke. "Mr. Hammell," he said in a low voice. Vincent stopped. Barrett made a gesture with his head and eyes back to the house. "Now you know, Mr. Hammell, what I meant when I used the expression to you, 'human relations.' Do you remember that I said to you on the occasion of our first meeting that I could be of help to you and you thought that I meant science. I said that the only help I could give you was in human relations. Do you happen to remember that?"

"Yes, I do remember."

The "assistant" made another gesture with his head back to the house. "That was what I had in mind. Those relations, Mr. Hammell, are not—harmless."

That moment when Buxton stood with Perdita, her hands in his, was too charged for Vincent for him to permit Barrett to intrude into it. Not harmless—as Barrett uttered those words, Vincent could suppose that they were accurate, that any human relation that Claudine Post presided over was not a harmless one, that what Claudine Post had brought to the moment to intensify it was precisely the possibility of harm.

But the sense he had had of life summarized in that moment was his own and he rejected Barrett's intrusion into it. So he dropped his eyes rather haughtily and said, "Indeed?" And then, to crush Barrett he said, "All human relations, Mr. Barrett, have their dangers, you know."

Barrett consented to be crushed. He shrank back into himself, humble, sorry and submissive. But having thus suppressed and effaced himself, he permitted himself to murmur, "Later, perhaps," and he gave Vincent a glance that was bolder than his words, a glance that had irony and knowledge in it and that seemed to say, "You are not yet ready for what you could know, but perhaps you will be."

But perhaps the glance was bolder than Barrett meant, for when Vincent had turned to go, Barrett came after him and said, "By the way, I should tell you that I am a typist and nothing would give me more pleasure—I assure you, nothing—than to make your task lighter by typing your manuscript when you are ready."

"That's very kind of you," Vincent said. "Thank you very much."

"Oh, don't thank me—it would be a privilege," Barrett said.

trilling's commentary

The time of the story is, let us say, 1937—or any time after 1929 and before 1939 in which it is possible to think about life without the *most* immediate reference to economic crises. There was a period then—no doubt it varied for individuals—in which this was possible.

The story follows the adventures of a young man, name of Vincent Hammell. He is a very young man, not more than 23 when the story opens. He is not "poor"—but he is the only son of a declining middle class family, his father an optometrist, once prosperous, now no longer so. He is a cherished child—I call him the child of hope and despair and it is that, perhaps, which gave him the sense of destiny, which is what chiefly marks him for us.

Young Vincent's social plight is not a bad one. From a base a good deal less secure than his, many young men have easily gone on to the study of one of the established professions and have done very well. But Vincent's choice has been that of the intellect. [Something should be said to this effect as the story now stands—that is, the profession of the arts should be treated in an even more matter-of-factual way. One advantage of this is to make the ordinary reader more at home, less likely to think that he is engaged with a book that has a merely private—professional—reference: he should be made to see that Vincent could just as well have chosen the profession of law, medicine, engineering. It might not be a bad idea here to say what is true of myself that Vincent could not imagine these professions for himself, but that at a later time he would easily see their attractions and his own ability to handle them. There really cannot be too much objective comment on Vincent's profession.][1] It is a choice that makes difficulties. For Vincent lives in a large mid-western American city: at present it is not named, but perhaps it should be named and it should be Cleveland, St. Louis, Cincinnati, Detroit, Minneapolis, some city which has its "culture" but not the kind of active intellectual life that would satisfy a young man of Vincent's sort.

Vincent's character does not need explanation here. It will, as living character, develop either without specific intention or not all. What is to be understood now is simply that the young man is attractive as a person, yet not too much so—people can be impatient with him, but on the whole they like him and can be devoted to him. He has a curious little internal force to which they respond; his manner and appearance are of a kind to make this little tough power appear.

As the story opens, we learn this about young Vincent: that he is deeply involved in the idea of moral "integrity" and that he is at the same time wonderfully drawn to personal achievement and success.

[The present treatment of the idea of integrity is too *tight*. It needs to be opened out more—treated more objectively (as with the profession of writing above) and communicated more to the reader. Perhaps names are needed; and that incredible Michel Mok "interview" with the drunken destroyed Scott Fitzgerald might very well serve for a center.]

This central moral fact of Vincent's life we learn about immediately in action. The story opens on a tennis-court, at the socially sound Tennis Club. Vincent is playing with his old friend, Toss Dodge. They have long been friends, but now they are growing apart, not merely because Toss is rich but because Vincent has become an intellectual. Vincent has just received a letter from Harold Outram, replying to one of his own about Outram's books. He makes a bet with himself—but the story gives it well enough and it does not need to be repeated...

Toss, with a kind of blind accuracy, sees the ambiguity of motive in Vincent's writing to Outram, the man who has lost his "integrity." This

---

[1] These brackets are Trilling's, as are all others in this commentary that enclose more than one word.

perception is repeated in the scenes with Vincent's mother and with Theodore Kramer, Vincent's former teacher: until Vincent himself must understand why he had written Outram.

The scene of the end of the friendship with Toss: "My youth is over."

The scene with Vincent's mother... to build up the economic and family background. Essentially as now. But more developed.

And in this development, more of the life that Vincent has been living.... His book more dealt with... why does he not run off to New York as so many young men do?... his neurotic feelings and inability to write.

[I think this is true of things as the job now stands: that there is not enough *spread*—there is too much economy. It is remarkable how much exposition a novel can stand, and of the crudest sort: all the reader really needs is a promise of story to come. The story so far is perhaps too "elegantly" told. The novel must always have the sense of chronicle—at least I like it when it has.]

His father's "place"...

The interview with Theodore Kramer... dramatically sets the situation of Outram and the nature of Outram's defeat.[2]

[Not enough is made in this scene of Outram's breakdown—Kramer should be more aware of it.]

This scene further establishes Vincent's moral situation, but it should show him as really a very nice person; his attitude to his old teacher should be in large part endearing, but not too much so. On the whole, I think this scene is reasonably well handled as is.

The scene with Outram, much as it is now: but, again, expansion is needed: they should not sit, as now, in one place—the bar or grill—but should go at least for a walk—the business of Outram giving Vincent a gift, as in an earlier draft, is good and useful and should be restored.

Very possibly the present unity of scene is wrong—makes too much happen in a short time—possibly a day should intervene between the first meeting and the dramatic climax of the offer, a day in which Vincent's hopes and anticipations are raised very high: this would give us

---

2 The ellipses are Trilling's. In the original they are of varying lengths, but I have used the conventional three periods.

the opportunity of saying a great deal more about his situation—right in the midst of an action—which I more and more think needs saying.

In any case the story makes its first step forward by Outram's offer to Vincent of the job of writing the biography of that remarkable man, Jorris Buxton. Same business, I am sure, of Buxton as a young writer who had little success, became at 40 a scientist, is now 80. But this should be built up from the present draft, there should be more told, or it should be told twice, or discussed—as it is now it is too pat and summary.

And so Vincent has his chance and, I think, dramatically enough. He is to be taken—lifted—out of his present depressed and depressing situation and put into a situation of brilliance, which—and I think we can begin to gather this—holds the promise of a moral situation of some weight.

Now we get the scene at Meadowfield, the class in creative writing, which should be kept. [But Meadowfield must be built up in a different way, through the various scenes, not told about. It should still be the reason for Harold Outram's visit to the city, however. But H. O. should not be shown directly there.] The scene of the class signalizes, as it were, Vincent's departure and freedom.

Then we have the day of departure—Vincent's scene with his mother: but this should be made more affecting: it is now MUCH too minimal and restrained; it should a little match the scene with the father; but since there ought to be an actual scene of departure at the station, the affectingness might well be kept for there; and on the whole I think it should be. Then there should be added the scene of Vincent in the Pullman—that scene of the young man on his first travel of adventure which is so much an American theme.

[Whether to have a passage on what is bound to be important to a young man, his arrival in New York, must be considered. I am not attracted by it as a matter of any length; yet it would perhaps seem odd in a realistic novel that it is not mentioned. It could of course be mentioned in retrospect, upon Vincent's arrival at Outram's house in the country.]

The arrival at the Outram house: The present scene is very adequate—the young man's confused and mistaken impressions—his first meeting with Mrs. Outram. His first meeting with Garda Thorne, of whom we have had as it were a spiritual glimpse in the scene of the class in creative writing.

Up to now, although reasonably dramatic, the story has been going along the ground. So long a stretch of taxi-ing must argue a long novel. We have to face up to this: the pace of what has occupied us until now can be the introduction only to a long story. We must give up all craven hope of making it short. If it is to be short, it must begin with Vincent's arrival at Outram's. But that isn't what you want. So best make up your mind to length.

Here the story begins to leave the ground for flight.

The plot actually *thickens*. Garda Thorne has an interview with Vincent in which, it is apparent, she is for some reason trying to take him into camp. She has a deep interest in the way Buxton's biography is to be written and she immediately reveals her reason for it: she has been Buxton's mistress and naturally would be concerned with how the crucial matter of their relationship would be treated. But as she talks, she cannot hide what is the specific worry for her—the somehow scandalous fact that she was only seventeen and Buxton quite fifty-five when the affair began. But she breaks off the interview with a cry of fear and horror as the fact is terribly borne in upon her that seventeen is now more than twenty-five years behind her. Vincent's feelings are by this and by other things about Garda, deeply and truly stirred.

The story, as it is now, goes forward the next day when we learn of the existence of a certain Claudine Post who has apparently some kind of control over Buxton. It is she who has prevented Buxton from coming to the Outrams' for dinner the evening before. It is clear that Garda deeply resents Mrs. Post and that so do the two Outrams. But when Vincent, naturally interested in a person so close to Buxton, asks about Claudine Post he is told by Outram that he had better find out for himself.

This reply—not in itself very significant, except for what it might say about Outram and about the curious tenseness of the social situation around Buxton—gives Vincent cause for offense. He is suddenly struck with the fact that he is being a little manipulated by Outram and he begins to wonder, angrily, why he, so very young, has been chosen to write the biography of so notable a man—a work that a much more established man would be glad to undertake.

[This, looked at now, suggests that the early scenes must deal with the job more objectively and in greater detail, so as to make the unlikelihood of the choice of Vincent the greater and also the more acceptable. As it now stands, it is all too summary. This would have the effect, in addition, of making richer and more dramatic the relationship between Outram and Vincent which at the moment is too thin.]

But Vincent's anger subsides in the charming life he is introduced to, most particularly the charm of Garda Thorne herself. In a scene at the swimming pool, a scene which has certain reminiscences of the Garda Thorne story which Vincent had read to his class, there is a kind of unconscious or rather unrealized sexual passage between them. It is immediately upon this—it is early evening—that Buxton arrives with Brooks Barrett, coming to the little dinner party that is being given by the Outrams.

We then have the scene between Brooks Barrett and Vincent and then the strange perception that Vincent has of the power of mind—that curious Aristotlean business. He has what may be the illusion of peace: but illusion or not it is a perception and it endows Buxton with a great meaning for him.

[The little relation between Garda and Buxton is pretty good. Also the little passage between Vincent and Brooks Barrett. Perhaps in the business between Buxton and Vincent something more could be done, though substantially it is sound.]

Then comes the dinner party. We now have the introduction of several characters—Philip Dyas, Julian and Linda Hollowell. Consider them presently.

The dinner party serves two purposes—it gives us the information about the Philip Dyas school and Linda's desire to have it; and it gives an example of the effect of Buxton on the people around him. Essentially the scene is adequate yet very likely it could be strengthened, not so much in dramatic point as in interest—in charm. The chapter should glitter rather more.

Then the meeting with Marry. Then the great storm with its disclosure of Buxton's mortal weakness and Vincent's handling of this situation. The point of that "handling" is that it brings Vincent to what is for the purposes of this novel maturity. We have now a grown man on our hands, yet still with all the weakness of a very young one. It is only that he has the possibility of being greatly involved—in life. He is not yet free from temptation and the possibility of destruction. But he has an edge now on all the other characters.

Here we have stopped [the set-piece description of the town is all right, but it is so set and fixed that nothing much can be thought about it except whether or not it fits usefully].

What has been done up to this point is a not inconsiderable achievement. I think we can say this: that it has point, immediacy, warmth under control, drama and even size. It seems to me a very decent third of the book. What is now needed is two other parts of equal length and similar but mounting intensity.

The question is how to handle—even how to produce the two parts. The bare bones of the story are there—and are sound bones.

But the intermediate part of the story does not present itself. Except in certain small flashes, most of which seem right.

The first part, after many approximations and failures, did grow into something. And it grew with a kind of unconsciousness. This unconsciousness was very beguiling and reassuring. One scene suggested another. Sometimes a few words in one scene suggested another. I think I am right in feeling that this way of creating incident is a right way. And I am experiencing discouragement because this kind of unconscious movement of the mind isn't now going on. But what I forget—as one always forgets certain parts of the writing process after the job is finished—is that for the first part I had in mind a very clear scenario; it was on this that the creation grew: it was the stick for the vine. True, the incidents I have finally used were not part of the scenario, but I knew this much very clearly: what kind of person Vincent was and what his situation was, same of Outram; and I knew the relation of Outram to Buxton; and I knew that Vincent was to be picked up by Outram and taken to the East.

The job for me was then simply to get from point A to point T in as interesting a way as possible, creating interesting points in between. I did get to point T as desired and on the whole the other points are interesting.

What is making the difficulty is that I have not yet got a new point at which to aim. That once got, I think I can depend on the unconscious process working out a series of connecting and interesting incidents.

The problem now is to get the second point. The third when we come to it; in general we know what it is.

But the first thing to discover is whether we are properly equipped with characters.

appendix

"The Lesson and the Secret"

The following collation is included for the convenience of readers interested in comparing the manuscript of the novel with the story Trilling published from it. In "The Lesson and the Secret,"[1] Trilling sharpened the principal theme of chapter 10 through foreshortening and dramatization. Vincent's reveries about the offer from Outram and other details relevant only to the novel are, of course, excised from the story, and the sympathetic Miss Anderson is not the source of Vincent's enlightenment about the women's dissatisfaction. At two points in the story, Trilling relies on discussion among the matrons both to individualize them and to establish the grounds of the antagonism toward their young instructor. The first such discussion immediately follows the opening paragraph of the story, which is quite similar to the opening paragraph of chapter 10. The second paragraph of the manuscript ("Of the nine women … supposed ideally to aspire.") follows. The other

---

[1] "The Lesson and the Secret" was first published in *Harper's Bazaar* in 1945; my source is Diana Trilling, ed., *"Of This Time, Of That Place" and Other Stories* (New York: Harcourt Brace Jovanovich, 1979), 58–71.

"new" conversation among the students follows the descriptions of the individual class members and Vincent's assumption that in the East, wealth would "make a better show." The short story ends with the sentence following Mrs. Stocker's question about Garda Thorne's commercial success as a writer.

Passages from "The Lesson and the Secret" reprinted below illustrate the new material and new sequencing of the story. Minor differences between the manuscript and the story—deletions or additions of a phrase or a sentence, transpositions, and changes in diction—are not included, only those that alter the meaning or composition of Vincent's classroom experience.

"The Lesson and the Secret"

The nine women of the Techniques of Creative Writing Group sat awaiting the arrival of their instructor, Vincent Hammell. He was not late but they were early and some of them were impatient. The room they sat in was beautiful and bright; its broad windows looked out on the little lake around which the buildings of the city's new cultural center were grouped. The women were disposed about a table of plate glass and their nine handbags lay in an archipelago upon its great lucid surface.

Mrs. Stocker said, "Mr. Hammell isn't here, it seems." There was the intention of irony in her voice—she put a querulous emphasis on the "seems."

Miss Anderson said, "Oh, but it's that we are early—because of our being at the luncheon." She glanced for confirmation at the watch on her wrist.

"Perhaps so," Mrs. Stocker said. "But you know, Constance—speaking metaphorically, Hammell is *not here*, he—is—just—not—here."

At this remark there were nods of considered agreement. Mrs. Territt said, "I think so too. I agree," and brought the palm of her hand down upon her thigh in a sharp slap of decision.

Mrs. Stocker ignored this undesirable ally. She went on, "Not really *here* at all. Oh, I grant you that he is brilliant in a theoretical sense. But those of us who come here"—she spoke tenderly, as if referring to a sacrifice in a public cause—"those of us who come here, come for practice, not for theory. You can test the matter very easily—you can test it by the results. And you know as well as I do, Constance, that—there—are—just—no—results—at—all."

Miss Anderson had gone through uprisings like this every spring and she knew that there was no standing against Mrs. Stocker. Mrs. Stocker would have her own way, especially since the group that opposed her was so small and uncourageous, consisting, in addition to Miss Anderson herself, only of Mrs. Knight and Miss Wilson. Young Mrs. Knight was extremely faithful and quite successful in carrying out the class assignments and this naturally put her under suspicion of being prejudiced in favor of the instructor. Her opinion was bound to be discounted. As for Miss Wilson, her presence in the group was generally supposed to have merely the therapeutic purpose of occupying her unhappy mind. It was not a frequent presence, for she shrank from society, and now she looked miserably away from the insupportable spectacle of anyone's being blamed for anything whatsoever.

Miss Anderson said, "But surely we can't blame that all on Mr. Hammell."

"No, not all," Mrs. Stocker conceded handsomely because it was so little to concede. "I grant you it isn't *all* his fault. But I think we have the right to expect—. It isn't as if we weren't paying. And generously, too, I might add. And there's nothing to show. Not one of us has sold herself."

Mrs. Territt gave vent to an explosive snicker. At once Mrs. Stocker traced the reason for the outburst to Mrs. Territt's primitive sexual imagination and said sharply, "Not one of us has sold herself to a single magazine. Not one of us has put herself across."

Of the nine women, all were very wealthy.

[The manuscript and story are quite similar for the next few paragraphs up to "a more firmly bottomed assurance, a truer arrogance." A new sentence—"Then, too, he could suppose"—concludes that paragraph, followed by another new conversation among the women in which Mrs. Stocker, rather than Miss Anderson, raises the subject of contacts and "the straight dope."]

Then, too, he could suppose that these women were the failures and misfits of their class, else they would not have to meet weekly to devote themselves to literature.

"I have nothing against Hammell personally, nothing whatsoever," Mrs. Stocker said. "What I think is that we need a different *kind* of person. Hammell is very modern, but we need somebody more practical. It seems to me that if we could have a literary agent, who could give us the straight dope, tell us about contracts and the right approach..." [ellipsis in original]

Mrs. Stocker had no need to complete her conditional clause. The straight dope, the contracts and right approach, went directly to the hearts of Mrs. Territt, Mrs. Broughton, and Mrs. Forrester. They murmured a surprised approval of the firm originality of the suggestion. Even old Mrs. Pomeroy raised her eyebrows to indicate that although human nature did not change, it sometimes appeared in interesting new aspects. To all the ladies, indeed, it came as a relief that Mrs. Stocker should suggest that there was another secret than that of creation. There was a power possibly more efficacious, the secret of selling, of contacts and the right approach.

Miss Anderson said, "But aren't all the literary agents in New York?" She said it tentatively, for she was without worldly knowledge, but what she said was so sensibly true that the general enthusiasm was dampened.

"But surely," Mrs. Stocker said, and her voice was almost desperate, "but surely there must be somebody?"

Mrs. Broughton, who was staring out of the window, said, "Here he comes," whispering it like a guilty conspiratorial schoolgirl. Mrs. Forrester closed her dark expressive eyes to the group to signal "mum" and the ladies composed their faces.

Could Vincent Hammell have heard the conversation of which he was the subject, he would have been surprised by only one element in it—the lack of any response to him personally. He knew he was not succeeding with the group, but he knew, too, that none of the instructors who had come before him had succeeded any better.

[two paragraphs roughly the same, up to] held in bondage by a great conspiracy of editors.

Vincent Hammell was carrying his brief-case... hope of better days. Vincent was glad of the brief-case, for it helped to arm his youth and poverty against the wealth and years of his pupils. He laid it on the plate-glass table, beneath which his own legs and the legs of the women were visible. He opened it and took out a thin folder of manuscript. Miss Anderson cleared her throat, caught the eye of member after member and brought the meeting to order. Hammell looked up and took over the class. It was only his entrance into the room that gave him trouble and now he spoke briskly and with authority.

"Two weeks ago," he said, "I asked you to write an account of some simple outdoor experience."

[At this point the story and the manuscript converge again; the discussion of Mrs. Knight's story about her lodge follows, ending with Mrs. Stocker's question about its "marketable value." The short new succeeding paragraph in "The Lesson and the Secret" shows Mrs. Knight's interest in the commercial potential of her story.]

There were little nods around the table as the spirit of the junta asserted itself once more, but there was a constraining sense of guilt now that Vincent Hammell was here. Mrs. Knight looked very conscious. She was humble about her writing and near enough to her college days to submit to the discipline of an assigned exercise, but she was naturally not averse to knowing whether or not she had produced a commodity.

"Now you take Constance's stories—Miss Anderson's stories, Mr. Hammell."

[The manuscript and story similarly recount Mrs. Territt's hostile question about writing "at all," Vincent's reading of the Garda Thorne story, the class's benign elevation, and Mrs. Stocker's deflating question as to whether Thorne's stories "sell well." The story concludes with the following one-sentence paragraph.]

At the question there was a noisy little murmur of agreement to its relevance as the eyes turned to Vincent Hammell to demand his answer.